THE FRONT PORCH PROPHET

RAYMOND L. ATKINS

Medallion Press, Inc.
Printed in USA

THE FRONT PORCH PROPHET

RAYMOND L. ATKINS

"THE FRONT PORCH PROPHET is a fine piece of southern fiction—by turns poignant and hilarious. Atkins knows his front porches; the rustics who inhabit his novel are real people who walk right off the page, but he's also had some book learning . . . in the rich, lucid prose, one finds moments of breathtaking elegance.

With a knack for storytelling, a sly sense of humor, and a Faulkneresque sensibility, Ray Atkins enters the literary scene with aplomb, and he plans to stay."

—Melanie Sumner, author of
The School of Beauty and Charm and *Polite Society*

DEDICATION:

To Marsha, of course.

Published 2008 by Medallion Press, Inc.

The MEDALLION PRESS LOGO
is a registered tradmark of Medallion Press, Inc.

Printed in the United States of America
Typeset in Baskerville
Title font set in KiraLynn

Library of Congress Cataloging-in-Publication Data

Atkins, Raymond L.
  The front porch prophet / Raymond L. Atkins.
    p. cm.
  ISBN 978-1-933836-38-6 (alk. paper)
  1. Georgia--Fiction. I. Title.
  PS3602.T4887F76 2008
  813'.6--dc22

                                      2008016013

10 9 8 7 6 5 4 3 2 1
First Edition

ACKNOWLEDGEMENTS:

Special thanks to Ken Anderson, who took the time to teach me to write. Thanks to the Wednesday night group—Jeanie, Jon, Jess, and Amelia (I wish there had been pie). Thanks to Kerry and Helen for the chance to live my dream.

THE APPALACHIAN MOUNTAINS MEANDER FROM the flatlands of the South to the Gulf of St. Lawrence. They were ancient when first discovered by the human species—venerable even as age is measured in geologic time—and have endured with injured grace the attentions of that destructive race. In its impetuous youth, the range was formidable. Now, wind and water have brought the mountains low, although they are, in their fashion, still as wild as their larger western cousins. Lookout Mountain originates in south-central Tennessee, wanders west across northwest Georgia, and terminates in the farmlands of northeast Alabama. It is considered by some to be the southernmost principal mass of the Appalachian chain. To others, it is home.

A thousand souls reside in the town of Sequoyah, Georgia, sixty miles southwest of Chattanooga. Located in a mountain valley surrounded by peaks, Sequoyah does not differ significantly from countless other small communities dotting the Southern landscape.

It has a store and a gas station, a diner and four churches. It boasts a school, a post office, a traffic light, and a town hall. There is a doctor, a lawyer, and an Indian chief—or at least, that is what he claims. Over the years, however, the settlement has developed a character unique to itself. The whole has exceeded the sum of the parts. The individuals who resided there have left traces, pieces of the patchworks of their lives. A child's name. A house. The lay of a fencerow. A snowball bush. This is the way of towns and of those who people them. These are the relics of security, for it is not human nature to live alone.

One such memento of Sequoyah's living past is A.J. Longstreet. His mother, Rose, succumbed to a venomous cancer when he was an infant. She was in hideous pain through much of her pregnancy but staved off the inevitable until her child was born. Her husband, John Robert Longstreet, was desolate. He paid the heavy price of sentience with his sorrow.

Time heals most wounds, but by no means all. On the day after Rose was laid to rest, John Robert quietly rocked his son. Rose had named the baby Arthur John after her father and her husband. It was a warm evening early in the spring, and the scent of wisteria pervaded the air. That aroma would sadden John Robert for the remainder of his days, the lying smell of illusory hope, the cloying sweetness forever tied to memories of the funeral parlor, the mound, and the gaping hole in the red Georgia clay. He sat with his mother, Clara, on the porch of the old family home place, in which had resided many generations of Longstreets. The sky to the west bled ruby into the night. John Robert sighed, kissed the baby, and offered him to Clara. She looked at him, discerned his fatal intentions, and refused the bundle.

"Take the boy, Mama," John Robert said woodenly, his voice a bottomless melancholy. He was not a coward but had chosen the craven path, and he had a long journey ahead to regain his place at Rose's side.

"No," she said in a voice as unyielding as frozen time. "That is not the way. We'll raise him together, but I won't do it alone." She spoke calmly and with finality, but a hard fear gripped her heart like an eagle's claw. She had just lost the daughter she never had and was now in danger of losing her son. Loneliness was her terror. She had become a widow many years earlier due to a freak accident involving a hay baler, a rock, and a young husband who was counting on many long years of happiness. So Clara raised John Robert alone, and she had been overheard to say on more than one occasion that she had done a fine job. But she was an old woman now and doubted her ability to repeat the task.

"Mama, it's time for me to go," John Robert insisted. He stood and placed the baby on the seat of the rocker. Clara was a woman with unalterable concepts of right and wrong, and was known to be spirited when crossed. She had heard enough.

"John Robert, there will be no more of this talk. Do you hear me? Not another word. That poor baby doesn't know what his mama went through to get him here, but he *is* here, and you can just set your mind to doing your duty by him." John Robert hung his head, but Clara was not through. "I have never heard such in all my days," she continued. "What would *you* have done if I had gone and jumped into that hay baler with your daddy?" She reached up and touched his unshaven chin. "What do you think Rose would say about all

3

this?" she asked quietly, saving the trump card for last.

And that had been that. The talk of joining Rose was ended. John Robert would be with her in good time, but first he had to finish the task they had initiated together.

So he and Clara commenced the raising of Arthur John Longstreet, and the joy that John Robert had lost upon his wife's passing was slowly replaced on a smaller scale by his son. He was subject to brief depressions for the remainder of his days, particularly early in the spring, but he never again allowed himself to be overcome. He never remarried, much to the chagrin of many of the available young women in the area—all of whom knew a fine catch when one swam by—but it appeared he was no longer interested in members of the opposite sex, which was a shame in a man so vital, handsome, and propertied.

Total disinterest was not quite the truth, however. John Robert had been comforted during his darkest days by a local angel of mercy, an iron-willed woman who had survived bleak times of her own and who had the uncommon talent of knowing her own mind. To her lasting credit, she determined to help this lonely and despairing man find solace, and as payment for her kindness she bore a son. Conception had not been her intent, but she knew a gift when she received one and recognized their scarcity in an indifferent world. So she was content with the outcome and burdened neither John Robert nor her husband with the details.

Arthur John Longstreet grew into sturdy, barefoot boyhood under the dutiful care of John Robert and Granmama. John Robert's lessons were those of hard work, duty, family, and respect. He told Arthur John of his mother, Rose, and the boy learned to hold her in reverence. There were several photographs of Rose Longstreet in the house, grainy black-and-white slices of a life that had been. His favorite depicted her in a cotton dress sitting by a pond, smiling at the photographer, her long hair windblown. Arthur John had been to that spot many times, always hoping to find her, always convinced that somehow he had just missed her. He could sense a presence there, as if her arms enfolded him across time.

While John Robert tended toward the larger issues of life, Clara was as practical in her upbringing of Arthur John as she had been with the raising of his father. She kept him clean and taught him manners. She read him stories and held him when he cried. She doctored his scrapes and made him eat his vegetables. She made him mind, and more than once found herself applying the business end of a hickory switch to his stubborn behind. She also took the boy to church each Sunday, but the weekly excursion was made without John Robert, who refused to go.

"It's a good idea," he told Clara when she first broached the subject. "Take the boy on down there. There's a lot of good to be had out of going to church."

"You ought to come with us, John Robert," she said.

"I expect I'll wait awhile. Me and the Lord don't see eye to eye these days. We'll get around to talking, directly." But they never did. The betrayal had been too great, the theft of Rose into the night too harsh. John Robert had looked deep into his heart and found no forgiveness. He knew he was a minute speck in the vastness of the cosmos, but he was the injured party and expected an accounting. But no bush on the farm burst into voice and flame to reveal why Rose's presence had been required elsewhere. Skulled specters did not trot in across the back pasture under a white flag of truce to clarify why her transition from here to there had been so ungodly cruel. So John Robert did not forgive. And he did not forget.

Arthur John became initialized early in life. Initialization is a Southern rite of passage akin to the Hebrew practice of circumcision, but it is sometimes less painful and does not always occur on the seventh day. So Arthur John Longstreet became A.J., and A.J. he has remained.

When A.J. was six, Granmama took him down to the school in town. It was a bright, sweet morning in early September, and A.J. was beside himself with excitement. He was decked out in stiff-as-a-board jeans, a blue cotton shirt, and U.S. Keds, black high-tops fresh out of the box. This was the big league, and A.J. knew it full well. After a brief, informal registration, he was remanded into the custody of Mrs. Williams, a sweet, blue-haired woman who had been teaching since John Robert was a child.

So it was that A.J. began his formal education. He loved the neat structure and implicit boundaries of classroom life and awaited his lessons with eagerness. He quickly and correctly learned all the material presented to him and always seemed hungry for more. He thought Mrs. Williams was a pearl and liked most of his classmates. His one problem was Hollis Battey, a bully from a long line of the same who took particular delight in harassing A.J. Hollis was seven and much bigger than A.J. The Battey clan esteemed only unemployment and alcohol above ignorance, and Hollis was in school solely because the county sheriff had insisted.

A.J. endured Hollis's torments for the better part of a month. He did so for two reasons. The first was that John Robert had always told him fighting was to be held as a last resort. Secondly, A.J. was afraid of the brutish boy. He knew without doubt that when it came to blows, he was going to lose. So he tried avoidance, but that was tough to pull off in a class of eleven. Then he attempted accommodation, but Hollis was not to be accommodated. A.J. even tried to make friends with the Battey boy, but the novelty of having a comrade did not appeal to Hollis. Finally, A.J. turned to his father for advice.

"If he was after you, John Robert, would you fight him?" A.J. asked, perplexed by the enormity of his problem.

"No, I wouldn't fight him," John Robert replied. "And I'll love you just the same whether you fight him or not." So A.J. went on to school without a definite solution to his predicament while John Robert put on his jacket and headed for the truck. It was his intent to drive out for a chat with Jug Battey, father of Hollis and, in John Robert's opinion, the root cause of the problem. Clara did not care for the plan.

"I'll not have you rolling in the dirt with Jug Battey," she firmly declared. "That man is as mean as a snake and as sorry as the day is long." Clara disliked Jug Battey as much as any Christian woman was allowed—perhaps even a tad more—and she did not want any members of her family near him.

"I'm just going for a talk, Mama," John Robert responded. "There won't be any fighting."

"What if *Jug* starts a fight?" Clara demanded. She knew there was a temper buried deep under her son's fabled composure.

"I'll finish it."

While John Robert was chewing the fat with Jug, an animated

discussion by all accounts, A.J. was arriving at a crossroad on the highway of life. It was recess, and Hollis had sought out A.J. and pushed him to the ground. Tears of anger welled in A.J.'s eyes. Then Hollis made an error in judgment and overplayed his hand. He told A.J. he ought to go cry to his mama, but that he didn't even have one to cry to.

"People without mamas are bastards," Hollis sneered. "You're just a crybaby bastard." A.J. had no clue this genealogical seminar was fundamentally in error, but he did know an insult when he heard one. He had had enough. He arose slowly, fists balled, and advanced on the bigger boy. He knew he could not win, but his anger made him momentarily fearless.

The combatants plowed into one another, and Hollis was surprised and a touch anxious at A.J.'s ferocity. Even so, it was only a matter of time before size became the determining factor, and soon enough A.J. found himself flat on his back with Hollis on top.

The drubbing was about to begin in earnest when a random factor presented itself. A small boy launched himself from the ring of spectators and landed on Hollis's head and neck, where he held on for sheer survival. Hollis released A.J. to concentrate on the removal of the new assailant. With his freed fists, A.J. pummeled the Battey midsection with such dramatic result that Hollis was relieved when Mrs. Williams arrived a few moments later and ended the fracas.

At supper that evening, A.J. felt elated. He had stood up for himself even though he had been afraid. The whipping he received had not hurt as much as he thought it might, and he wore his faint shiner with pride.

John Robert's black eye was a bit more pronounced. The talk with Jug had not gone well, its outcome inconclusive. Granmama was bustling around, slamming crockery onto the table while apologizing to the Lord on behalf of her son and grandson, stating she had done her absolute best.

It had been a day of meetings for A.J. He had met and mastered his fear. He had met John Robert as an equal, fresh from the field of battle, and they had met Granmama's wrath in tandem. And he had met a small boy who had saved him. He had met Eugene Purdue, who was destined to be his lifelong friend.

I'm dead, and I can <u>still</u> whip your ass.
—Excerpt of posthumous letter from
Eugene Purdue to Hollis Battey

TO THE EAST OF SEQUOYAH LIES FOX MOUNTAIN, also known as Eugene's Mountain in honor of its owner and sole inhabitant, Eugene Purdue. The elevation came into the possession of the Purdue family soon after the conclusion of the Great War of Northern Aggression, also called the Civil War by certain scholars and historians. Upon his return from that conflict, Eugene's great-great-great grandfather, Clayton, acquired the tract during a game of chance with Charles Fox, the last surviving member of the Fox family. Clayton Purdue was a rascal who claimed gambling as his vocation. Charles Fox was a drunkard and a fool, inalienable rights at that time of the sons of the gentry. The game was Five Card Stud, and the betting on the final hand was heavy. When Charles Fox drew his fourth jack with his fifth card, he wagered the mountain. Clayton Purdue had a great deal of money on the whiskey barrel and was bluffing a busted royal flush. Ever the sportsman, he drew his trusty Navy Colt and called the bet with finality. The dealer and only witness, Spartan Cook, swore under oath at the inquest that Clayton had acted in self-defense when he shot Charles Fox. In return for this middling perjury he received five-hundred dollars and subsequently relocated to the Oklahoma Territories to practice law. The judge at the hearing, Clayton's cousin Samuel, ruled that the demise of Charles Fox was lamentable but unavoidable. He then awarded the mountain to Clayton after first advising him to refrain from attempting to draw inside to a straight. Both the mountain and the Navy Colt have remained in the Purdue family to this day.

A.J. Longstreet arrived at the foot of Eugene's Mountain after driving the dirt road that wound eight miles from the state highway. It was noon on a Saturday. He parked his old pickup under the hanging-tree near the trail that snaked up the mountain to Eugene's cabin. The trail had once been a road, but due to a bitter family disagreement, Eugene no longer had access to his father's bulldozer and thus was unable to keep the roadway in good repair. The falling-out had occurred when Eugene inherited the mountain from his grandfather, A.R. Purdue. The inheritance had passed over Eugene's father and on to Eugene because of a difference of opinion regarding a choice of brides.

When Eugene's father, Johnny Mack, returned from the Big War back in 1946, he had in tow a beautiful French woman, Angelique, and her young son, Jacques. A.R. Purdue was charmed by Angelique and took right to little Jackie—*Jacques* was a bit too European for his taste—but all hell broke loose when he discovered that both newcomers bore the *Purdue* surname. He had been under the mistaken impression Angelique was a souvenir of sorts, along the

12

lines of a Luger or a bayonet, but prettier.

"Did you think I just walked around France till I found one I wanted?" Johnny Mack asked, amazed at his father's crystalline stupidity.

"What about that boy?" A.R. demanded, pointing at the child like he was a sack of meal. "Is he yours?"

"He is now," Johnny Mack replied, looking at his father with disdain.

So Johnny Mack and Angelique set up housekeeping in the face of significant opposition. A.R. continued to rant and rave and pitch a general fit over the audacity his son had exhibited by marrying a damn foreigner, and a Catholic damn foreigner at that. These on-going tirades caused Johnny Mack's mother to take to her bed with a case of nerves destined to last for years. The newlyweds ignored the histrionics and plowed ahead undaunted, and Johnny Mack figured that sooner or later A.R. would come the long way around to reason. He was quite surprised at the eventual reading of the will to discover the old man never had.

Regarding the relationship between Johnny Mack and his younger son, Eugene, the inheritance of the mountain was almost the straw that broke the camel's back. Almost, but not quite. They had not gotten along for some time and took opposing views on most issues. Johnny Mack was stern and pious, and had imposed harsh discipline throughout Eugene's formative years. Eugene, on the other hand, held nothing sacred, and he took particular delight in antagonizing his father. Still, they eventually might have struck an uneasy truce for the sake of Angel, formerly known as Angelique, whom they both loved. They might have, but the week after Eugene inherited the mountain, his cannabis harvest was found curing up in the rafters of the well house of the Hog Liver Road Primitive Baptist Church. Johnny Mack was a deacon out at the church, and the incident proved to be a religious liability to him.

"What in hell were you thinking?" Johnny Mack growled around the unlit cigar clamped in his jaw. He had given up smoking and cussing as a younger man after accepting the Almighty into his bosom, but the well house incident had caused him to backslide. "You were raised up better than this!" he continued. "W.P. is running around like a damn fool telling everyone that he has been touched by the hand of the Holy Spirit!" He was referring to W.P. Poteet, unpaid janitor and unofficial watchman at the church. W.P. had discovered Eugene's marijuana when he went into the well house to get his lawn mower, with which he intended to touch up a few graves. The unfortunate combination of W.P.'s agricultural background, poor eyesight, and lack of mental acuity had led him to assume some local farmer was drying a cash crop of burley up in the rafters. Since he had not enjoyed a good *fresh* smoke in about forty years, he tamped his pipe and fired up. Sweet Baby Jesus had revealed Himself shortly thereafter.

"I can't help it if W.P. is a damn fool," Eugene had replied coolly. "And what raising I got was Angel's doing, not yours. Before you get too holy, I know about that half gallon of bourbon you have stashed in the stove. It would be a damn shame if the brethren found out about it!" The threat was clear. He was referring to the church's potbellied wood heater, used for warmth on cold mornings and as a liquor cabinet by Johnny Mack during more temperate weather. Johnny Mack kept the sour mash around in case of pleurisy. A cautious man, he stored an additional half gallon under the tractor seat at home and even took the occasional preventive dose to be on the safe side.

Eugene knew all of this but was overcome with emotion and had spoken rashly. In his defense, his entire harvest of homegrown had just drifted up in smoke during the Evils of Satan bonfire and picnic held at the church the day after the well house discovery. Also destroyed were two Rolling Stones albums, a *Hustler* magazine, a hula hoop, and any hope of reconciliation between Johnny Mack and his wayward, errant son. There was some fireside discussion concerning the hula hoop, and many of the less zealous parishioners voiced doubts about its inclusion. But Myrtle Ellsbury was adamant, having apparently been drawn into mortal sin by one when she was a young girl, and Rabbit Brown finally chunked the foul instrument onto the pyre so Myrtle would hush.

Myrtle has long since gone to claim her reward for vigilance, Johnny Mack eventually overcame the stigma of having a spawn of Lucifer for a son, and the following year Eugene grew more dope. But Eugene and Johnny Mack never spoke again, and the road suffered greatly as a result.

A.J. got out of his truck and stretched for a moment. Then he reached behind the seat for his old Louisville Slugger, which he would need for his long walk up to the cabin. His intent was not to play baseball. He was there because Eugene's ex-wife, Diane, had delivered an invitation from Eugene. The bat was for snakes, of which he had a lifelong terror. And for Rufus, should the need arise.

A.J. had encountered Diane down at Billy's Chevron, where she was pumping gas into the tank of her 1977 Ford LTD. It was long, yellow, and arguably the worst-looking vehicle south of the Mason-Dixon Line. She had taken to driving the relic after her divorce from Eugene. In the settlement, she had received child support, a small but nice house in town, and a nearly new Buick, which later turned up missing, until it was discovered at the bottom of Lake Echota by some scuba-diving Eagle Scouts from Atlanta. So Diane's father fixed up the old LTD and gave it to her until she could see a little better.

Actually, her eyesight was fine, but her salary down at the glove mill wasn't, and Eugene was always behind with his child support payments so Diane had to be careful with her budget. Her lawyer had twice threatened Eugene with garnishment, but these were empty gestures, since most of his income was unreported and stemmed from his brokerage of alcoholic beverages in a county where the enterprise was officially frowned upon.

Eugene's slow payments to Diane were not the result of a problem with cash flow, since large quantities of it flowed right into the house down by the county line where he conducted business. Rather, it was to him a matter of principle to be late. He did what he wanted to do when he wanted to do it. He resembled Johnny Mack in that respect but did not like to have the similarity pointed out.

Diane informed A.J. of Eugene's request for a visit as she was finishing pumping her gas. She then cast him a questioning glance and asked if he intended to visit *the shit head*, a term of endearment she used when referring to her ex-husband. Eugene and A.J. had not seen each other for quite some time since exchanging hard words one bleak evening after Eugene accused A.J. of having the hots for Diane. This was not unusual behavior for Eugene, because he was a jealous man and Diane was an attractive woman.

To be honest, Diane and A.J. had been somewhat attracted to each other in high school, where they had once attempted to consummate their relationship. Technically speaking, both had still been virgins afterward thanks to the high state of excitement achieved by A.J. during the short foreplay period, and a rematch had never been attempted.

"What do you suppose Eugene wants?" A.J. asked, leaning on the fender of Diane's car. It was a calm, cool autumn day. He needed to be heading on to work but had no great urge to do so. He hated his job only slightly less than he would hate watching his children starve. He was not politically astute in the workplace, and the lack of diplomatic acumen had not had an enhancing effect on his career. He was relegated to the nether realms and occupied the position of permanent night shift supervisor at the sawmill.

"He wouldn't say what he wanted," Diane replied. "You know how he is. He just said to tell you that he really needed to talk to you." She leaned up against the LTD beside A.J., sipping on a cold Coke. She was a little over five feet tall and was ten pounds to the right of slim. She was pretty, not beautiful, with the coal-black hair, almond-shaped eyes, and high cheekbones that were common traits in the area. The high valley was once Cherokee land, until Old Hickory himself—Andrew Jackson—had decided the proud mountain and forest tribe would be happier romping on a government reservation in the Oklahoma Territory, which was where he sent them. They left behind their names, their genes, and some of the prettiest country ever stolen by the white eyes.

"Anyway, what are you doing talking to Eugene?" A.J. asked.

"Did hell freeze over?" At the divorce hearing, Diane had specified that date as the next time she would willingly lay eyes on Eugene. She had then gone out to his Jeep parked in front of the courthouse and shot out all four tires plus the spare to finalize the arrangement. The incident caused a stir, but Eugene declined to press charges and the judge admired a spirited woman, so no legalities ensued. Diane had not seen Eugene since. His intermittent child support payments arrived courtesy of the U.S. Mail, in a manner of speaking. Eugene would periodically drive down to the highway and hand over an envelope full of cash to the town's ancient postman, Ogden Abney. Ogden would personally deliver the envelope to Diane later in the day after first removing one dollar for postage.

"No, it didn't freeze, but I could have waited," she said with a ghost of a smile. "The boys wanted to see him." Diane had loved Eugene when they married, but fifteen years of life with him had laid that love in an unmarked grave. She had endured the marriage for the sake of the children until the day Eugene's occasional verbal abuse turned physical and he slammed his fist into the wall beside her head, breaking three knuckles and creating a fairly large hole in the wall. Then he had stormed out of the house.

He had returned three days later feeling sheepish, a feeling that intensified exponentially upon his discovery of a totally empty house. Diane and the boys were gone, as was the furniture, the carpets off the floor, and the light bulbs from the fixtures. Eugene contemplated the sorry state of affairs while consuming a fifth of bourbon and arrived at the conclusion that it was no longer possible to find a good woman, one who would stick by a man. Then he burned the house down. When Diane heard the news, she was

18

surprised to discover that she really didn't care. Her life with Eugene was over. It had ended during the fight when she saw Eugene's fist change trajectory ever so slightly right before it whizzed past her left ear. His gaze at that instant was lethal, as if his eyes were made of cobalt.

"How did the visit go?" A.J. asked Diane. "You didn't shoot out his tires again, did you? I loved that." He smiled and punched her softly on the shoulder.

"No, I didn't have to shoot anything," she replied. "He behaved himself all day. We rode up there last Saturday on Jackie's horses. The boys were really excited about seeing their father."

"I don't guess *you* were all that excited," A.J commented. He looked up and noted a small flock of geese tacking across the azure sky.

"You know for a fact I didn't want to go up there," she replied, shrugging. "But I can't keep the boys away from him forever. It was a strange day. He actually spoke to me a little, and he was good with the boys the whole time. They went fishing down in the canyon, and later on he showed them how to shoot. Do you remember his matched pair of shotguns? The ones he bought in Memphis? He gave one to each of the boys. Later, when we got to the bottom of the mountain, Cody handed me an envelope. He said his daddy told him to give it to me after we were down." She looked over at A.J. "There was five thousand dollars in that envelope and a note telling me to make sure the boys had a real good Christmas." She shook her head. Her long hair blew gently in the breeze.

"You're sure you were at Eugene's place?" A.J. asked. "Maybe you went up the wrong mountain." A.J. thought it was unlikely, but so was the Big Bang, and it had certainly received its share of the press.

"No, it was him," she replied. "I know the face. He looked bad, though, like maybe he's been sick." They were quiet for a moment. Then she spoke again. "I'm just not used to him acting nice. It hasn't come up that often."

"Maybe he's trying to win you back," A.J. suggested. "A girl could do worse than a nice cabin, two custom shotguns, and envelopes full of money lying around everywhere."

"The cabin is not that nice, there are not enough envelopes in the world, and I'd end up using both shotguns on him. No thanks." She seemed adamant.

"Well, I guess that's your choice," A.J. said dubiously. He shrugged. "So, what did you do all day while Eugene played with the boys?"

"I sat on the porch and read my book. Rufus sat and watched." The book in question was Diane's dog-eared copy of *The Happy Hooker*, a cult classic she had been reading for about fourteen years. A.J. once saw her finish the saga, shut the book for a moment, then open it back up to page one and begin again. Out of curiosity, he had also read the book, and although it contained some compelling passages, he was relieved to discover he had no compulsive urge to reread the tome for eternity.

"Rufus was there?" A.J. asked. He disliked Rufus and had heard he was dead. He was disappointed to hear it wasn't so. "You're lucky that dog didn't drag off one of the horses."

"I don't know why you don't like Rufus," Diane replied, opening the car door and climbing in. "He's really a pretty good dog."

"Call me sensitive," A.J. said, shutting the door for her. "I don't like him because every time I see him he tries to kill me." It was true. Rufus had been the scourge of the food chain up on Eugene's Mountain for a long, long time, but the only human he ever bothered was A.J. Small children could ride the dog like a pony, but he transformed into the Hound of the Baskervilles if he ever caught A.J.'s scent.

"He *doesn't* seem to care for your company all that much," Diane agreed, firing up the old LTD. It chugged quietly, sending up light blue exhaust to foul the clear mountain air. "Maybe you could take him a biscuit or something," she proposed. "You know, make friends with him."

"I'd rather just keep on hating him," A.J. said. "We're both used to it, and I don't like new things."

Diane waved and motored off.

A.J. crossed the cracked concrete in front of the garage. He raised the lid of the old cold drink box, dropped in two quarters, and retrieved a grape Nehi that was mostly slush. He sat on the weathered bench in front of Billy's to sip and consider. A.J. put a lot of store in fate, and as fate would have it, the bad blood with Eugene had been heavy on his mind. He had already decided prior to his encounter with Diane that a visit to his old friend was in order. It was time to bury the hatchet.

I see a new preacher in your future.

—Excerpt of posthumous letter from Eugene Purdue to

the deacons of the Hog Liver Road Baptist Church

A.J. STOOD UNDER THE HANGING-TREE AT THE FOOT
of Eugene's Mountain on the early autumn Saturday morning. It
was cool, almost brisk, and the sky that could be seen through the
canopy of trees was clear. He leaned the Louisville Slugger up
against the hanging-tree and lit a cigarette. For whatever reason,
he had decided to go see Eugene.

The hanging-tree was a huge old oak with a large limb jutting
perpendicular to the trunk about twenty feet from the ground. Legend had it that two Yankees had gotten themselves hung there back
during the unfortunate period of time when William Tecumseh
Sherman, the Anti-Christ, was burning Georgia to the ground. A
local farmer and his wife had been murdered, and two young men
unlucky enough to be wearing blue and unwary enough to be sleeping away from their weapons had been apprehended by several of
the local worthies and charged with the murder. The fact that both
men and their regiment had been fighting sixty miles to the north

at Chickamauga when the crime was committed did not alter the outcome of their trial, although a pause of several seconds occurred when the information was revealed.

The dilemma was resolved by Spartan Cook, unofficial prosecutor at the affair. He had acquired a great deal of legal expertise during his many court appearances, and even though he had always been on the receiving end of justice, he was deferred to on matters of law at the current proceedings. It was decided the two villains had no doubt murdered several farmers and their wives up in Chickamauga, and they surely would have committed the local crimes, as well, if someone had not beaten them to it. The fair and speedy trial had concluded shortly thereafter.

A.J. began his slow journey up to Eugene's cabin. The battered but proud Louisville Slugger was his walking stick as he made his way. He moved silently through the north Georgia mountains, as quiet as a stolen kiss. It was a talent he had always had, to pass unseen and unheard through the wild places. His father attributed the knack to the trace of Cherokee blood flowing in A.J.'s veins, and a rustle and a shadow were all that marked his passage. As he reached the midpoint of his journey, he tightened his grip on the bat and swung it up on his shoulder. He was sure Rufus was already stalking him and had no doubt his perennial foe would join him presently. He listened carefully, and as he rounded the bend in the old road he heard a twig snap. He whirled and assumed the batter's-up position. Running straight at him from behind was Rufus. Their eyes met, and they froze.

"Come on over here, boy, and get some of this," A.J. said quietly, not taking his eyes off the hound for an instant. Rufus lowered to a crouch, teeth bared. His eyes emanated malice. Then he blinked and lowered his head to his front paws, conceding the round to A.J.

Rufus's specific lineage was unclear, but he appeared to be a cross between a Great Dane and a bear. He was as big as a small Shetland and covered with scars. His hair grew in patches around the scar tissue, and his eyes were yellow and bloodshot. A.J. likened the dog to a creation by Dante on LSD. He was a hound from hell, and A.J. had no doubt that if Rufus ever got hold of him, there wouldn't be much left to bury, except maybe a half-eaten shoe or a few small pieces of the Louisville Slugger.

A.J. backed up slowly, then turned and headed on his way. Rufus stayed where he was and watched. It was always that way, as if the dog was just letting A.J. know he was still around, waiting for the day when his foe forgot to be cautious. For the life of him, A.J. couldn't remember any incident that might explain the dog's ire. It didn't really matter much, anyway. The ritual of defending his life had evolved into a routine nuisance, akin to paying taxes, going to the dentist, or listening to his neighbor, Estelle Chastain, talk about the hard old days when her long-suffering and now-deceased Parm had gone off to fight the Hun, leaving her, a mere girl of seventeen, pregnant but still petite, mind, to fend for herself for two long, cold, lonely years.

A.J. entered the homestretch, the last quarter mile of his trek to Eugene's home. Just ahead was a wide place in the trail, and parked there, rusting peacefully, was The Overweight Lover. It was a 1965 Chrysler Imperial with fine Corinthian leather interior and a 440 cubic-inch motor. It sat where it had finally died and, in A.J.'s opinion, this was hallowed ground. The car was green and wide, and it had *The Overweight Lover* hand-painted in Gothic script across the tops of both the front and back windshields. Eugene had purchased the Lover complete with lettering back in the days when pre-owned vehicles were simply used cars. He made the acquisition because he needed another motor for his little hot rod, but his plans changed dramatically when the old Chrysler hit 128 mph during the trip home. Eugene held great admiration for speed in those days, and since the Lover handled better than his Dodge Charger ever had, he parked the smaller car in favor of the touring sedan.

"How long would you say this car is?" A.J. had asked Eugene upon his first glimpse those many years past. "Thirty, maybe thirty-five feet? Nice wide whitewalls, too." He was standing by the car, hands in pockets, lightly kicking at one of the tires as if he were a potential buyer.

"Don't talk about my car," Eugene had replied from under the dash. He was in the preferred position for eight-track tape-player installation, upside down with his legs hanging over the back of the front seat.

"What name would you put on this shade of green?" A.J. had continued, running his hand down the front fender. "I've seen this before, somewhere." He was enjoying himself. He had been listening for some time to Eugene's derisive comments about his own humble vehicle, a 1963 Chevrolet Impala that Eugene called the Hog Farm. So A.J. had been praying for a vehicle of the Lover's pedigree to appear.

"I told you to quit talking bad about my car," Eugene said, sitting up while he plugged in a Led Zeppelin tape to try the stereo. Jimmie Page and Robert Plant sounded like they were gravely ill.

26

"Led Zeppelin is a little raw for an automobile of this stature," A.J. had observed, reaching into the ice chest for a beer. Eugene gave him a hard stare. Then he secured a beer of his own and began to wash the car. When he got around to the windows, A.J. noted that they could probably scrape the name off with a razor blade.

"You have got to be kidding," Eugene had said, looking at A.J. with disbelief. "The name is the best part."

A.J. emerged from his reverie of times dead and gone and smiled a little wistfully as he passed. He felt strangely happy to see the old Lover again. It was a monument to simpler days. Even now, long past her glory and rusting away on the side of Eugene's Mountain, The Overweight Lover was one of a kind.

A.J. entered the clearing that held Eugene's cabin, a euphemistic term for an assortment of structures and objects that had been tacked together over the years. The core of the abode was a Ford school bus he and Eugene had accidentally acquired late one night many years upstream of the present. They were seniors in high school, and they were busy on that fateful evening borrowing a little gasoline from each of the school buses parked behind the school gym.

This activity was considered to be entrepreneurship rather than theft by all the local boys, and Eugene and A.J. were up in the rotation on the night in question. As they were siphoning the last bus, Eugene discovered the keys hanging in the ignition. They both pondered the development briefly before deciding to borrow and hide the bus for a couple of days prior to easing it back into the bus line when no one was looking. They agreed that this course would be a good joke on Slim Neal, the local policeman, who would be quite upset by a missing school bus. In retrospect, it turned out to be one of those deals that looked really good on paper but in actual fact should have been reconsidered.

But A.J. and Eugene were young and foolish, so they took the bus. A.J.'s partner in crime suggested the perfect place to hide it would be in the big clearing up on top of the mountain. The road had been recently scraped, and they figured they should be able to get the bus up there. Eugene drove, and A.J. followed along in the Hog Farm, and they were both nearly overcome with the hilarity of it all.

When they arrived at school the next morning, they were faced with the realization that some people did not have their appreciation for fine humor. Slim Neal was livid, and there were times during the day when it seemed he might combust. He had called in the county sheriff, Red Arnold, to help with the investigation.

Red was a law enforcement official from the old school and had acquired the reputation over time of shooting first and not bothering much with the questions later. The state police arrived before noon, and the Georgia Bureau of Investigation rolled in shortly thereafter. Slim had waited all of his life for the opportunity to use his CRIME SCENE—DO NOT CROSS tape, so the area was roped off and diligently patrolled by an armed and dangerous Leon Neal, Slim's brother and erstwhile deputy for the day.

Around one o'clock Slim started talking about bringing in a brace of bloodhounds, and Eugene and A.J. knew they had a deteriorating situation on their hands. Their joke had developed significant technical difficulties, and when they heard that a citizen's patrol had been organized to keep an eye on the gas tanks, they realized it was going to be no easy task to return the bus. Both of their fathers had joined the patrol, and they figured that Johnny Mack, at least, would have them sent down to the state prison at Reidsville as a character-building exercise if he caught them. So, since there appeared to be no other viable options open to them, they kept the bus.

"What the hell are we going to do with it?" Eugene asked a few days later. They stood in the clearing on the mountain and viewed their handiwork.

"We could turn it into a snow-cone stand, but I don't know how much business we'd get up here," A.J. replied, staring at that yellow embodiment of ten-to-twenty if they got caught. "Maybe we should run it on into the woods and cover it up with brush," he continued, thinking this action might prove useful should Slim decide to use aerial reconnaissance.

"I can't believe we stole a school bus," Eugene said, shaking his head. But there it sat, quiet testimony to questionable judgment and bad luck.

As time passed, it became fairly common knowledge around town that the master bedroom of Eugene's cabin was the infamous missing bus. It was a tribute to Slim Neal's investigative expertise that he was perhaps the only person in north Georgia who had no idea where it was, although Eugene considered it sporting to give him the occasional hint.

As the bus became absorbed into the cabin, architectural necessity dictated the removal of some of its parts. These extra pieces would invariably work their way down the mountain and onto Slim's front porch. A.J. had urged Eugene to discontinue the practice, but the temptation was too strong. Thus, every so often, Slim would step out with his morning coffee and stumble over a tire, or perhaps a fender. One time the engine was sitting there, cold black oil oozing all over Slim's *Protected by Smith and Wesson* doormat. He invariably had a bad day after one of these discoveries, and it was best to avoid him until he had regained his composure.

As A.J. neared the cabin, he saw Eugene sitting on the ramshackle front porch, rocking gently in an old rocker. He was methodically loading the Navy Colt his grandfather had left him, the same one that had dispatched Charles Fox in the previous century. Loading the Colt was a complicated business, and he did not seem to notice A.J.'s arrival.

Eugene's appearance was startling. His shoulder-length white hair was in desperate need of a combing. His long white beard hung to his chest and was reminiscent of Rip Van Winkle's whiskers. There was translucence to his skin, as if the full light of afternoon was shining through. As he sat there on his front porch, he reminded A.J. of an Old Testament prophet, a modern-day Elijah perched atop Mount Eugene, preparing to read the Law to the unworthy and to enforce it, if necessary, with the Navy Colt.

A.J. cleared his throat to warn of his approach, then stepped up on the porch. Eugene continued loading, and A.J. viewed his surroundings.

An old wooden cable spool sat between the two chairs on the porch and served as an end table. Its contents included a quart of bourbon, several pill bottles, a scattering of loading supplies, one of the Lover's hubcaps that was spending its golden years as an ashtray, and an open can of gunpowder. A cigarette was burning in the hubcap like a slow fuse. A.J. reached down and removed the cigarette from the vicinity of the gunpowder. Eugene looked up from his work and gestured at the other chair, an oversized rocker. He had taken a liking to it one night on Slim's porch and had swapped a bus hood for it. A.J. sat.

Eugene finished loading the cylinder and slid it into the pistol. He raised the big pistol, cocked it, and took careful aim at the hackberry tree across the clearing. A.J. was gently tapping the porch rail with the bat while keeping a casual eye on the revolver. Eugene squeezed off a round at the hackberry tree. Bark flew.

"Ten dollars says I can hit that tree six out of six times," Eugene said. He rocked gently in his chair. A.J. looked at the tree. It was riddled.

"Why are you shooting the tree?" A.J. asked. Eugene shot again. It was a hit.

"That's two," he said. He took a short sip from the bourbon bottle before lighting a replacement cigarette. "So how about it? Ten dollars on six out of six? I'll even shoot left-handed." He had won a tidy sum over the years with this inducement. Since he was left-handed, it was not the sporting proposition it appeared to be.

"A ten-dollar bet would put you under too much pressure," A.J. observed. "If you missed, you might decide to shoot me to get out of paying. But if you need the money, I'll give you ten dollars to shoot Rufus."

"It would take a cold son of a bitch to shoot his own dog for ten dollars," Eugene said, again putting his cigarette down in the hubcap and drawing a bead on the tree. He fired four more shots. The doomed hackberry shuddered, as if it could see its own short, sad future. "Make it twenty and I'll call him up here." He removed the spent cylinder and slipped a loaded replacement into the pistol. His movements were sure.

"How about if I pay you the twenty and just shoot him myself?" A.J. asked, reaching over to again remove a lit cigarette from the vicinity of the gunpowder. Eugene was a grown man and could blow himself up if he wanted to, but it would have to wait until A.J. left.

"You know," Eugene said, lighting yet another one, "if you're out of smokes, I'd be glad to spot you a pack." He took a deep drag before placing the cigarette in the hubcap. A.J. realized he was dealing with an immovable object so he picked up the can of gunpowder and moved it to the opposite end of the porch.

"No, I've got cigarettes. I just don't want to get fried. Also, I'd like to find out why you called me up here. Have you decided to forgive me for whipping your tail?"

"Whipping *my* tail? Shit, what are you talking about? I was all over you like a cheap suit. I was on you like white on rice. I whipped you so bad your *kids* had black eyes." He leaned back in his chair, obviously enjoying his own use of metaphor.

"You forgot *like a dog on a pork chop*," A.J. replied. "I must have given you a concussion."

In truth, it had not been much of a fight at all. A.J. and Eugene had been at the annual volunteer fireman's barbecue and beer bust, and the leader of the organization, Honey Gowens, had done his usual excellent job of arrangement. Many fine young hogs had unwillingly given up their ribs to fuel the day's events, and there was enough cold beer in the keg to extinguish a three-alarm blaze. Honey had arranged for a bluegrass band to play and had gone to the trouble to bring in his brother-in-law as a guest speaker. He was a real fireman down in Birmingham and had come up to give the men a talk on current firefighting techniques. The information was critically important to the members of the squad, since their usual method of dealing with a fire was to arrive late and stand around, slowly shaking their heads while the affected structure burned to the ground. Occasionally they would drag out the hoses and keep an adjacent building from going up, but by and large they were pitiful when it came to putting out fires. Captain Honey—who had made his fortune by marrying it and who had paid for the fire truck—was getting fairly disgusted and had put the squad on probation. If they didn't get some flames extinguished soon, he was going to trade the truck in on a Winnebago, and he and Jerry Ann were going to head out for Yellowstone and all points west.

It may have been the pressure of being on fire probation that caused Eugene to lose his perspective that day, or it may have been the large quantity of cold beer he had consumed. Or it could have been the fact that he was often foolish, a theory many felt held water, A.J. chief among them. In any event, A.J. was talking to T.C. Clark and Skipper Black, accomplished fire-watchers both, when up stormed Eugene with murder in his eye.

"Right here in front of the whole damn town," he said, voice full of menace. "Did you think I wouldn't see? Did you think I didn't know what was going on?" He had moved in close to A.J.

"What do you think is going on?" A.J. asked. He figured Eugene was drunk, which he was, and that he was having his little joke, which he wasn't.

"Don't try that shit with me!" Eugene spoke loudly. A small crowd had gathered. "I saw you and Diane together. I saw you touch her arm!" Now A.J. knew what the fuss was about. Eugene had seen him talking to Diane a few minutes earlier. During the conversation, A.J. had apparently inadvertently touched her arm. It was Eugene's opinion that payment for the transgression was due.

"You're not serious, right?" A.J. asked. "I touched Skipper's arm a minute ago, too. Do you think I'm screwing *him*?" Skipper was uncomfortable with this analogy and brushed at his arm as he edged away.

"What I think is that I'm going to break your damn head!" Eugene yelled, sounding like he meant business.

"Eugene, nothing happened," A.J. said emphatically. "Diane was asking about a job for her brother. Period." Diane's brother had a history of being discriminated against by various employers, most of whom seemed to unfairly want some work out of him between paydays.

"Period *this*," Eugene said as he swung a roundhouse right that loosened one of A.J.'s molars but did not knock him down as Eugene had intended. Then Eugene had troubles of his own as A.J. smacked him open-palmed over both ears before dealing him a sharp blow to the sternum. Eugene hit the ground hard but was back up in a moment, barreling into A.J.'s midsection. A.J. went over backward with Eugene on top, and they rolled around and swore at each other for another minute or two until several of the boys hauled them apart. Slim Neal arrived and sent them both home; he wanted to run them in, but the big storage room in back of the library that was used as the lockup was occupied at the moment by all three members of the Ladies' Literary Society, who were having their weekly book chat.

Now, three years later, A.J. was sitting on Eugene's porch, and they were slowly becoming accustomed to being in each other's company again. "I may have been . . . hasty . . . at the barbecue," Eugene said, coming as close to an apology as he was genetically able. He looked away as he spoke, up at the sky over the clearing. The moment passed by silent agreement, the tension dissipating like leaf smoke in the fall, an acrid memory on the wind.

"Forget it," A.J. said, realizing the magnitude of Eugene's gesture. "But next time I'm trying to tell you something, listen."

"There won't be a next time," Eugene said vacantly as he continued to study the sky. Then he turned and looked at A.J. "How about a drink of bourbon?" he asked.

"No, it's a little early in the day." Eight to ten hours early, in fact.

"How about a beer, then?"

"A beer would be all right," A.J. said. He really didn't want anything, but his grandmother had raised him to observe the social niceties. He went inside to get the beer. He came back out with two and handed one to Eugene, who opened it and downed about half.

"Nice housekeeping," A.J. said as he sat back down and opened his beer. "There's something alive in the sink. I would have killed it, but I thought it might be a pet."

"It's hard to get good help these days," Eugene explained. "I tried to get Diane to straighten up while she was here the other day, but she didn't seem interested in the idea."

A.J. choked on his beer.

"I bet she loved that," he said, coughing. He watched while Eugene topped off his half-empty beer bottle with most of the remaining bourbon. He then opened up two of the pill bottles,

35

removed several tablets, and washed them down with the alcohol. A.J.'s curiosity got the best of him. "Got the flu?" he asked. Eugene's answer was evasive.

"I have to take them every four hours. Doc Miller said it was very important to be punctual." Eugene was gazing again, seemingly preoccupied. A.J. could not fathom what was on his mind, but he supposed Eugene would spill the beans in his own good time.

"What did Doc say about washing the pills down with boilermakers?" he asked Eugene.

"We didn't actually cover that," came the reply.

"Probably just as well," A.J. conceded. Doc was known to have a touchy streak. "So what's the deal?" A.J. waited for his answer. The silence grew long and oppressive.

Finally, Eugene sighed. When he spoke, his voice was lifeless, as if a rock were talking.

"I have cancer. I'm rotten with it. It's terminal." Eugene stared at his lead-poisoned hackberry tree. His words hung over the clearing like a gas attack over the Argonne. A gentle breeze blew through the branches, but the words would not dissipate. Overhead, a contrail made slow progress against the backdrop of soft sky. A.J. heard Rufus down the mountain, barking. The scene etched itself into his consciousness, the sights and sounds permanently fixed in blacks and whites and shades of grey, as if Currier & Ives had come to high Georgia to find a little work and had walked up to the clearing in their tight Victorian pants and top hats to capture the moment forever. A.J. did not know what to say, so he said nothing, and stillness reigned.

Finally, Eugene took a ragged breath and turned to A.J. "But

I'm not dead yet," he said. He began fumbling with his reloading supplies. A.J. was subdued as he retrieved the can of gunpowder for his friend. Eugene quickly and efficiently reloaded the spent cylinder. Then he offered the Colt to A.J. "Ten dollars says *you* can't hit the tree six out of six."

"I don't feel like shooting your tree," A.J. said. He knew he should respond to Eugene's revelation, but his mind was blank. Impending death was not his strong suit, and the episode had taken on aspects of the surreal. He looked over at Eugene, who was staring down at the Colt in his lap.

"How long?" he asked. It was the inevitable question.

"Six months," Eugene replied. "Maybe less. Doc Miller says he can't be sure. It started in my pancreas, but now it's all over." He spoke matter-of-factly, like he was talking about an outbreak of crabgrass. He looked at A.J. "Of all the things in the world that could have killed me, I never thought it would be my fucking pancreas."

"You're not taking Doc's word for all of this, are you?" A.J. asked. He felt the need to find a solution for Eugene's problem. "You need to let someone else take a look."

Doc Miller was the local physician. He was pushing eighty and still a pretty fair hand at setting a broken arm or sewing up a cut leg. He had relocated from somewhere in New York about thirty years ago, and the people of the town had been so overjoyed to have a doctor they chose to overlook the fact that Doc was a Yankee. Over the ensuing years, vile rumors worked their way south, tales of bitter lawsuits and large malpractice settlements. The townspeople's view was that nobody was perfect, and Doc had always taken pretty good care of all of *them*. Still, medical science had made great strides in fifty years, and it was A.J.'s hope that Eugene might receive a different diagnosis and a less-final prognosis from someone who had attended medical school *since* the Roosevelt years.

"No, Doc sent me down to Emory for tests." Eugene swallowed before continuing. "It's official. I'm dead. I just haven't fallen over yet."

There was no panacea for his malignancy, and he had come back to his mountain to die on his own terms. A.J. watched as Eugene drew a right-handed bead on the hackberry tree and fired. Ambidexterity with firearms was not one of his strengths, and a hole appeared in the windshield of his Jeep.

"Shit," he said. He switched hands and put the other five rounds into the tree.

"You never told me why you're shooting the tree," A.J. said, changing subjects to allow himself time to assimilate.

"It was Doc's idea. He told me that I should have a hobby to take my mind off my troubles."

"I bet he had something like stamp collecting in mind," A.J. said, eyeing yet another cigarette that had slipped in close to the gunpowder. He picked up the can and placed it once again out of harm's way. He thought it was a mercy that Eugene had not decided upon doctor shooting as an alternative pastime. He envisioned the scene. Eugene would walk into the lobby down at Emory with the big Colt stuck in his belt, right up in front like Billy the Kid used to wear his. He would saunter up to the Pink Lady at the information counter. "Oncology, please," he would say, and then all hell would break loose.

"Stamp collecting?" Eugene said, sounding slightly appalled.

He shook his head. "No, I've got a good hobby." He dumped his spent cartridges and began looking around for the gunpowder.

"Your hobby is going to get you blown up," A.J. said.

"I can think of worse ways to go," Eugene replied with certainty, as if he had given the matter considerable thought. A.J. wondered if Eugene was entertaining the notion of getting it over with, just a boom and a flash, quick and clean.

Eugene arose and left the porch. He moved unsteadily across the clearing toward his violated Jeep. A.J. followed. Eugene stood by the Jeep and looked at the hole in the windshield.

"I can't believe I shot my own damn Jeep," he said softly. He looked at A.J. with a slight smile. "If anyone asks, we'll tell them that Slim did it."

"Well, they'd believe that," A.J. said as his own smile appeared.

They were referring to the time Slim Neal had shot the front and back windshields out of John Robert's pickup truck. Eugene and A.J. had been boys of sixteen, and they were riding around one summer night drinking hot beer because they didn't have any ice and hoping the six cans they had would be enough to get the job done. They had just finished a short pit stop up a dirt side road when the misunderstanding occurred. As they were pulling back onto the highway, the back glass exploded in a hail of gunfire and several holes appeared in the front windshield. A.J. slumped down and floored it, heading for town and the protection of Slim. Eugene was hunkered in the right floorboard, cursing and bleeding from a small wound in his left earlobe. It seemed that the pale rider was upon them. Then they heard a siren, and a blue light began to flash. The car chasing them was Slim's cruiser. A.J. pulled over, and Slim was all over them.

"Freeze!" he hollered, approaching the truck slowly behind the barrels of the largest shotgun A.J. had ever seen. Slim eased up to the truck and jerked open the door. Confusion replaced his fierce expression when he realized who occupied the truck.

"What the hell were you boys doing up that road back there?" he demanded, keeping the shotgun aimed in their direction.

"We were taking a leak," Eugene growled from the floorboard. "I can't believe you just shot me for pissing on a dirt road."

"You weren't stealing pigs?" Slim asked, lowering the ten-gauge a little.

"Do you see any pigs?" A.J. asked. He had a lot of fairly unexplainable truck damage to explain when he got home and was becoming cranky now that another sunrise seemed to be in his future. "Eugene, you got any pigs down there with you?"

"Nope."

"Goddamn," Slim said quietly. He lowered the shotgun all the way. "A.J., take Eugene down to Doc Miller's and get his ear fixed. I'll go talk to your folks."

It turned out there had been a rash of hog thefts in the area, and Slim had received an anonymous pork tip earlier in the day. He was a man who would not tolerate pig theft, and even *suspected* pig theft would be dealt with harshly. When A.J. and Eugene pulled up the side road that led to Rabbit Brown's barn, they had no idea they were under Slim's zealous scrutiny. When they stopped to relieve themselves, he had vaulted into action. The real swine thief was busy at the time stealing fifteen hogs from Slim.

When Slim attempted to explain the mishap to Eugene's father,

Johnny Mack spoke no word. He simply stepped into the house for a moment and returned with his twelve-gauge and a box of shells. Slim executed a quick retreat as Johnny Mack stood on the porch, slowly loading the pump shotgun. The luckless constable fared no better when he talked to A.J.'s father. John Robert Longstreet was a man of few syllables and spent only one on Slim Neal.

"Git," he said, pointing to the road. Slim got.

Slim was fired over the incident, but he was reinstated two months later when no one else could be found to take the job for what it paid. The town council extracted his solemn promise to only shoot at confirmed perpetrators in the future. Then they returned his badge after knocking from his wage the price of the new glass in John Robert's truck. Johnny Mack attempted to whip Eugene over the incident, because the boy should have been home reading the Bible and not out peeing on Rabbit Brown's pigs. The whipping didn't go well, however, due to Eugene's objections over being punished for getting shot while urinating on a dirt road. John Robert didn't try to whip A.J., but the incident indicated to him that the boy had way too much spare time on his hands. Thus A.J. spent all his free time during the following several weeks replacing rotten fence posts around the back field at the farm.

"If you get to needing to pee while you're out there, just drag her out and let her rip," John Robert said, chuckling at his merry joke. "Just make sure your granmama's not around."

But those were the old times, long gone and mostly forgotten. Eugene and A.J. stood by the Jeep in the clearing and admired Eugene's handiwork. Rufus trotted up and flopped down, panting. He seemed tired, and A.J. supposed he had been killing something large. The dog eyed A.J. for a moment, dismissed him, and laid his head on his paws. In the distance they could hear the thrum of a freight train. The haunting sound of shave-and-a-haircut echoed as the engines approached a crossing.

"I guess you need to be going," Eugene said.

"Yeah," A.J. affirmed, "I don't want to get caught in the woods after dark by your dog." A.J. was feeling an overwhelming urge to place distance between himself and the general vicinity of doom. The clearing held too many problems for him to handle at present. He required time to absorb and consider.

"I need for you to do me a couple of favors," Eugene said, his halting cadence indicating the difficulty he had asking A.J. for help.

"Sure," A.J. said. "Anything you need." It was uncharacteristic of Eugene to request an indulgence. A small dread settled on A.J., a premonition of crisis.

"I would like for you would come back next week," Eugene said. "I don't get much company up here, and it gets a little quiet. You can take the Jeep so it won't be so much trouble getting back up the road."

A.J. felt bad for Eugene.

"Now, that's odd," he said. "I was just about to tell you that I might come up next week and check on you." He was shaking his head as if he could not believe the coincidence. Eugene couldn't believe it, either.

"When it comes to lying," Eugene said, "you really suck."

"You mentioned two favors."

"The other one is kind of large."

"The first one was kind of large," A.J. pointed out. "What is it?"

"When it's time, I want you to kill me." A.J.'s head snapped around as if he had been slapped.

"Run that one by me again." Maybe it was Eugene's idea of a joke.

"You heard me," Eugene said. His tone was so flat A.J. knew it was no jest. They stared at one another momentarily. Then they both looked away. A.J. felt slightly nauseous, as if he had been hit hard in the solar plexus.

"How the hell can you ask me to do that?" he asked.

"I'm asking."

"You must be crazy. If you want to shoot yourself or blow yourself up, go ahead. But leave me out of it." A.J. felt like he was breathing mud. "I know ten or fifteen people who would be happy to accommodate you. Hell, Diane's daddy would *pay* you to let him do it."

"I'd do it for you," Eugene said quietly.

"I'd never ask you to," A.J. said with certainty.

"Never say never," Eugene said with a small sigh. "You don't know what might come up."

"I've got to go," A.J. said abruptly. He had heard enough. He walked across the clearing to retrieve his bat from the porch. Eugene meandered toward the cabin and met A.J. when he returned. They stood like Lee and Grant at Appomattox. Eugene swayed. His pupils were dilated.

"Are you coming back?" he asked.

"Yes," he said. "I'll come back, but I won't kill you."

"Well, I'm batting .500 at least." Eugene said. "Take the Jeep. I'm high all the time, now, and I can't drive it. If I wasn't dying, I'd be having one hell of a good time."

"No, you keep the Jeep. You might run out of something to shoot. I'm going to borrow a bulldozer and clean up that road. Winter is coming, and it's already a mess." A.J. had decided on the spur of the moment that fixing the road was his best alternative to a series of long walks in the Georgia mountains.

"I assume you'll be borrowing the dozer from Jesus Junior," Eugene said, referring to Johnny Mack.

"He's the only one I know who has one," A.J. replied. Eugene seemed to consider this for a moment. Then a smile crossed his face.

"Good luck with that," he said as he walked back onto the porch. A.J. headed on across the clearing and down the trail. As he neared the Lover, he heard six shots ring out, and he knew that Eugene's faithful Jeep, like its owner, had entered its final days.

I got the bus.
—Excerpt of posthumous letter from
Eugene Purdue to Slim Neal

A.J. MADE QUICK WORK OF THE WALK DOWN THE
mountain. He was unsettled. The afternoon had been like a trip
into the Twilight Zone. So much so, in fact, he wouldn't have been
much surprised to find Rod Serling standing in the road, wearing a
black sport coat with narrow lapels, chain smoking and eyeing him
with intensity. He decided to stop at Billy's Chevron for a Coke and
some non-apocalyptic conversation. A dose of normalcy would do
him good after the recent festivities up on the mountain. The establishment sat at the crossroads right outside of town.

"You'll be needin' some tires soon, Will," Billy said, peering at
the rubber on A.J.'s truck. Billy called his male patrons *Will* and his
female customers *Missus*. He was ancient and grizzled. At the moment he was shaking his head, as if he found it hard to believe that a
grown man would run around on such a pitiful set of tires.

"You sold me that set last month," A.J. said, sipping his cold
drink. Billy was an old country boy who had done extremely well

for himself by adhering to the simple belief that every vehicle had some problem that should be repaired by Billy.

"Well, they're wore some," Billy said stubbornly. "Maybe we need to line her up and rotate these front tires while there's a little life left in them."

A.J. was now fully alert.

"We 'lined her up' when we put the tires on," A.J. noted. "Maybe your alignment machine was out of whack." Billy was squatted down, looking at the tires. He scratched his head and lit a slightly bent cigarette. Confusion was etched on his grainy features. As A.J. watched, he saw Billy nod his head twice and look up with certainty in his eye. A resolution had been reached.

"Here's what we need to do, Will," Billy said, standing and dusting his hands on his pants. "Bring her in next week and I'll line her up and rotate those tires. You must've run over a pothole or something and knocked her out."

Actually, it had been a curb. A.J. had vaulted it while avoiding one of Estelle Chastain's more erratic driving maneuvers. But he wasn't telling Billy that.

"Don't you worry," Billy continued. "I'll fix her up good as new."

Ironically, at that moment, A.J. saw Estelle's aged Ford motoring up the highway, running astraddle the broken white line in the middle of the road. All that could be seen of Estelle were two white gloves clenched on the steering wheel and the top of her head, complete with pillbox hat. She peered with myopic eyes in A.J.'s general direction, and he knew it was time to go. He exited after pointing out the danger to Billy, who was no fool and took cover. When Miss Estelle came to town it was every man for himself, vehicular

Darwinism based on survival of the quickest.

In his rearview mirror, A.J. saw Estelle swing into the Chevron in a long, slow arc that left her parked with her right front tire up on the pump island. Billy came out from hiding and squatted in front of Estelle's car—elevated for convenience—and when the venerable mechanic began to slowly shake his head, A.J. knew the game was again afoot.

It was dusk when A.J. arrived home, exhausted. He sat for a moment and gazed at Maggie's Folly, his name for the family manor. He and his wife, Maggie, had bought it thirteen years ago, an abandoned Victorian dwelling that had seen better times. It was built during the days when the wealthy kept summer homes in cool mountain valleys to escape the heat of the city. This particular structure was built by a carpetbagging entrepreneur who had traveled to Georgia in 1866 with the intention of stealing a fortune and living the good life, both of which he managed to do before being shot fatally in a bawdy house by the estranged husband of one of the employees of the establishment. As A.J. sat, he remembered the first time he and Maggie had seen the house.

"I want it," Maggie had said as they walked through the creaking, moldering foyer. "Look at that stained glass! Look at that stairway!" She turned and looked at A.J. "We have to buy it." A.J. thought that ten or fifteen skilled craftsmen could have it whipped into shape in a couple of decades or so, if their luck held and it didn't rain too much.

"Who are you going to get to fix this dump up?" he had asked, but it was token resistance. The deal was done from the moment they walked through the door, and he knew it.

"I didn't marry you for your good looks," Maggie replied, folding her cruel arms around his poor, doomed neck. The house continued its decline momentarily as she kissed A.J. Then they drove down to the bank and arranged to buy it.

They found the bankers to be motivated sellers; they had been in possession of the property for several years and had pretty much given up on ever finding buyers. Then in had walked A.J. and Maggie. The Longstreets signed a promissory note stating they would pay the bank some money every year if they could manage, and that the house should be paid for in twenty years, if that was convenient.

Now a sense of calm descended upon A.J. as looked at the old place. The anxiety brought about by his reunion with Eugene drifted away. He was in his element. He got out of the truck and walked slowly to the house, which had shaped up well. Maggie had been a stern taskmaster while bringing the Folly back from the brink of ruin, and they both had put in many long hours on the project. She stood double duty as construction superintendent and general laborer, and A.J. did everything in between.

A.J. walked past the porch and patted one of the columns. He rounded the corner and saw Maggie and their five-year-old son, J.J., planting chrysanthemums in the side yard. Gardening wasn't coming naturally to the boy, and Maggie was down on her hands and knees trying to help him. Several of the unsuccessful attempts lay scattered about.

It was a Longstreet family tradition to butcher fifty or sixty dollars' worth of flowers each fall and again each spring. These ritual sacrifices were not a pagan rite marking the passage of the seasons. Maggie just wanted a pretty yard. Unfortunately, the ground in the vicinity of the Folly stubbornly refused to support any plant that might possibly bloom. A.J. was the son of a farmer and took personally the fact that he could not get anything worthwhile to grow around his house. He had fertilized, aerated, rotated, watered, and chopped, and still no flowers. Finally, he gave up.

"This must have been an ancient vampire execution ground," he had told Maggie. "The earth has been scorched and sown with salt." He went on to suggest that they continue to buy the plants, anyway, and then just throw them away on the way home, thus cutting out all the work in the middle. "Some farm boy you turned out to be," had been her reply.

"What's up?" A.J. asked as he sat on the ground. Maggie turned and smiled.

"We're killing these flowers," she explained, gesturing with her trowel. "And what we haven't murdered outright," she continued, hiking a thumb in J.J.'s direction, "he has tried to eat." At the moment, J.J. was intent on tamping the dirt around his latest attempt.

"How did the flowers taste?" A.J. asked his son.

"They tasted nasty," the boy answered.

"They probably needed salt," A.J. said, tousling his son's long blond hair. "Run on in and wash up. We'll kill more flowers tomorrow, but right now I need to talk to Mama." J.J. frowned and crossed his arms. Going in was not what he had in mind. A.J. looked over at Maggie. "This boy needs a haircut," he said conversationally. At the mention of the dreaded word, J.J. jumped up and ran toward the house. His little arms were over his head in a protective gesture.

"He sure hates a haircut," A.J. observed as they watched their son go.

"I've never seen anything like it," she replied. They heard the screen door slam. "Except maybe when it's time to take Harper to the dentist." Harper Lee was their eight-year-old middle child and, unfortunately, her first dental experience had been painful. Thus, all subsequent visits to the dentist were like pulling teeth. The problem was so severe the Longstreets had been referred to a pediatric dentist, which is a regular dentist who charges more due to an ability to work on screaming children. They had been faced with this necessity when they discovered Harper Lee was blacklisted at every dental establishment within a fifty-mile radius. "You can't rely on people with slim hands," A.J. had noted upon discovering his daughter had become a *persona non grata* in the dental community.

"You're right," he said, back in the yard with Maggie. "Taking her to the dentist is worse. It's your turn next time." He laid back on the grass to watch the sunset. The sky to the west was passing from dark blue to black. A chill crept into the air.

"How could I forget?" Maggie responded, lying next to him. Together they watched the light fade over the magnolias.

Night fell, and a lone cricket warmed up. It was late in the season, and soon he would be gone. A.J. had briefly forgotten about Eugene's short, bleak future, but now thoughts of him crept in like ghosts. A.J. wondered what Eugene was thinking now that night had descended. He silently wished him well. As if she could read his mind, Maggie spoke.

"Tell me about your visit with Eugene. Was it a social call, or did he want to accuse you of sleeping with some other member of his family?" Maggie did not generally succumb to petty commentary, but she had not cared for the misunderstanding at the barbecue and had made no secret since then of her opinion that Eugene was primarily responsible for the whole sorry affair. Not that A.J. had escaped unscathed. He had caught the rough side of her tongue over the incident and had listened in abashed silence to an hour-long monologue peppered with many a succinct observation.

But the fight was long ago, and Maggie's anger did not last, although references to the event occasionally surfaced as instructional aids. She had even sent A.J. off with her blessing earlier in the day. Of course, she had also given him benediction to brain Eugene with the Louisville Slugger if the necessity arose.

The Longstreets lay there in the deepening darkness, and as the stars flickered into their nightly patterns, A.J. related the details of his visit. He spoke of how Eugene had looked, how he had sounded, and what he had said. But not all of what had been said. He did not mention the second favor Eugene had requested. There was no real reason to withhold this information since he had no intention of complying with the wish, but he could not voice the words. They were too bold and terrible, too cold and final. When A.J. finished the story, they were both quiet.

"Well," Maggie said, breaking the silence. "I don't know what to say." She paused for a moment and then continued. "I haven't had much use for him for a long time. You know that. I think he has been a horrible father to those poor boys and the worst excuse for a husband I have ever seen. He has driven away everyone who ever cared about him, including you. Still, for all of that, I feel really bad for him." She sighed.

"He's been no saint," A.J. agreed. A memory popped into his

head to support the opinion.

They had been at a Little League game, and Eugene had taken it as his fatherly duty to coach his oldest boy on the finer points of the game. This action would have been normal behavior for any father in that setting, but Eugene added a twist when he drove his Jeep through the fence and out to center field to give the boy instruction and encouragement. He was in his cups that day, and it had seemed too far to walk. A.J. had sprinted out and sent the mortified youngster to the dugout with a pat and a reassuring word. Then he had turned to Eugene.

"Do you know what hubris is?" he had asked.

"No," Eugene had said. "What is hubris?"

"Hubris," A.J. had replied, "is when God screws you over for being a smartass. Move the Jeep." The words A.J. had spoken in the outfield now rang in his ears.

"Who knows about this?" Maggie asked.

"I get the impression that you, me, Doc Miller, and the Emory boys are the long list," A.J. said.

"Do you think he intends to tell his family?" Maggie asked. "He can't just die and disappear. Diane and the boys need to know. He owes them a chance to say good-bye."

"Who knows what he's thinking?" A.J. was privy to Eugene's strategic plan, but he was unclear on the smaller, tactical details, and Eugene tended toward a random logic that made his actions difficult to predict.

"When you go back up to see him," Maggie said, "try to find out what his plans are for informing his family." A.J. was silent. "Whoops," she said, looking at him. "I'm sorry. I was assuming you were going back. Are you?"

"I suppose I am," A.J. said with reluctance. "I don't want to, but I said I'd do it. To be honest, I don't want anything to do with this. I don't want to see him dying, and I don't want to see him dead. I must be a coward." He had developed a bad headache, his lifelong habit when dealing with cosmic no-win situations. He rubbed his temples in the darkness.

"Well," she said after a moment, "I'd really be worried about you if you were looking forward to it. And you're not a coward. You're just a little more honest than most men." She reached over and patted his chest. "Which isn't saying that much, really."

As he was about to respond, they were interrupted by a commotion coming from the house. The screen door slammed and Harper Lee's voice came to them across the gloaming.

"Mama! Emily says I'm adopted." Emily Charlotte was the Longstreet's oldest child at eleven years. In a break with a tradition that had been handed down from mother to daughter for generations in Maggie's family, Emily Charlotte was named after not one but two of her mother's favorite authors, the Bronte sisters. A.J. was unaware of this unusual family tradition when he married Maggie but probably would have taken her to love, honor, and obey anyway, had he known. The other two children, Harper Lee and J.J. (short for James Joyce, much to A.J.'s dismay), had to resign themselves to being living tributes to only one of Maggie's cherished writers. Emily took every opportunity to point out this literary shortcoming to her siblings, because it was her job to torment her younger brother and sister. It was a duty she took seriously.

Maggie, born Margaret Mitchell, had been named by her

mother, Jane Austen Callahan, after the celebrated author of *Gone with the Wind,* a self-help manual that dealt with the subject of how best to cope with Yankees when they venture south.

"Mama? Daddy? Am I adopted?" Harper's voice had a small quaver in it.

"Absolutely not," A.J. replied. "We got you the regular way. Mama and I went down to the hospital and picked you out. Emily, on the other hand, we bought from a roving band of Gypsies. We gave nineteen dollars for her, back when that was a lot of money. We wouldn't have paid so much, but we really wanted a son. Emily was the only boy they had, so they charged extra."

"But Emily is a girl'" Harper protested.

"Well, sure, now she's a girl. But she was a boy when we bought her. She changed when she caught the chicken pox right after we brought her home. I looked all over for those Gypsies to get my money back, but they were long gone."

"Really, Daddy?"

"Absolutely. I have a receipt around here somewhere." Harper was very quiet. Then Maggie and A.J. heard the screen slam as she ran inside to discuss genealogy with her older sister. A.J. got up from the ground and dusted off. Then he offered his hand to his partner in child procurement.

"I wish you wouldn't tell her things like that," Maggie said as she stood beside him. "She believes every word you say." They walked toward the house.

"I guess we had better feed them before they turn mean on us," A.J. said. They stopped on the porch.

"Are you feeling better about Eugene?" she asked.

"A little better," he replied. "Not great, but better. I will do what I can. It wouldn't be decent to leave him hanging. Thank you for straightening me out."

"I've been straightening you out since the night we met," she observed. "I view it as my life's work. I just wish it paid a little better."

Maggie and A.J. first met fresh out of high school while working the third shift at a cotton mill famous for its denim products and its abuse of the hired help. A.J. could recall these days as clearly as if he were watching a Movietone Newsreel of his own life, complete with humorous clips, mugs for the camera, and narration by Lowell Thomas. The clarity of his memories was no doubt influenced by the altered states of awareness he achieved throughout most of the period. Unlike Eugene, he did not favor drugs; his main weakness was alcohol, and between the ages of sixteen and nineteen he had been attempting to drink himself to death before his invitation arrived to visit exciting tropical climes and get shot. Luckily for A.J. and Eugene, Richard Nixon was, at this point in history, coming to the belated conclusion that it was not possible to subdue Asiatic peoples through warfare by attrition.

A.J. was sober the night he met his future wife. He had seen Maggie around the mill previous to their first meeting and had admired from afar her obvious grace, intelligence, and poise, all of which he had inferred from the way she filled her blue jeans. He had been hoping that the chance to introduce himself would arise, and when that opportunity presented itself, he was quick to realize his time had come.

A.J. was operating his forklift on that fateful evening when he noticed Maggie engaged in a discussion with the shift supervisor,

Clyde Cordele. She seemed to be agitated, but Clyde was smiling and nodding and did not seem perturbed in the least. Then Clyde reached over and touched her shoulder. A.J. walked toward the pair. As he neared their vicinity, Maggie knocked Clyde's arm out of the way, and he again reached over and touched her shoulder. Maggie again knocked the offending arm away, then balled her fist and drew it back. It was this defiant gesture that caused A.J. to fall in love with her, or at least that's what he always said. She cut a fine and formidable figure. A.J. was close enough by then to hear her next words, and they were eloquent.

"If you touch me again, Pillsbury," she said, "I'll knock your teeth down your throat." There was cold steel in her voice and fire in her eye. All of Clyde's employees called him *Pillsbury* due to his uncanny resemblance to the famous doughboy of the same name. It was a tribute to Clyde's intellect that he never realized the insult and believed instead the name was a term of endearment.

There was never much doubt in anyone's mind, excluding upper management, about the shortage of anything vaguely resembling common sense in Clyde Cordele. Any shred of confusion lingering on the subject was cleared up on the night A.J. first met Maggie. Clyde stood facing her, smiling and mulling his alternatives. He had been warned and should have retired from the field. But it is one of Nature's immutable laws that a snake does not know how to be anything but a snake, and Clyde could not overcome his own DNA. So he reached over for one more try. He was one surprised doughboy, however, when he realized it was a different shoulder he was holding. A.J. had slipped between Maggie and Clyde at the opportune moment and was now looking into the latter's confused eyes.

"You had better let go of my shoulder," A.J. said. "You know how people around here talk."

"Longstreet, you goddamn hippie," Clyde hollered with color in his cheeks, "get your ass back on your job, and get it over there now! This ain't none of your affair!" A.J. had been suspecting his budding career in textiles wasn't truly important to him, so it was with no great distress that he decided to plow into Clyde like a Massey-Ferguson tractor into a new row.

"She isn't interested," A.J. said. "She probably has religious convictions against consorting with farm animals." That one really got to Clyde. His face turned blood red, and his mouth began to make random movements. At that moment, he resembled the Pillsbury dough fish. Behind A.J., Maggie cleared her throat. Then she lightly tapped her uninvited hero's shoulder.

"Uh, look, whoever you are," she said, her soft drawl a melody of syllables to A.J.'s ears, "I appreciate that you are trying to help me, but I can take care of this. Really." A.J.'s shoulder tingled as if burned.

"I know you can," A.J. said, not removing his eyes from his opponent. "But let me." He had arrived at another crossroads, but none of his possible avenues were clearly marked.

"You're going to get yourself fired," Maggie said in a dubious tone, but the nobility of his action was strangely appealing. White knights had all but gone the way of the passenger pigeon and the two-dollar haircut, and the novelty of meeting a real live one at 3:00 a.m. in a cotton mill was refreshing.

"He's not going to fire me," A.J. said, although in his heart he didn't believe it. But the die was cast, and there would be no turning back. If it came down to unemployment before dishonor, then so be it.

"You're fired!" Pillsbury hollered.

"I probably am," A.J. said, "but you're not going to be the one to do it. I want to sit down with Howard Hoyt in the morning and talk to him. If he says I'm fired, then I'm fired." Howard Hoyt was the mill manager. He had been known upon occasion to be a fair man, but he was not obsessive about it.

"*I* said you're fired, goddamn it, and I'm callin' Security right now to get your ass off the property!" Clyde was panting.

"Go ahead," A.J. responded. "Call Uncle Luke down here and let's see who he decides to shoot." His mother's oldest brother had been the night shift security guard at the mill for years, which left his days free for farming. Unfortunately, A.J. was not his favorite nephew due to a boyish prank that had once cost Luke one of his barns. A.J. hoped Clyde would not call his bluff, because he sensed it could go either way upon his uncle's arrival. Luke had really liked that barn.

Pillsbury was quiet for a moment. Then he turned abruptly and walked toward his office.

"Both of you be in Howard's office at eight o'clock!" he hollered over his shoulder as he stomped off, as if it had been his idea all the time. A.J. felt another tap on his shoulder and turned to greet his Lady Guenivere. He intended to be humble and assure her thanks were not in order; he would have done it for anyone.

"That certainly went well," she said. There was a tone in her voice he could not identify, one that did not sound like undying gratitude. "You came barreling in here like a wild bull to defend the honor of a total stranger, got in a fight with our boss, and got yourself fired. Probably me, too. Did I miss anything, or does that cover it?" Her manner was arch and her arms were crossed.

"I guess if you want to take the short view, then that about covers it," A.J. replied, abashed. He wondered what was happening. This initial meeting was not going as he had hoped. He would be the first to admit his plan had been skimpy, but it had been a plan, and Pillsbury was no longer bothering her. He was hard pressed to understand why she seemed miffed. He decided he should just leave, but he could not take his eyes off of her.

She was tall with piercing green eyes that radiated intelligence. Her shoulder-length brown hair was curly and thick, and A.J. wanted nothing more out of life at that moment than to reach out and touch it. Luckily, he realized—even as smitten as he was—that this would have been a grave error given the circumstances. Her beauty was a positive energy that flowed from within. Hers was an old soul, and a fine one, and it had without question been around the wheel many times.

"It's not that I'm locked into taking the short view," she told A.J. "I'm just having trouble seeing the bigger picture." She looked at him another moment, then let him off the hook. "Since we're going to be fired together in a couple of hours, I think we should introduce ourselves," she said. "My name is Maggie Callahan." She was smiling as they shook hands.

"Yes, ma'am," he replied, seeking the haven of civility, a time-honored tactic of Southern men when confronted with formidable women. "My name is Arthur John Longstreet," he said, "but everybody calls me A.J. Except old Clyde. You heard what he calls me."

Maggie smiled.

"You don't like him?" she asked.

"You must be psychic," he said, shaking his head in admiration of her exceptional observation.

"Neither do I," she admitted. "I should have been promoted to day shift three months ago, but he keeps holding me back."

"He's a real gem," A.J. said. He looked into her eyes, and it was like looking into green eternity.

"Well," she said, "we will deal with him in the morning. Or try to, anyway." She shrugged. "We should get back to work, although I don't suppose it matters much now. Thank you for trying to help me." She stood on tiptoe and kissed his cheek, and then she was gone. The sweetness of that one kiss lingered and would be with him until he was no more.

Many problems were resolved when Howard Hoyt arrived the next morning. He sat and listened to all three versions of events, and then he efficiently made short work of the whole situation. He first told Maggie she must have misunderstood Clyde's intentions and apologized on his behalf for any unpleasantness the confusion may have caused. Then he told her that the day shift job she was seeking was not going to be filled at present, after which he sent her home with an admonishment to refrain from spreading unfounded rumors. She sat quietly through her portion of the chat, but as she stood to leave, she calmly informed Howard that she did not consider the matter resolved. Having watched her glare throughout his monologue, Howard had no doubts he would be hearing from the Callahan girl again.

After Maggie left, Howard turned to Clyde and began to chew

him loud and long on the apparently related subjects of compromising positions and absolute stupidity. A.J. sat there and thought it odd that he was being given the opportunity to view the show. But he was fairly quick on the uptake, and it took only a moment to figure the score and realize which long-haired forklift driver was on the losing team. Still, he had expected it, so it did not trouble him greatly. He settled back and enjoyed the scene as Clyde was drawn and quartered by Howard Hoyt. After about thirty minutes of verbal abuse, however, even A.J. began to feel bad for Clyde. He would not have thought this possible and figured he would get over it presently.

Howard continued his tirade until his voice became hoarse. Then he sent Clyde home with instructions to return the following morning. He was now first shift supervisor so he could be watched.

Howard and A.J. sat alone in the office. Howard looked up at him over glasses that had slid down to the tip of his nose. "I let you hear that because I wanted you to know your former supervisor was dead wrong," he said. "You risked a great deal to do the right thing." A.J. looked at Howard, and the mill manager could not hold the gaze.

"But I'm fired, right?"

"You're fired," Howard agreed. He picked up a pad and pen and wrote down a name and a phone number. "This man is a friend of mine who runs the little mill over at Dogtown. Call him later today. I'll have it arranged so you can start work tonight."

He handed the slip of paper over to A.J., who took it because he didn't know what else to do. It seemed Howard was going to great lengths to soften the blow, and he appreciated it, but the fact loomed large that the man who should have been axed had just been promoted to day shift. It was a poor excuse for justice, a sort of anti-justice that A.J. did not understand. He was tender in years and had not yet learned all he needed to know.

There were several postscripts to the episode. Maggie went home and over coffee told her mama, Jane Austen, of the events that had transpired. Janey was sympathetic and told her daughter not to let it worry her. She also told Maggie to be sure not to mention the problem to her father, Emmett, because they both knew how he would react. Ironically, Emmett agreed that his wife had given their daughter some sound advice. He was sitting in the next room working on an ingrown toenail with his pocketknife when he overheard the conversation. Without a word, he put his knife in his pocket, slipped on his shoe, and took a drive to the mill. Right was right and wrong was wrong, and Emmett had a history of explaining the difference between the two to people like Howard Hoyt.

Emmett Callahan had no tolerance for shades of grey, and he didn't like anyone harrying his girls, as A.J. would find out presently when he began to court Maggie. In later years, A.J. amused himself by imagining the look that must have been on Howard Hoyt's face when he saw Emmett filling the door frame, looking as hard as a bar of iron. The two of them conferred privately, and although neither ever spoke of the conversation, the phrase *Come back down here with my shotgun and blow away everything wearing a damn necktie* was overheard by Howard's secretary, Mrs. Hicks.

Maggie was surprised to learn upon her arrival at work that night that the job she desired had been awarded to her. When she later discovered what had led to her promotion, however, she confronted her father in anger and told him in no uncertain terms that when she wanted his help, she would certainly ask for it. Emmett listened in silence. Women were a mystery to him.

Clyde Cordele did not fare well on first shift. A smarter man would have acknowledged a near miss and vowed to change. But this sanity was beyond Clyde, and he never skipped a beat as he slammed into the day crew like a tidal wave. Ironically, Clyde's ultimate downfall occurred over a set of circumstances eerily similar to those that had gotten him sent to day shift in the first place. Karma will find a way.

Not long after his arrival on his new shift, Clyde became enamored of Beatrice Beaufort England, a weaver otherwise known as Betty B. Although she in no way encouraged Clyde, he took every opportunity to present his attentions and to make a general nuisance of himself. This situation continued for some few weeks until the fateful day of Clyde's professional and very nearly personal demise arrived.

On that day, Clyde finally became completely overwhelmed with desire and actually reached out and touched one of Betty B.'s breasts. No one would argue the fact that they were dandies, a point that formed the core of Clyde's defense. But dandies or not, his urge constituted sexual harassment even by the extremely liberal standards of the textile industry of the day.

Betty B.'s husband, Rocky, was the day shift forklift driver, and he was not known for his tolerance where his wife's breasts were concerned. When Howard Hoyt and Security arrived, Clyde was bound head to foot in a length of winding and was standing on a pallet raised ten feet in the air by Rocky's forklift. There was a strip of heavy denim looped around Clyde's neck, the other end of which was tied to a ceiling joist directly above. Rocky had decided to hang the scoundrel, which was better than he deserved, and Clyde had not handled this reversal of fortune well. Luckily, cooler heads prevailed, although it appeared at the time that Howard left Clyde standing on tiptoe somewhat longer than was absolutely necessary before he was cut down and fired. Rocky had to go to the regional hospital for an evaluation but was pronounced sane. He was allowed to come back to work with a write-up in his file and a stiff warning about hanging management.

As for A.J., he had enjoyed his fill of textiles and did not take advantage of the employment opportunity that Howard Hoyt had offered. Eugene urged A.J. to come help him run a little import business he had started, and A.J. was intrigued at first. But ultimately he took a pass when he discovered that Eugene's fledgling enterprise consisted of high-speed runs in the Lover to Denver, where the old Chrysler was loaded with as many cases of Coors beer as it would hold for transport back to Cherokee County for resale at three times its purchase price.

"You're missing the boat," Eugene said in an exasperated tone when A.J. informed him that he appreciated the offer, but he felt he wasn't cut out for the occupation. Instead, he hired on dragging slabs at a little sawmill down in the valley. The work was unpleasant but not intellectually demanding, so he had plenty of time to think. And what he thought about was Maggie.

Don't investigate my demise too thoroughly.

—Excerpt of posthumous letter from Eugene Purdue to

Red Arnold, Cherokee County Sheriff

IT WAS LATE AFTERNOON ON THE FOLLOWING SAT-
urday when A.J. rolled into the clearing for his second visit with
Eugene. He parked Johnny Mack's old bulldozer next to Eugene's
Jeep, which had deteriorated appreciably during the previous week.
He left his bat on the dozer and climbed down. He and Rufus had
already enjoyed their reunion for the day, and it had gone poorly for
Rufus. The big canine left the encounter visibly shaken, as if the
sight of A.J. banging the Louisville Slugger against the track of the
Cat while yelling *It's showtime!* had upset him. A.J. had not intended to offend his foe's sensibilities and almost certainly would have
veered away before impact, but Rufus hightailed it before A.J. had
the opportunity to explain. For a large dog, Rufus was extremely
fleet of paw when the need was upon him.

It had taken most of the day to reclaim the road, and A.J. was
tired. He walked slowly to the porch where Eugene sat, quietly
rocking. The scene appeared much as it had the week before, with

one notable exception. The Navy Colt lay on the cable spool with its barrel split and flared. The proud old gun's Jeep, tree, and Fox shooting days were over. They had come to an end as all things eventually must, saddening A.J. in a way he could not readily explain. He sat down heavily next to Eugene, who was busy loading his replacement weapon of choice, a twelve-gauge pump shotgun that looked vaguely familiar.

"What did you do to Rufus?" Eugene asked conversationally. "He came tearing through here awhile ago like he was on fire." He raised the shotgun and sighted down the barrel. "Pull," he said. Then he shot the Jeep.

"Rufus doesn't like the bulldozer," A.J. explained, reaching for a beer in the cooler on the floor. "I may need to make Johnny Mack an offer on it."

"Pull," Eugene said, again shooting his faithful vehicle. "You need to quit scaring my dog like that. He might get skittish, and I like a dog to have plenty of spirit."

"No problem. He's loaded with spirit." A.J. took a sip of his cold beer. "What happened to the Colt?"

"I guess it was too old to work for a living," Eugene said. "It was a fine gun, and I hated to see it go." He sounded melancholy. "Pull," he continued, blasting away at the Jeep. "You want to take a crack at it?" he asked. "You used to be pretty good with this shotgun." A.J. thought he had recognized it, and now he knew from where.

"Is that it?" A.J. asked, accepting the shotgun from Eugene. He hefted the gun and sighted down the barrel. "Yeah, this is it. I had almost forgotten about that night," he said absently, remembering. He looked over at Eugene. "You nearly got us both killed."

66

"Killed? No. Seriously injured, maybe."

"I should have just shot *you*," A.J. said. "I could have told everyone it was an industrial accident."

"An industrial accident with a shotgun?" Eugene asked dubiously.

"We were in Sand Valley, Alabama. I could have sold it."

On the night in question, Eugene and A.J. were cruising the Lover across the state line in Alabama where, everyone knew, the romantic pickings were easy. They were young bucks at the time and accepted as hard scientific fact the supposition that Alabama girls put out. Alabama boys knew better and were all trolling in Georgia where, in theory, the damsels were waiting impatiently for love.

Eugene and A.J. rolled into Sand Valley around midnight, having heard about a set of twins living in that small town who were wild and could not be satisfied. The boys weren't equipped with names or addresses, but such is the nature of the decision-making process when optimism and testosterone are involved. They were apparently of the impression that these girls would be at the outskirts of town, holding a sign written in lipstick that read: FRISKY TWINS LOOKING FOR GEORGIA BOYS—NO EXPERIENCE NECESSARY, or something to that effect. Unfortunately, this had not occurred. Quicker Georgia boys seemed to have beaten them to it, so they ended up parked by the depot splitting a bottle of very cheap wine before they undertook the long ride home.

After they finished the bottle, A.J. stepped behind the depot for a moment to relieve himself. While he was indisposed, he began to hear strident conversation from the front of the depot. The discussions seemed urgent, but their raucous tone did not prepare him for the scene that greeted him when he returned to the Lover. There in the middle of the street was Eugene, engulfed by four of Sand Valley's farm-raised, corn-fed finest.

The misunderstanding had occurred over remarks made by Eugene regarding the boys' mamas and sisters. These comments had been good-natured jest, an icebreaker of sorts, but the boys took it all wrong and hostilities ensued. Eugene was briefly holding his own, but sheer weight of numbers was destined to bring his downfall. A.J. had to act quickly, so he reached into the Lover and removed Eugene's old twelve-gauge pump shotgun from the back floorboard. He cocked and shot it in the air, twice. Then he aimed at the melee in the street. All was quiet in Sand Valley, Alabama.

"Let him up," A.J. said. He was in deep water, but no better ideas had occurred to him, so he guessed he was stuck with the one he had. The largest of Eugene's assailants disengaged himself from the pile and stood. He and A.J. recognized each other at the same moment.

"Longstreet," he said, drawing the name out slowly like an incantation, his voice dark and full of menace. "You're Longstreet."

"Yeah, you big son of a bitch, I know _you_, too," A.J. replied with his shotgun still leveled at the crowd. The other three continued to hold Eugene down. "I told you to let him up." A.J. spoke in a quiet tone that in no way reflected the panic he was feeling.

He was on enemy turf facing Mayo Reese, who stood six-feet, six-inches tall and weighed about two-hundred eighty pounds on the hoof. They had encountered each other on one previous occasion, when Sequoyah met Sand Valley on the gridiron in a preseason exhibition arranged by their coaches. The match was semilegal since the teams were from different states, but Southern high school football coaches are entities unto themselves provided they posted winning seasons, and both coaches decided the game would be a good way to toughen the boys up.

They had squared off on a hot and humid August night. Sequoyah dressed out seventeen gladiators for the game including the three boys who never got to play, so it was another iron man night for A.J. and Eugene, offensive and defensive right guard and tackle. The Sequoyah Indians kicked off, and Sand Valley returned the ball to their own thirty-yard line. The trouble began on the first play from scrimmage. Big Mayo hit his stance about five yards behind the line, and when the ball snapped he lumbered straight for A.J. When he plowed into old number nine, A.J. knew he had been hit. To make matters worse, as he ran over A.J., he slugged him hard in the solar plexus. A.J. grabbed Mayo's leg when he went by, and when the play was over he found himself under a pile of sweating, swearing country boys with Mayo on top of him biting his calf. A.J. knew he was in for a long game.

The first half was a study in pain, with A.J. doing everything he could think of to keep his opponent at bay. Even so, Mayo sacked the Sequoyah quarterback five times during the first half and spent most of the rest of his time chasing the beleaguered general all over the backfield.

"A.J., you've got to stop that motherfucker," Booger Brown told him during one huddle. "He's gettin' here faster than the ball is." Booger was the quarterback. Luckily, he was a fast one or he would have already been killed.

"I could shoot him," A.J. growled, "but I'm afraid it would just piss him off." He was in sad shape and not receptive to criticism.

Sequoyah was down twenty-eight points at halftime, and Coach Crider was not happy with the way the first two quarters had gone. "I don't know what you pussies think you're doing out there, but you're damn sure not playing football! Hell, I could dress your *mamas* out and do better than this! This is the most pitiful excuse for a football game I've ever seen!"

Football was very important to Coach Crider. He had played professionally for two years with the Chicago Bears back in the days when a good lineman made twenty-five thousand a year and was proud to get the work. Unfortunately, he had received two torn ligaments in Cleveland and a bus ticket home shortly thereafter, which was how the pigskin used to bounce in the National Football League.

Homing in from the general to the specific, Coach Crider turned his attention to A.J. "Longstreet, just what the hell do you think *you're* doing out there? I've seen legless nuns in wheelchairs hit harder than you're hitting that damn hog." A.J. was lying on his back on the floor wondering why he was playing football at all and where, exactly, Coach had seen legless nuns play. He supposed it was one of those Chicago things. His nose was smashed. His jersey was ripped, and his pads were hanging out. He had what felt like a cracked rib, and his arms were solid blue, just two long bruises. He was bleeding from several bites, and his left thumb was broken and taped to his hand. Mayo had beaten him like a drum.

"You want to go hit him?" A.J. asked wearily, holding up his helmet to the coach. He was beyond fear or caution, even with Coach Crider. He felt that nothing anyone could ever do to him again could possibly compare with what Mayo had already done. He had underestimated. Coach got down on his hands and knees

70

and positioned his face about an inch from A.J.'s.

"Get your weak, sorry ass up and go out there and take that big piece of shit *out*! You get him, or you'll be running laps until your feet are gone." Coach had a dynamic effect on the boys, and they were always eager to please him. A.J. climbed to his feet and went and stood, uniform and all, under a hot shower, preparing himself mentally for one final attempt.

It was and is a Southern tradition to send adolescent boys to men like Coach Crider to learn to play the game of life. A.J. was not particularly *interested* in the game of life at that point, but neither was he yearning to run laps for the next three decades or so, and Coach was not prone to idle talk. After the kickoff for the second half, Sequoyah returned the ball to their own twenty-three-yard line. In the huddle, A.J. outlined his plan.

"Booger, take the snap and lie down. Eugene, hit him in the nuts as hard as you can. I'm going to hit him in the throat. If we're lucky, he'll die."

It was a simple plan, but it had potential. The ball was snapped, and they executed Operation Mayo. He came thundering in, and A.J. and Eugene fired like cannonballs at their targets. Charlie Trammel, the Sequoyah center, got a mean elbow into Mayo's kidney for good measure.

After the play, everyone got up but Mayo Reese. He was in the fetal position, vomiting while trying to swear at A.J. and Eugene. They were both standing there shaking their heads, as if it were just a darned shame the young athlete had been hurt and was now being dragged to the bench by his coaches. He wasn't terminal, but he was out for the game. Unfortunately, so were A.J. and Eugene,

71

thrown out for unsportsmanlike conduct. As they approached the bench, Coach Crider came up to them. They figured they were in for it for sure.

Then Coach smiled and said, "Now *that's* some goddamn football." Sequoyah went on to lose forty-two to nothing, but Coach Crider didn't seem to mind. He kept looking over at his boys, benched in disgrace. They reminded him of himself back in the golden days when he, too, had been a warrior, eager for the taste of battle and the sound of leather slapping flesh.

So A.J. and Mayo had history prior to their encounter in Sand Valley. While A.J. was willing to let bygones be bygones, Mayo seemed to feel the need to linger over old times.

"Let him up," Mayo said to his companions. He pointed to A.J. "That's the one we want."

A.J. stood his ground with the shotgun aimed at the crowd. He eased the weapon to his left so it pointed at Mayo.

"You won't shoot," Mayo sneered. "You're afraid you'll hit him." He pointed at Eugene, who was clambering to his feet. Mayo was correct in his assertion, but A.J. hoped he didn't know that he was for certain.

"You'll get most of it," A.J. replied, wishing he had stayed behind the depot. Eugene shoved his way past Mayo and asked him how his sex life was these days. Recognition flickered across Mayo's features when Eugene arrived back at the Lover.

"Start the damn car," A.J. said tensely. Eugene gave his recent companions a gesture before doing as he was told. A.J. backed up slowly and got in, still holding the shotgun on the group in the street.

"I'll be seeing you," Mayo said, eyeing A.J. with raw hate.

"Not if I see you first," A.J. replied as they fishtailed off with tires squealing. The Sand Valley rowdies made an attempt at pursuit, but the Lover was more than a match for their old Ford Galaxie, and soon Eugene and A.J. were just bad memories in the night. A.J. had acquired a headache during the ordeal and wanted a quiet ride home. Eugene, however, wanted to talk.

"Man, that was something," he said, shaking his head and smiling. "I've never seen anything like it. I didn't know if you were going to shoot or not."

"I wasn't going to shoot," A.J. said, rubbing his temples. "Shut up and drive." He was disgusted. All he had wanted to do was take a pee. But, no, Eugene had to run his mouth.

"No, you wouldn't have shot," Eugene rattled on. "You didn't really have the stomach for it." A.J. turned to Eugene.

"I didn't have the shells for it. The gun was empty." He closed his eyes and pressed his eyelids with his fingertips. Eugene absorbed the new information. The Lover slowed to a halt in the middle of the highway.

"You backed those pieces of shit down with an empty gun? Man. A.J. the badass. Man." There was awe and respect in his voice.

"Just shut up and drive," was his hero's reply.

As A.J. thought back to that night long past, a sense of the unreal descended upon him. It was as if he were considering the foolish exploits of a young man in a faraway land rather than walking down memory lane. *What a dumb ass*, he thought. He shook his head and looked about him. The scene on the porch was much the same as it had been the previous week. He noticed the current incarnation of the eternal cigarette was burning in the hubcap. He picked it up and flipped it out into the yard.

"You're not going to start that shit again, are you?" Eugene asked.

"Absolutely," A.J. replied. "How do you feel today?" Eugene laid the shotgun across his lap and rocked slowly, reminding A.J. of Judge Roy Bean, Law west of the Pecos.

"I feel like shooting Johnny Mack's bulldozer with this shotgun," Eugene said, the old rocker creaking. He looked over at A.J. "I guess you'd rather I didn't." A.J. doubted any damage would occur but saw no point to the exercise.

"Johnny Mack's jacket is behind the seat," A.J. said. "I'll hang it up on the Jeep, and you can shoot *it.*" It seemed a reasonable alternative.

"No, that's okay," Eugene said sadly, holding up his hand. "It wouldn't be the same."

"Maybe later," A.J. suggested, but Eugene had already moved to another topic.

"I bet you had hell getting the dozer from Johnny Mack," he said with a little smile.

"You know Johnny Mack better than I do," A.J. said, shrugging. "You already know about how it went."

"Come on. You can't deny a man in my condition. I want to hear about it. Did he throw some Scripture on you? Did he get huffy? Did you have to kick his ass?" Eugene was truly excited, so A.J. relented and told the tale.

He had encountered Johnny Mack down at the Jesus Loves Tater Tots Drive-In, the current week's name for Sequoyah's only eating establishment. In actual fact it had no real name and was not a drive-in at all, except for the time that Estelle Chastain misjudged the impact of momentum upon a moving Ford and ended up in the middle of the dining room. Luckily it had been a slow Thursday morning, and no fatalities were reported.

The restaurant appeared to change names weekly due to the haphazard placement of signs in the front window by the firm's owner, cook, and advertising consultant, Wilson Crab. Wilson preferred to be called Hoghead for reasons unknown and was an extremely pious but nearly illiterate man who liked to letter slogans of a religious bent onto pieces of cardboard and tape them up in the front window of his diner. Unfortunately, he also advertised his weekly specials in the same small pane, and often the close proximity of the two distinctly different types of messages produced unintended results, particularly when overlap was involved.

Thus, at various times the beanery had been the God Will Save Ham-N-Eggs Drive-In, the Jesus Is Corndogs Drive-In, and the infamous The Road to Hell Is Paved with Country Fried Steak Drive-In, to name but a few. A.J.'s personal favorite had been the well-meaning Christ Died for the Best Fried Chicken in the County Drive-In, of which he was fortunate enough to get a snapshot before the signs were personally rearranged by the Reverend O'Neal Tanner. The pastor had stopped by for a cup of coffee and had almost gone on to his reward upon reading of the Savior's previously unknown weakness for the local delicacy.

A.J. sat by Johnny Mack at the counter and ordered a cup of Hoghead's foul brew, which he loaded down with as much cream and sugar as the mug would hold. He normally took it black, but Hoghead's coffee was best when disguised. Hoghead had served twenty-three years in the Navy as a cook, and his wretched, scalding, painfully strong concoction had kept many a sailor alert during the midnight watch. But Sequoyah was not the icy North Atlantic, and it was only recently and with great effort that the coffee drinkers in town had prevailed upon Hoghead to discontinue his practice of tossing a handful of eggshells and a pinch of salt into each potful.

"A.J., how have you been?" Johnny Mack asked pleasantly, stirring the contents in his cup. "Is your family all right?" He placed his spoon on the counter and reached for a homemade doughnut, referred to as *collision mats* by Hoghead and kept handy on a plate.

"Everyone is fine, Johnny Mack," A.J. replied. "I need to ask a favor. I need to borrow the Cat this weekend. I've got a little job I need to do."

"You can use it anytime you need it," Johnny Mack said. "It's already loaded on the trailer and hitched to the dump truck. Just come on out and get it. Angel will be happy to see you." He took a sip of his coffee. "You getting around to fixing that bank behind your house?" Johnny Mack was not being nosy, much. He just seemed to be interested, and A.J. was of the opinion that it was a bad time for the old man to be developing social skills.

"No," A.J. replied. "I need to borrow the Cat to clean up the road on the mountain." There was an uncomfortable silence. Finally, Johnny Mack spoke.

"Are you talking about *his* road?" he asked.

"That would be the one," A.J. replied. Johnny Mack's shoulders tensed. His hands formed fists that resembled small hams.

A.J. watched Johnny Mack strive with his demons. It was his theory that every person had a few snakes in the head, but it seemed to him that the Purdue variety was a more evolved breed of reptile. Finally, Johnny Mack's fists unclenched, but his features were still grim. From the kitchen came the clatter of pans and a high-pitched noise that may have been Hoghead whistling a tune.

"You can't borrow the Cat," Johnny Mack said. "Not for him. You know how I feel."

"I'm not borrowing it for him. I'm borrowing it for me."

"The last I heard, you boys weren't getting along," Johnny Mack observed. "I heard you roughed each other up pretty good at the firemen's barbecue. Why are you all of a sudden worried about his road?"

"I just need to fix the road. It's hard for Diane to get the boys up there to see their father."

"So Diane asked you to fix it?"

"Not in so many words."

"A.J., you are trying real hard not to tell me something. I've known you since you were a boy, and I know when you're not saying something that needs to be said."

A.J. opened his mouth to speak but noticed the quiet and immobile form of Hoghead. He had been wiping the counter but was now poised in mid-wipe, listening raptly.

"Hoghead, this is sort of private," A.J. said, gesturing toward the kitchen while raising his eyebrows. Hoghead looked confused. Then his eyes lost their glazed look.

"You don't need to worry about a thing," he said, winking at A.J. and giving him the A-OK sign with his hand. "There's nobody back there. You go right ahead and tell Johnny Mack what you need to tell him." There he stood, as immovable as the smokestack of the old *U.S.S. Blackhawk*, aboard which he had served faithfully for many a year. It was no mystery to A.J. why the old cook had never risen to the rank of Admiral of the Ocean Sea. Exasperated, he pointed first at Hoghead, then at the kitchen. Hog got it that time, but he seemed hurt as he shuffled back to his domain, muttering as he progressed that you didn't need to hit *him* over the head with a board, that was for sure.

Back at the counter, A.J sighed and waded in. "Eugene is very sick," he began. "He's not going to get well. I've promised I'll come see him from time to time, and I need to be able to drive up the road to do that." It was quiet in the diner. Johnny Mack was staring at the floor. Finally, he swallowed loudly and looked at A.J.

"I'll let you use the Cat," he said. "But it's you I'm letting use it, not him." There was tension in the words and in the air when A.J. responded.

"Do you understand what I just told you?" he asked. "Eugene is about to be rowed across the river. He's waiting to catch the big bus. If you were ever planning to get over it, now wouldn't be a bad time."

"'They have sown the wind, and they shall reap the whirlwind.' Hosea chapter 8, verse 7."

"Johnny Mack, don't do the Scripture thing," A.J. said. It was Johnny Mack's habit to quote the Holy Book during times of stress, but A.J. wasn't in the mood.

"The Bible doesn't lie," the senior Purdue admonished.

"Right," A.J. allowed. He really did not want to argue with Johnny Mack. He just wanted the keys to the damn bulldozer.

"'Be sure your sin will find you out.' Numbers 32:23," Johnny

Mack added. He had been raised a staunch Baptist, and his God didn't mess around. It was His way or the highway, and that was that. A.J., on the other hand, was a Methodist, and his conception of the Almighty leaned more toward that of a good pal.

"Johnny Mack, don't do the Scripture thing," A.J. repeated. He was getting a headache.

"'For what is a man profited,'" Johnny Mack asked, "'if he shall gain the whole world, and lose his own soul?' Matthew 16:26." A.J. restrained himself from pointing out that inheriting a stolen mountain and opening a beer joint hardly constituted gaining the world, impressive though it was by local standards.

A.J. looked at his watch and saw it was past time to be heading to work. It was just as well. He had secured the use of the bulldozer, and there was no point in continuing to be Johnny Mack's straight man while he was in the mood to quote King James. It was a venture in futility, a journey to nowhere. A.J. stood abruptly and made for the exit. At the door he stopped and turned. "I appreciate the loan of the bulldozer," he said. "I'll be by for it Friday evening."

"It will be ready for you," Johnny Mack said woodenly. A.J. nodded his head and left. He could not comprehend an animosity such as that which existed between Eugene and his father. It was foreign to him, as unfathomable as Latin.

"It sounds to me like he whipped you," Eugene commented after hearing the tale. During A.J.'s rendition he had washed down some medication with a little Jim Beam and was feeling mellow.

"Yeah, he tore me up," A.J. said. "And I got out while I was ahead. He was about to haul out the big guns. He had that Revelation look on his face."

79

"Yeah, that would have been it," Eugene agreed. "When he gets into that mean shit, no one can touch him. When I was a kid, he used to fill me full of that Pale Rider of Death crap. There was always a lot of smiting going on. On the other side, I had Angel telling me about Jesus loving the little children. I liked her stories much better. I remember once I asked her about Lot's wife right after Johnny Mack told me the story. Even a stupid kid like me could see she got a raw deal. You know what Angel said? She told me not to worry, because God didn't do mean things like that to people anymore. I loved that. She and Johnny Mack had a big fight that night after I was in bed. She was hollering at him in French and throwing dishes. He removed himself from my religious instruction right after that." He lapsed into silence. A.J. smiled.

"I wish I had heard Angel cleaning Johnny Mack's clock in French," he said.

"It was something," Eugene agreed. "One thing's for sure. She never took any of his shit. She thought he was too rough on me and Jackie, though, and she didn't like it." He was quiet for a moment. "If she had known how rough, she probably would have shot him."

"Bitch, bitch, bitch," A.J. said. "The man went to a lot of trouble to get you raised up right, and all you can do is gripe about it. No wonder he won't loan you the bulldozer. You have no gratitude. Hell, I wouldn't loan you my bulldozer, either."

They were silent for a while. The afternoon was strolling casually toward evening. "You know," Eugene said after a time, "I never understood why Angel and Johnny Mack got married. I understand it from Johnny Mack's point of view. She was a real catch for a hayseed like him. What I have never been able to figure out is what she got out of the deal. She could have done a lot better than him."

"I don't know," A.J. replied. "Maybe she could, maybe she couldn't. There weren't too many live ones left to choose from by the time Johnny Mack showed up. Who knows what the appeal was? Love? Security? A way out? Maybe she was just hot for him in his soldier suit."

"No, I think she just felt sorry for him."

"Charity sex between Angel and Johnny Mack?"

"I'm not talking about sex. They have never had sex."

"So the stork brought you?"

"I don't know who my father was," Eugene said. "But I know it wasn't Johnny Mack. He stepped on a land mine right before entering Paris. It was mostly a dud, but it took out what counted. It was actually Angel who helped nurse him back to health." Eugene calmly related this as if telling an interesting anecdote about two strangers.

"You're telling me Johnny Mack stepped on a mine and, uh . . ." A.J. was caught by surprise.

"He blew his dick off," said Eugene matter-of-factly. "She married him anyway, and I was born ten years later. The math is not that hard."

"Maybe they did artificial insemination," A.J. offered, piecing his way through this mystery.

"They didn't have that back then," Eugene said, as if he actually knew. "Anyway, there's nothing to work with. It's all gone." All A.J. could do was shake his head. He had always known that Eugene was a bastard but hadn't realized it was the literal truth.

"When did you find this out?" A.J. was morbidly curious. He

recognized this shortcoming in himself and vowed to change. To-morrow.

"I'd had my suspicions for years. You just don't grow up in a house with a man who has no dick and not get the feeling something is wrong. You ever take a shower with John Robert when you were a kid, or maybe take a leak on a tree together?"

"Sure."

"We didn't do that sort of thing. I've never seen him with his pants off. I sat down with Angel one day and asked her what the deal was. She hemmed and hawed but finally came across. She wouldn't tell me who my father was, but she admitted the dastardly deed. She thought I would be upset. I told her it suited me just fine that Johnny Mack wasn't my father. As a matter of fact, I was hap-pier." Eugene began to hum a quiet tune. Eventually he turned to A.J. "Cat got your tongue?" he asked.

"Since you brought it up, if Angel married a man she knew couldn't dance the waltz with her, why did she dance the waltz later with someone else?"

"Dance the waltz? Come on, Victoria. If you mean *fuck*, say *fuck*."

"We're talking about your mama. Have some respect."

"Boy Scout," Eugene said, rolling his eyes. But he seemed to take the point. "I have a theory. Angel got Jackie the hard way courtesy of a Nazi. So I don't think. . . dancing was very high on her list when she met Johnny Mack. She may have even married him because he couldn't dance. I don't know. Later on, her biology caught up with her, and she began to want to do the old two-step again."

"Who all knows about this?" A.J. had until tomorrow to be

morbidly curious and wanted to find out more while there was time.

"You, me, Angel, Jackie, and Johnny Mack. Assuming, of course, he understands how these things work. My real father, who-ever he is, may or may not know. Who can say?" Eugene stood up, stretched, and started toward the yard, stumbling a bit when he stepped off the porch. He walked to the bulldozer, climbed up, and started it.

"I'll be right back!" he hollered as he headed down the trail. A.J. walked to the remains of the Jeep for a smoke. The porch was still too combustible for his comfort. He wondered what Eugene was doing. He knew he would have issues to address with Johnny Mack if the Cat went off a cliff. He heard Eugene down the trail, making a great deal of noise. Then the Cat hove into view, and A.J. was amazed at what he saw. Eugene was pushing the Lover up the path. As he got closer, he waved A.J. to the side and shoved the old Chrysler right in beside the Jeep, as if he had been looking for a good parking spot and finally found one.

"Tell me you're not going to shoot it," said A.J.

"I'm going to shoot it."

"Why?"

"I don't want it to outlast me," Eugene replied as he climbed down from his perch. The effort winded him. A.J. had almost forgotten the central issue during the discussion of Angel's unusual dancing habits. Now it was back on his mind, and it was depressing. Still, he hated to see the old Lover end up like the Jeep and the tree, riddled and abused.

"It's your car, but it deserves better," A.J. said.

"Don't we all?" came the reply. A.J. looked at the Lover, the

Jeep, and the remains of the tree across the clearing. He thought of the Navy Colt.

"If you keep getting rid of things that might outlast you, I'm going to get nervous," A.J. observed. "Maybe I ought to hog-tie Rufus and get us both out of here before it's too late." Eugene looked at him with an odd smile.

"You're getting paranoid. I *would* like to see you hog-tie Rufus, though. I don't know which way I'd bet on that deal. You're smarter, but his teeth are sharper. If you use your bat, I think you might have a little edge."

"If I use your shotgun, I might have a bigger edge."

"That would be poor sportsmanship. What would Coach Crider say?"

"Coach Crider dropped dead, which saved someone the trouble of killing him," A.J. said. Coach had died of a heart attack while expressing a difference of opinion with a referee. He had spit in the official's face a bare moment before he collapsed, so it was actually the first time in Georgia high school football history that a dead coach was ejected from a game for unsportsmanlike conduct. It was a sad moment, a true low point for the team, and the boys had not played well the rest of the contest. "Anyway, I have never claimed to be a good sport."

"No, you haven't," Eugene said. "But you are." He lit a cigarette. "What are you going to do with Rufus after I'm gone?" The question caught A.J. off guard.

"I wasn't planning on doing anything with him. Why don't you give him to someone? Maybe Jackie. He has a lot of dogs." It was a sure bet that A.J. didn't want him.

84

"No, Rufus would kill all of them, and some of them are good dogs," Eugene said. "Jackie would have to keep him tied. I'd rather see him dead."

"What do you mean by that?" A.J. asked, suddenly wary.

"After I'm gone, I want you to shoot Rufus. Nobody is going to want him, and he's getting too old to live wild. I don't have the heart to do it myself." A.J. sighed.

"Last week you asked me to kill you. This week, it's Rufus. Next week, you'll be wanting me to gun down Diane and the boys. Why are you doing this to me? I don't like killing. I don't even hunt! If Rufus walked up right now and keeled over, I wouldn't shed a tear, because I really hate your dog. But I don't want to kill him!" A.J. had become upset. "Why do you keep bringing up this kind of shit?" he demanded.

"Because you're all I have," Eugene said quietly, meeting A.J.'s eye. "Because I need the help." He paused for a long moment. Then he continued. "Because I know you can do it when you have to." A.J. stiffened. The clearing was as silent as the grave. A.J. walked to the bulldozer and climbed aboard. He fired up the old machine and sat there momentarily. Then he climbed down and walked back to Eugene.

"You son of a bitch," he said in a quiet voice that roared like a train. "You swore on everything you held sacred that you would never talk about that. You're a lying son of a bitch."

"No, I'm not," Eugene said. "I just don't hold anything sacred anymore." He sounded as if he might cry.

A.J. headed for the dozer. Without another word, he left the clearing.

Your coffee killed me.
—Excerpt of posthumous letter from Eugene Purdue to
Hoghead Crab, restaurateur

A.J. WAS HAVING A BAD WEEK. EUGENE HAD INITIATED
the process on Saturday by reminding him of an incident he had
tried to forget. The human mind was a devious organ, however,
and it chiseled in stone that which would be best left unrecalled. In
fairness to Eugene, he had not dredged a memory that had been
successfully entombed. It was always with A.J., coming to him in
the quiet moments. Still, Eugene had sworn never to mention it,
but mention it he had. In this regard he had proven faithless, and
his breach of trust had upset A.J. For Eugene possessed the truth.
Of the two of them, one was a killer. Of the two of them, one had
beaten two men to death with the Louisville Slugger and had shot a
third. Of the two of them, A.J. owned the bat.

Most people never foresee their dates with destiny, and A.J. was
no exception on that fateful day years past. He and Eugene had
decided to try their luck at a trout stream that ran on the mountain
to the north of Sequoyah. Their wives were both out of town, and

Eugene and A.J. had decided on a fishing trip to while away the afternoon. Actually, Eugene had proposed another plan, a scenic tour of some of the finer topless clubs of Atlanta. But A.J. vetoed the idea, although it had been touch and go for a moment when Eugene described the Panther Club, a bistro that featured nude interactive water volleyball.

They met early in the day. It was a fine morning, and the air held a hint of summer. They left their vehicles and began the long hike to the trout stream. Eugene carried the rods and a large tackle box. A.J. ferried his bat and a backpack loaded with food and a six-pack of beer. They walked briskly, exchanging easy conversation.

"I can't believe it," Eugene said. "We could be chest deep in wet, naked women right now. But no, you want to go on a fishing trip. I can't believe it." He sounded disgusted.

"You're married," A.J. responded. "If you want wet, naked women, take a shower with Diane." He swatted the bat at a movement in the leaves beside the trail.

"This is different," Eugene explained. "A little variety in wet, naked women never hurt anybody. These are nice girls. Girls just working their way through college. Girls helping their sick mamas. It's a look-but-don't-touch deal. If you touch, some big guy breaks off your hands and throws you in a dumpster." He had a patient, instructive tone.

"So we drive to Atlanta," A.J. recapped, "pay a twenty-five dollar cover charge, rent a bathing suit for another twenty-five, and get in a pool with naked but pure college girls with sick mamas who want to play volleyball?"

"There! Now you've got the idea!" Eugene seemed excited.

"Send Diane to college, and then take a shower with her," A.J. suggested. "Her mama's already sick."

"I don't know why I even try," Eugene said, disgusted again. "You're hopeless. Saint fucking A.J. I don't know why I even try." He shook his head.

"I'll take off my shirt while we fish," A.J. said, "but that's as far as it goes. If you touch me, I'll have to break off your hands."

They walked until they entered a small depression not far from their destination, where they decided to take a break. A.J. passed a sandwich and a beer before securing his own. They could hear the rush of the stream in the distance. It was a pleasant scene, a moment of peace in a world of bother. A.J. reclined, intending to let the trout work up an appetite. The aroma of marijuana floated from Eugene's side of the swale. He closed his eyes and drifted.

His eyes snapped open when he heard voices from beyond the ridge at his back. Then he heard a shrill scream followed by loud cracks of rifle fire. He bolted to his feet and looked at Eugene. Then he grabbed his bat and scrambled to the top of the small embankment with Eugene matching each step.

The scene in the clearing below burned into their corneas. They saw three hard-looking men in camouflage garb armed with automatic weapons. They were ranged around a young woman who sat on a log in front of a small tent. About ten feet away sprawled a motionless figure, the apparent recipient of the rifle shots. The woman was staring at the remains of her companion.

"Goddamn," whispered A.J. "They shot him in cold blood." It was unclear whether the man had been running or fighting, but it was a moot point since dead is dead, and he was certainly that. The largest of the scoundrels walked to the poor boy and nudged him with his toe, then laughed and rejoined his companions. They all three looked down at the girl. "Oh, shit," A.J. breathed.

"What are we going to do?" Eugene hissed.

"I think we are going to die," A.J. said.

"The next time I want to go to the titty bar, we're going to the titty bar," Eugene whispered fiercely. "Wait for me. I've got a gun." He slid down toward their trappings.

A.J. knew good advice when he heard it and was going to wait, but delay was removed as an option when one of the men grabbed the girl's long, black hair and dragged her to her feet. With his other hand he clawed her shirtfront, violently exposing her. She struggled and was backhanded to the ground. Then he dropped to his knees and held her wrists with one hand while fondling her with the other. The second man knelt and began to undo her jeans while the third unzipped his own.

A.J. knew the time for waiting was past. Live or die, Eugene or not, he couldn't stand by and watch the scene unfolding below. With no conscious thought, he was up and moving toward the campsite. He ran fast and quiet and was among them before they were aware of his presence. Upon his arrival, their cognizance increased dramatically.

A.J. came in screaming and swinging. The man who had ripped the girl's shirt turned just in time to receive all of the Louisville Slugger across the bridge of his nose. He was dead when he toppled over. A.J. then swung in the opposite direction and caught the second man in the temple. He was fueled by fear and rage, and he was a big man swinging hard ash. The smack of the bat echoed through the forest, and the man knelt lifeless for several seconds before gravity brought him low. The lone survivor started for his rifle, but at that moment Eugene began shooting his .22 pistol. The shots confused the brute, and he stopped. A.J. threw the bat at him and knocked him down. The man came up with a rifle, which he tried to aim at A.J., who grabbed one of the weapons no longer needed by the departed and beat his adversary to the draw by a whisper. Their eyes met and they froze, the other's rifle partially raised and A.J.'s locked, loaded, and aimed at the black heart of his quarry. He had the drop, and to his right, Eugene also held a bead.

It was silent on the killing ground. The acrid smell of cordite lingered with a richer, coppery aroma. A.J. heard the pounding of his own heart.

"Give me a reason to shoot you," he said through clenched teeth. "Any reason at all will do it."

The reprobate lowered his rifle. A.J. saw in his eyes a soul of darkness. He beheld an animal that deserved to die, yet he hesitated to shoot lest he become what he destroyed. The villain mistook what he saw in A.J.'s expression for a lack of resolve and began to laugh. A.J. couldn't believe what he was seeing. Without conscious thought, he shot. The M-16 was on full automatic, and the man was cut to pieces. When it was over, Eugene came to pry the rifle from A.J.'s hands. He still had the trigger depressed, although the magazine was empty.

"Easy," Eugene said. "Let me have the gun." He removed the M-16 from A.J.'s hands and threw it down. He was not a man who was easily jarred, but there was no mistaking the fact that they had a mess on their hands.

A.J. sank down next to the prone, inert woman. She was staring straight up with fear in her eyes. Her lips moved silently. He wiped spittle mixed with blood from her chin. Her mind seemed to have disengaged from harsh reality, and A.J. thought that this, at least, was a small mercy. He bent his head down between his knees and vomited.

Eugene inspected the two who had succumbed to acute wood poisoning. There was no point at all in checking the third and not much left to examine anyway. He came and stood in front of A.J. and his mute associate. In a gesture of tenderness uncharacteristic of Eugene, he kneeled and gently fastened her jeans. Then he raised her to a sitting position and eased her onto the log beside A.J. He reached into the tent and brought out a blanket, which he draped over her exposed torso.

"Those boys are dead," he said to A.J. "You swing a mean piece of wood." A.J. was silent. He was in danger of departing reality and joining his log mate. Eugene saw this and grabbed his shoulders, shaking him. "Wake up, Babe Ruth. Don't get weak in the knees on me now."

A.J. blinked slowly a couple of times, then met Eugene's gaze.

"Did you say the other two are dead?" he asked quietly.

"You can't get any deader," Eugene replied. "What I don't get is who these guys are. Excuse me, were. There are some survivalists living on the other side of the mountain. I know *them.* They seem okay, and they buy a lot of beer from me. But I've never seen these three."

A.J. viewed his handiwork. He had no idea what the next step was. He thought it odd that he felt very little remorse about killing the men. His only regret was that he had not arrived soon enough to save the young woman from suffering such trauma. He looked

92

over at his trembling female companion.

"I think she's in shock," A.J. said. "It could kill her. We need to get her into town." He leaned close to her ear. "Can you hear me?" She made no sound and continued to stare at the horizon. He looked over at Eugene. "I don't think she's going to be walking out anytime soon."

"We'll carry her," Eugene said. "We don't need any more bodies up here. They're going to have to haul them out in a truck as it is." He reached down and pulled the K-Bar knife from the sheath in one of the dead men's boots and looked at the razor sharp blade. "These guys had all the toys," he said. Then he chuckled softly. "Man, don't you know they would be pissed if they knew they got wiped out by a guy with a baseball bat?" A.J. glared at him, and Eugene took the hint. "I'll go cut some poles," he said. "We'll make a stretcher out of the tent." He headed from the camp to find some suitable material. While Eugene was gone, A.J. dug around in the tent and came up with a shirt. The woman stiffened when he gently removed the remnants of her original.

"Easy, now," he said. "You've had a bad day, but I'm not going to hurt you. Those people won't bother you anymore. We just need to get you covered up." She remained stiff but did not otherwise resist. It was like dressing a large doll. When he finished, he wrapped her back up in the blanket. "That's much better. Just hang in there a little while longer. We're going to get you out of here and take you to town." She continued to sit motionless.

Eugene came back dragging two long saplings. He stripped them of branches and fashioned a workable conveyance using the tent plus the dead men's bootlaces. When he finished, he viewed his creation and nodded in satisfaction.

"Are we ready?" he asked. A.J. looked at him for a long moment.

"How much prison time do you suppose I'll get?" he asked, gesturing in the direction of the deceased.

"It was self-defense. You won't get anything."

"He wasn't self-defense," A.J. said, pointing at the man he had shot. "I looked him in the eye and murdered him."

"No, see, that's where you're wrong. He was about to blow you away, but you got him first."

"That's not what happened. You know it, and I know it."

"Yeah, and nobody else knows it. So, if you'll keep your mouth shut about that 'looking him in the eye' shit, everything will be just fine." Eugene spoke in an exasperated tone. "I knew you were going to make a big deal out of this. I just knew it."

"Well, damn, it *is* a big deal," A.J. noted, gesturing at the carnage. "We won't be dealing with Slim on this. There will be big boys involved. I better just tell the truth and hope they take the circumstances into account." Eugene sighed.

"The only thing I hate worse than a hero is a stupid hero. If you hadn't killed them, I would have. Now, quit worrying. And for Christ's sake, let me do the talking when we get to town." He squatted down in front of the woman. "Lady," he said loudly, as if she were deaf, "we're going to put you on this stretcher and carry you out of here. Nothing bad is going to happen." He spread the makeshift palanquin next to her. She blinked, looked at Eugene, and screamed.

He was caught off guard and jumped back, tripping over his own feet and falling in the process. It would have been a comic display if the situation had not been so bleak. "Lady, *please* don't do that again," he said. She was sobbing quietly. A.J. put his arm around her shoulder to comfort her.

"Let's get her out of here," he said to Eugene. He stood and stepped behind her. He reached gently under her arms while Eugene got her feet, and they carefully positioned her on the litter. Without comment they raised their burden and began the long journey to less lethal climes. When they reached the top of the ridge, Eugene told A.J. to stop a moment, and he placed his end of the stretcher on the ground.

"I forgot my gun," he said.

"Leave it," A.J. replied, but it was too late. He watched in irritation as Eugene ran back to the campsite. He turned his attention to his remaining companion while waiting for Eugene's return. He hoped she was going to be all right. For that matter, he held similar aspirations for himself. There were serious explanations due regarding the mountain man he had shot, and even if he could avoid too much trouble with the law on that score, there was still Maggie to deal with. She did not condone killing in any form, save a selection of flowering plants twice a year, and he was going to be hard pressed to explain the pile of victims, particularly the one he had diced with the automatic rifle.

Eugene came hustling back up the hillside, panting. "Got it," he said. They resumed their journey to the land of the relatively sane, walking in silence for a while. Then Eugene spoke again.

"That was wild," he said from his position on the rear. "I thought you were a bad son of a bitch that night in Sand Valley, but that was nothing. I am going to have to keep a closer eye on you. We don't want this John Wayne shit to get out of hand." It was one of Eugene's most annoying habits to talk about subjects best left alone. He could home right in on the last thing in the world a person wanted to discuss and linger there indefinitely. It was a knack.

"I don't want to talk about it," A.J. replied.

"Took out three armed men with a ball bat," Eugene continued with an admiring tone in his voice, oblivious to A.J.'s wishes. "Went through those boys like Sherman went through Georgia. That last one would have had you if I hadn't distracted him."

"I don't want to talk about this," A.J. repeated, wishing he had gone to Atlanta for participative water sports. A question occurred to him. "And what took you so long getting down there? Did you stop for a smoke? Maybe take a leak?" These were ungracious questions, but the niceties were temporarily beyond him.

"Everybody's a damn critic," Eugene responded. "What do you mean, *what took me so long?* I had to run down the back of the ridge, get the gun, run back up the ridge, and then come down to where the action was. You were supposed to wait. You almost got killed."

"I couldn't wait," A.J. said.

"Yeah, I know you couldn't wait," Eugene replied. "But you should have waited anyway."

"Quit talking," A.J. said. They walked on in silence while he mulled what he intended to tell Slim. He was mentally reviewing and rehearsing, editing the story to its most explainable form. He was from the old school and deemed it important to present multiple murders in the best possible light.

"Bad son of a bitch," Eugene muttered every so often, mostly to himself, replaying in his mind the charge of the bat brigade.

Upon reaching their vehicles, they decided to split forces; one would take their ward straight to Doc Miller while the other went to fetch Slim.

"Take her to Doc," Eugene said. "I'll go get Slim and meet you there." It didn't matter to A.J. A cloud of doom had engulfed him during the trip home. Any way he cut it, he knew he was screwed. He would go to jail, where he would have to kill some big, lonely felon named Sonny or Lukey in defense of his honor in the showers, and then he would never get out. He would lose his wife. She would divorce him and in her shame marry an insurance agent or an accountant, a city boy with soft hands and pale, bony legs who would move her to Atlanta and frown at her in rebuke if she ever exceeded her grocery budget.

They placed the woman into the cab of A.J.'s truck. She stayed put. Her catatonia had not improved appreciably, but there seemed to be a little more expression in her eyes. A.J. climbed into the driver's seat and motored in the direction of the local equivalent of civilization with Eugene following along in his Jeep. When they reached town, A.J. made a beeline to Doc Miller's. Doc practiced out of his home, and as A.J. pulled into the drive he turned and spoke gently to his passenger.

"I'm going to leave you here for about two seconds while I step in and get the doctor. Don't get excited. Everything is going to be fine." A.J. realized the words were ludicrous. It would be a long time before everything was fine for her. Still, he meant well, and that ought to count for something. He patted her leg in a reassuring manner and reached for the door. She grabbed his arm and held it tight. The move surprised him. He looked over at her. She held

97

him in a hard stare, her brown eyes tearful and intense. The bruises on her cheek and jaw were livid.

"Where is . . . ?" She didn't finish but kept her gaze focused on her savior. A.J. had participated in some tough conversations in his time, but he figured this one was going to win, hands down. He wanted to avoid it altogether and had thought to leave her with Doc, who could break all the bad news in his own good time. Doctors were trained for that sort of task; it was why they got the big slice of pie. And A.J. knew he needed to be getting about the business of hiring a lawyer or fleeing to Mexico.

He sighed. Why, after all, should this part of the day be any better than the rest of it? It was not a reasonable expectation, and he knew he had been foolish to hope for respite from the fishing trip from hell.

"My name is A.J. Longstreet," he began slowly. "My friend and I found you in the woods. I have brought you to the doctor to get checked out." She continued to stare at A.J.

"Where is . . . Kenneth?" she asked quietly. She seemed to be missing some facts, and A.J. wondered if she had amnesia. He assumed the dead boy was Kenneth. Maybe he was her beau. A.J. was on ground he did not want to plow.

"Is that the guy you were with at the campsite?" he asked. She nodded. A.J. knew he couldn't delay the inevitable. "I am sorry to have to tell you this, but he's dead." The words ricocheted around the truck cab like shrapnel. The girl blinked and recoiled as if slapped. A.J. watched her closely, wondering how much detail of the morning's events would return to her now. His first concern was for her well-being, but running a distant and nearly inconsequential second was the flickering thought that a little friendly testimony couldn't do him any harm.

"I remember . . . those men. Then Kenneth tried to run . . ." She whispered before stopping abruptly. "He tried to run," she said again. A.J. had saved her honor and her life and had dressed her and hauled her down a mountain, but he really couldn't say he knew her well. He could, however, identify *pissed* when he heard it.

"Don't be too hard on him," A.J. advised. "You ran up on three really bad guys. He never had a chance."

"He tried to run," she said, reemphasizing a point that was a kernel in her craw. "He was going to run off and leave me. To them. They shot him. Then someone tore my shirt off . . . and hit me." Her hand strayed up to her bruised face and she winced when she touched it. "Then you told me we were at the doctor's." She spoke slowly, piecing the puzzle as she went. She seemed to be missing the big part after the backhand but before Doc's driveway. A.J. supposed that the less she remembered, the better it would be for her. He would just have to rely on Eugene to back up his story.

"Let's step inside and see Doc," he suggested. Her face was turning an ugly shade of purple, and he was aware of several scratches on her chest that needed attention.

"I don't feel like I've been raped," she said, almost vacantly. She pulled the front of her shirt away from her body and briefly inspected her chest. "All bruised up and scratched," she said, as if she were commenting upon apples down at the fruit stand. She looked over at A.J. "My shirt was ripped off. Now I have this one on. I should have been raped, but I'm not. I should be dead, but I'm not."

"You've had a rough time," A.J. said. "I think you were in shock. We should go on in and let the doctor check you out." He had done his duty and was ready for the handoff. But she wasn't moving. At least before, he could put her where he wanted her, and too much gab had not been an issue.

"Someone knocked those men off of me. My shirt was ripped. There was shooting. Then . . . then you and some other guy dressed me." She was still looking his way, but he could not meet her gaze. She had been in need of clothing, and he had taken the chore as a matter of mercy. He had thought nothing of it then, but now it seemed a little personal. He was embarrassed.

"I'm sorry, but . . ."

"Sorry? Are you kidding? You saved my life. Thank you is not enough, but thank you." She paused. "Those men are dead?" she asked. A.J. nodded.

"Yes, they have passed away," he said, not prompting her.

"Good. I hope it hurt," she said simply. A.J. suspected it probably had, especially the last one, but he did not enlighten her. "Where's that other man, the one who helped you?" she asked. "And which one of you killed those men?" She hadn't talked a great deal when they first met, but now she seemed committed to making up lost ground.

"We need to go on in," A.J. said. "Your face is really bruised." He got out of the truck and stepped around to open the door for her. She got out slowly and tested her legs. Then they walked up to Doc's door and entered. His living room had been converted into a waiting room, and Doc was sitting in a Naugahide chair by the wall reading a medical journal disguised as *Field and Stream*. He looked up as they entered.

100

"A.J., how have you been?" he inquired.

"Been better, Doc. This lady needs some attention."

Doc stepped up close and viewed the facial contusion.

"Yesss," he said absentmindedly as his expert fingers gently felt for broken bones in the area of the bruise. "Mrs. Jackson," he said loudly, calling the woman who had been his landlady, nurse, and companion for many years. When they were alone he called her Minnie, but this was business. "Let's get this young woman ready for a complete medical exam." Doc's trained eye had also noted the deep scratches that began at her throat and disappeared under her shirt.

"What is your name, dear?" Mrs. Jackson asked as they left the lobby, but the door swung shut before A.J. could hear the reply. He supposed he should have inquired before now, but the opportunity had not presented itself, and she hadn't volunteered. Doc and A.J. were left in the lobby.

"What's the story, A.J.?" Doc asked.

"Eugene and I found her in the woods. She hasn't been raped."

"How do you know that?"

"I know. Eugene is on the way here with Slim. When he gets here, we'll tell the story. Go check her out in the meantime. I think she was in shock when we found her." Doc was looking at A.J. hard. He knew that an abundance wasn't being said.

"I'll be wanting some answers soon, A.J.," he said.

"You'll have them. Oh, and Doc? When you get through with her, get your coroner stuff ready. The woods are full of dead people." Doc was on the way to the examining room. He stopped and slowly turned.

"I assume you are speaking euphemistically?"

"Nope."

Doc just stared.

"A.J., what in hell have you and Eugene gotten into?"

"We have wandered into a metric ton of shit," A.J. replied, and he meant every word. The old physician shook his head and left to tend his patient. A.J. stepped outside and waited for Slim and Eugene to arrive. His heels weren't kept cooling for long. The pile of cigarette butts at his feet had only grown to three when he heard the siren on Slim Neal's cruiser. Slim was usually as subtle as a B-52 raid and did not disappoint on the current occasion. He came sliding down Doc's driveway with all four wheels locked and leaped out. Eugene, A.J. noted, was sitting in the back where the prisoners go.

"Where is the girl?" Slim asked, excited and out of breath.

"She's in there with Doc," A.J. replied. Slim made to brush past A.J., who did not move from the door. "They won't be long," he continued. "Let's let them have their privacy." He couldn't precisely explain it, but he had become a little protective of her. The idea of Slim shining his flashlight at her private parts while looking for clues was unacceptable. Given Slim's history, it was not inconceivable that whole sections of her body would end up roped off with yellow tape, and A.J. wasn't going to have it. "Why don't you take my statement?" he suggested to Slim.

"I don't need your statement. Eugene has confessed. I know everything." Knowing Slim as he did, A.J. found that hard to believe.

"What, exactly, has Eugene confessed to?" he asked, looking toward the backseat of the police car. Eugene shrugged.

"To killing three men up on the mountain, of course. Said he beat two of them to death with your bat and shot a third one." Slim oozed exhilaration. "He says it was self-defense. Sure sounds like it was to me, but I've got to talk to that girl and check it out." Slim spoke proudly, unaware that the biggest case he had ever unraveled was solved incorrectly.

"Slim, that's not what happened," A.J. said. "I killed those men."

"A.J., A.J., A.J. Everyone knows Eugene is your buddy, and everyone knows you're going to stick up for him. Hell, even Eugene said you'd try to take the blame. Said you told him to just shut up and let you do the talking. I understand these things, but if you try to lie to the county sheriff when he gets here, you're going to get into trouble." Slim was patting A.J. on the shoulder and speaking in a tolerant tone.

"Can I talk to Eugene a minute?" A.J. asked tightly.

"Well, I don't know." Slim thought about the idea. "I guess it would be all right, but I'd have to put you in the backseat." He led A.J. to the car and shut him in. Eugene was sitting there, wearing handcuffs.

"What are you doing?" A.J. asked, getting right to the issue.

"Hell, A.J., the man wore me down. Had some of those hot lights shining on me. Beat me with a hose. I confessed. He also made me admit that I was the second man on the grassy knoll and he may have me pegged on the Lindbergh baby." Eugene had a faint smile on his lips.

"This is not funny. Tell him I did it, and quit playing around." A.J. was angry. It wasn't that he wanted to take the blame, or the credit, depending on the point of view. But right was right, and Eugene didn't do it. "If Slim is eating out of the palm of your hand,

103

why are you wearing the handcuffs? I'm telling you, you're loading yourself up for trouble you can't handle."

"Sorry," Eugene said. "It's my word against yours. You are a piss-poor liar, and I'm taking the rap. We were knights in shining armor on this deal, but four guys are dead. The shit heads shot one of them, and the two you brained with the bat were clearly self-defense. That leaves the one you made into dog food. A.J., I know you, and I know for a fact you were going to fuck that one up. You were already starting to warm up to that cold-blooded-murder shit. Now me, I can lie all day. Slim already knows that the man was just about to cut down on me and the girl, but I got him first. You had gone on ahead to find us a good spot to fish. By the time you got back, it was all over. As for the cuffs, do you know how long Slim has been waiting to slap these on somebody? Hell, I couldn't let him down. How often does he get to be in on a quadruple murder? Have a little compassion."

"There's a problem with your plan," A.J. said. "The girl remembers." It was a lie, but it might provide the necessary impetus for Eugene to recant.

"No problem at all," was Eugene's reply. "She was in shock. You prompted her because you're a hell of a guy and didn't want to see your buddy take the fall." He paused a moment before offering the kicker. "Here's the deal. You are a prince among men, and everybody knows you'd try to help me out of a jam. It's just something you'd do. Me, I'm a piece of shit. I've never done a noble thing in my life. Why would I start now?"

A.J. mentally acknowledged that Eugene seemed to have thought it through.

"Anyway," Eugene continued, "I'm a bootlegger. This will be great for my reputation. Might help get some of the larger bills cleared up. Maybe even discourage competition from some of the younger boys just taking up the trade." A.J. didn't know what to say. The abnormality of the conversation dovetailed with the absurdity of the day. They were a matched set, color-coordinated insanity.

"We'll take polygraph tests," A.J. offered, stubborn as a bulldog and losing ground. "I'll prove I did it."

"Those things won't stand up in court, and mine will come out better than yours, anyway. I lie better than I tell the truth. It's one of my strengths." Eugene was set on his course.

"Eugene, why are you doing this?" A.J. wasn't giving up, but he had to admit he had lost momentum.

"I'm doing it because I'm your friend. I can get away with this. You can't." Eugene was silent for a moment. "Besides, you would do it for me. Who knows? Someday I may need a favor."

The aftermath of the day's events was complicated. The girl's name was Regina Deberry of the Atlanta Deberrys, and she was a senior at the University of Georgia. Her declared major was anthropology, but her long weekend in the mountains had dampened her fascination with primitive cultures, and as soon as she returned to Athens she adjusted her academic focus toward psychology.

But there was one small blemish to clear up before she returned to scholastic life. Found among the ruins of the camp—in Regina's sleeping bag, to be exact—was five pounds of high-quality black Jamaican marijuana. The cache was discovered by Slim, and Regina's partial amnesia conveniently extended to cover the origin of the substance. So although she had been almost raped and nearly killed, Slim held her pending investigation of the drug charge.

"Any one of four dead guys he could nail, and Slim tries to hang it on the girl," Eugene said when he heard the news. He was disgusted. "Hell, I wish *I* had found it. It damn sure wouldn't be a problem now."

A.J. had no doubts on that score, and he found it unusual that Eugene had missed the stash when he had dashed back to retrieve his gun, because he hadn't overlooked anything else. He had re-claimed his pistol and its spent shell casings as well as retrieving A.J.'s fingerprints from both the bat and the M-16. He had replaced them with his own.

Regina's father, Mr. Deberry, Esquire, was a man of repute in the legal community, and he roared into town with the full intention of "straightening some country ass out." He spent exactly seven-teen minutes with Slim, and when he emerged from the town hall, he had his daughter. Slim remained inside. Mr. Deberry—*Deeb* to his friends—then sought out Eugene, who had succeeded in taking full responsibility for the killings despite A.J.'s best efforts to shift the blame to its rightful owner. Deeb found Eugene down at the beer joint, and they quaffed a couple while he thanked Eugene for sav-ing his daughter. Eugene was free on a property bond pending the outcome of the inquest, a guarantee posted by John Robert Long-street because Johnny Mack wouldn't sign. Deeb told Eugene his legal woes would be handled as soon as he got back to Atlanta, and he proved to be a man of his word.

As for the departed in the woods, they were dead first and fore-most, and not a great deal more could be added. The three A.J. had dispatched were the intended buyers of the marijuana. Kenneth was Regina's muscle on the deal, and Regina was the purveyor. The problem had been one of league. She was accustomed to dealing a little doobie down at the hallowed halls, and in that venue dissatisfied customers did not as a general habit rape and then kill their suppliers.

Playing with the big boys proved to have its own set of rules, but Regina was an intelligent woman who did not have to be told twice. She contracted with Eugene—whom she mistakenly believed would kill for her—to distribute all the black Jamaican she could provide, and since he warranted she would make a fair profit and not be ravaged or terminated, a partnership was born that lasted for several years.

This left the loose end of A.J. and Maggie. One of his main concerns—aside from Lukey in the Reidsville shower stall—was how Maggie would react when informed her beloved had killed more people than Lee Harvey Oswald, James Earl Ray, and Sirhan Sirhan, if that was his real name. But he told her anyway and was surprised to discover her thoughts on the affair were similar to Eugene's.

"Eugene was right. He could get away with it. *You* they would have hung." She spoke in a sardonic tone. "Anyway, he really wanted the credit. Can't you tell? He gets to be a hero without being a hero." And that was that, except for her comment on the act itself. After describing to her the scene at the campground, Maggie's response was cool and measured.

"Good. I hope it hurt."

Establish a scholarship in my name with the enclosed $5000.00.
—Excerpt of posthumous letter from Eugene Purdue to
the management of The Panther Club

A.J.'S WALK WITH MAYHEM WAS ANCIENT HISTORY, but it had taken center stage in his consciousness when Eugene had chosen to refer to the incident, and A.J. had been in a foul frame of mind ever since. His mood remained sour until the following Wednesday, when he was summoned to the mill for an early meeting. At that point, his disposition really decayed. He normally reported at 4:00 p.m. and turned logs into boards until 2:00 a.m. the following morning. He called it the Bermuda Shift, because many hapless souls had wandered onto it over the years, never to be seen again. He was sitting at the kitchen table drinking coffee with John Robert when the phone call came.

"A.J., there's a meeting at two o'clock," said Marie Prater. She had been an institution at the sawmill for many years. "You have to be here." Marie was John McCord's secretary, and John McCord was president and general manager of McCord Lumber. She was a formidable woman, seldom wrong and rarely challenged. Her husband, Randall, was disabled, having suffered from a bad back since about the time he was old enough to perform any work. This affliction was hereditary and had stricken his father and grandfather, and others before that. Marie's children—four teenaged boys with bad backs—amazed A.J., because he could not envision Randall expending the energy necessary to father them. In truth, none of the boys favored Randall much, and one of them was the spitting image of John McCord, so perhaps Marie had been forced to make other arrangements.

"What's the meeting about?" A.J. asked, still groggy. The previous evening's sawmill outing had been challenging, and he hadn't been up long. He hated early meetings and had pointed out on numerous occasions that if they were periodically scheduled for 3:00 a.m., then the day staff would be afforded equal opportunity to come in a couple of hours early. This suggestion had yet to be acted upon.

"I'm not supposed to say, but what the hell?" Marie replied. "John sold the mill. The new owners want to meet all the supervisors and managers." Rumors had been flying around the mill for weeks that a large lumber conglomerate was eyeing the property, and A.J. felt a stir of apprehension. The scuttlebutt had apparently been well-founded.

"Oh, shit," he said into the phone.

"You'd be surprised how many times I've heard that in the last couple of hours," was her reply. *"Oh, hell,* and *goddamn* have also been popular. All of you boys need to be watchin' that language." Marie was teasing A.J. in an attempt to lighten the moment. She was known throughout the Southeast and in three foreign ports for

110

her richly descriptive turn of phrase.

"Sorry about that, Marie," A.J. replied. "You know I don't think of you as a woman at all. You're just one of the guys to me." His mind was on the news she had imparted.

"Thanks a lot. Two o'clock," she said before hanging up. A.J. took a swig of coffee and sat quietly, thinking. Although the news at face value was not necessarily bad, he had a feeling that it would turn out to be so. He didn't know a great deal about Big Business, but he knew enough to realize he had just made the transition from big fish in a small lake to small fish in the middle of the ocean, if he was lucky, and dead fish in the creel if he was not. He turned to John Robert, who was watching him.

"McCord sold the sawmill," he told his father. "I have to go in to see who owns me now." John Robert digested the information for a moment.

"Well, he's older than I am," he offered. "I guess it's time for him to retire."

"Hell, he's already rich," A.J. said. "Why does he want to be richer?"

"Don't get upset until you know what you're dealing with," John Robert replied while refilling A.J.'s cup. "These new people will know a good man when they see one. You'll land on your feet."

John Robert had moved in with A.J. and Maggie six years previously after suffering a near-fatal heart attack. Luckily he had been in town and not somewhere out on the back forty when the bell tolled, so help was quick to arrive when he keeled over while having a cup of coffee and a couple of collision mats down at The Meek Shall Inherit the Chili-Mac Drive-In.

"That heart attack should have killed him," Doc Miller told A.J. when they met in the emergency room in Chattanooga, the location of the nearest hospital of consequence. He seemed shaken. "His heart stopped on the way here in the ambulance. All you could hear was that long, steady tone coming from the monitor. Before I could do anything, and believe me, I was moving fast, his own fist slammed into his chest, and he yelled *No!* I'll be damned if his heart didn't start beating again." Doc shook his head. "I've been a doctor for fifty years, and I've seen a lot in my time. But I've never seen anything like that."

"Nobody tells John Robert what to do," was A.J.'s reply as he watched his father through the glass of the ICU. "Not even God."

John Robert's recovery was slow, and he almost died again during the bypass surgery that followed his attack. It was the surgeon's skill rather than his own stubbornness that saved him that time, although to hear John Robert tell it, the man had nearly done him in. This trace of acrimony was due to a talk the doctor had with John Robert that was not altogether to the elder Longstreet's liking. During the conversation, the physician extracted a promise from John Robert that the Pall Mall he was currently smoking would be his last. This was no small demand to make upon a man who had thoroughly enjoyed the two packs a day he had smoked for the last half century. The doctor explained that anything less than full compliance would be fatal. John Robert eyed him coolly for a moment. Then he stubbed out the item in question in a handy potted plant and quit on the spot.

Having survived two brushes with death and the loss of his favorite and perhaps only vice, John Robert should have been out of the forest. But he had one last blow to sustain. Upon his release with a clean bill of health, he and A.J. sat down on a cold winter afternoon and tallied the medical bills that had been piling up in the knife drawer for two months during John Robert's convalescence. Life is cheap in many instances, but in John Robert's case the price of continued existence was in excess of one hundred thousand dollars, not small change except to those who spend the public monies.

A.J. called Charnell Jackson to seek financial advice. Charnell was the only lawyer in Sequoyah and one of John Robert's oldest friends. They had been boys together, and John Robert hadn't held it against Charnell when he had chosen to read the law. Charnell looked over the debts and viewed the available assets. Then he advised John Robert to file for bankruptcy. John Robert's reaction was negative, as if he had been advised to kick a good dog.

"I'm not broke," he said. "I have a little money in the bank, and I own the farm outright."

"The point is not what you have, John," was Charnell's patient reply. "The point is what you get to keep."

"The point is, I owe the money. They did their part, and now I have to do mine." He was quiet for a moment before rendering his decision. "Charnell, see if you can find a buyer for the farm. It ought to more than cover what I owe. Fix it so I can keep title to the cemetery plot and always have use of the road up to it. I'll need to tend to Rose and Mama." He looked at A.J. "I'm sorry about your inheritance."

"I already have a house, John Robert, and I can't farm for shit." He smiled at his father, trying to make him feel better. "You're doing me a favor."

"When the farm sells, I'd like to come stay with you and Maggie. At least for a while." A.J. was surprised John Robert had even brought it up; he and Maggie had been trying to talk him into moving in with them since Granmama had passed away.

Thus it came to pass that John Robert retired from farm life. The day after the farm sold, he arrived at the Folly with a truckload of belongings and was quickly incorporated into the household. A.J and Maggie had the impression John Robert was simply coming to live with them, but the elder Longstreet had more than mere occupancy in mind. The house was spotless before the first week was over, and three square meals per day began to grace the table. Maggie and. A.J. protested that he needed to relax and enjoy his golden years, but John Robert paid scant heed. Jobs that A.J. had been putting off were completed. John Robert washed windows, waxed floors, painted cabinets, mowed the yard, and did the shopping. He even dispatched the venerable repository known as the sewing barrel, into which many a torn item had been placed and forgotten.

"If I had known this," Maggie observed one Saturday, "I'd have peeled you off years ago and married John Robert."

"If *I* had known this," came A.J.'s reply, "I would have burned the farm and given you away at the wedding." He paused. "But I still make better lumber than he does."

"Of course you do," she replied, patting his leg absently as she turned the page of the book she was reading.

But all of that was long ago and far away, and A.J. was thinking of none of it as he prepared to depart for work to meet the new owners. He told John Robert to brief Maggie on what was up when she arrived, gave J.J. a kiss, and headed out into the wild, bad world, which was licking its chops as it awaited his arrival.

As was his custom, A.J. was working up to an agitated state, although his calm exterior gave no hint. He did not like uncertainty or change. He was a pessimist by nature, so by the time he drove into the sawmill parking lot, he had succeeded in losing all objectivity concerning the upcoming meeting. As he left the truck, he considered taking the Slugger with him in case he encountered a snake or two at the meeting. But he rejected the notion in favor of going for that good first impression.

A.J. had an itchy spot between his shoulder blades when he entered the conference room. He noticed the rest of the staff members were already there, looking nervous. John McCord was sitting in the front of the room with three somber men wearing nice suits. John wore blue jeans, as did the remainder of the attendees. The most solemn of the three newcomers looked pointedly at his watch as A.J. sat down. He was on time, but arriving fashionably early had apparently become a new company standard during the last couple of hours, and no one had informed him.

He had a bad feeling about the man with the watch. He leaned over and whispered to Ellis Simpson, his counterpart over at the planer mill. "I bet you five he's wearing red suspenders to match that tie."

"Shut up, A.J.," Ellis hissed back. "This shit is serious." Ellis had the habit of squinting one eye when he spoke, like Popeye. He was a good supervisor, and he, his nine children, and his wife, Raynell, all liked to eat three times a day.

"Boys," John McCord began, "I have sold the sawmill, and I am retiring. The man to my left is Mr. Ralph Hunter. He is vice president in charge of lumber operations for Alabama Southern. You now work at that corporation's fifteenth sawmill. They also own four plywood factories, a particleboard mill, two paper mills, and three chip mills. They are the big dogs. I believe Mr. Hunter has a few words to say."

As John McCord sat down, his gaze met A.J.'s, and in that instant, A.J. knew. John looked old, and he looked tired, but more than that, he looked guilty. McCord averted his eyes quickly, but the truth had been revealed. A.J. realized with certainty his sawmilling days were drawing to a close. He grasped that a long career with Alabama Southern was not ahead. What he did not yet know was how he felt about that.

Ralph Hunter removed his jacket before addressing the troops. His red suspenders gleamed, and the way A.J. saw it, Ellis Simpson now owed him five dollars, although collection might prove difficult.

"Gentlemen, I bid you a good afternoon, and welcome to Alabama Southern," he began. His manner was brisk, his voice atonal. He was looking no one in the eye, which in A.J.'s opinion was a bad sign.

"As Mr. McCord has indicated," Hunter continued, "Alabama Southern is a diversified corporation whose primary focus lies in the direction of responsible fiber usage. We are a *Fortune 500* company. We believe in the optimum interplay of our natural and human resources, which, when combined with strong strategic support from upper management and modernization of our physical facilities, guarantees our continued success as a leader in our industry."

A.J. believed that holding a man to his word was difficult if he spoke in code. He looked around the room. Half the boys were clearly lost, and John McCord was looking at the tops of his shoes. He looked up, and A.J. was staring at him with intensity. John looked back down at his brogans. He had started the mill from scratch forty years ago and had labored hard and long to make it fly. He expected hard work and loyalty, and he paid well for good employees. He had always favored A.J. because he got the job done. Actually, A.J. reminded McCord of himself in his younger days. And A.J. had always liked and respected John, but he didn't like him all that much today.

"At Alabama Southern, we believe that management is a team concept," Hunter droned on. "Some of you in this room have achieved exceptional results." He was looking at A.J., who looked right back. "Others in this room seem to be struggling." This time he was looking at Harry Ford, who looked like he wished he were elsewhere and who most likely would be before long. "Regardless of how each of you is currently performing, let me make myself clear about your status. You will be scheduled to meet with Mr. Kramer, our human resources manager." He gestured to the pallid individual sitting to his left. "He will interview you, and based on the outcomes of those interviews, you may be offered employment." A.J. took a long look at Mr. Kramer, who appeared to be a humorless soul. Ralph Hunter continued. "You will each be interviewed, and it is my hope you all will be offered continued employment at Alabama Southern Number Fifteen. Mr. McCord has spoken highly of you all and has recommended to me that you all be retained. I have noted his suggestion, and we shall see what we shall see. Are there any questions?" There were probably no more than five or six thousand potential queries, but anonymity had become suddenly attractive and no hands were raised.

This was a group of men who had made money for John Mc-Cord over the years by running his business well. They were all family men with many obligations and had paid their dues the hard way. To A.J., the current situation had an odor about it that made sitting in the room an effort. He took another long look at Kramer. Then A.J. shrugged. He wasn't going to survive the purge anyway, so he raised his hand. He hated set pieces. They tended to get his dander up. He believed that people's lives were more than file folders and numbers on balance sheets.

"For those of us who don't get offers, what do we take with us?" A.J. asked quietly.

"All of this will be covered by Mr. Kramer in the interviews," Mr. Hunter began, "but in general it will work like this. Whether you stay or move on, each of you will receive your vested retirement in the form of a lump sum settlement. For those of you who leave, Mr. McCord has insisted upon an additional ten-thousand-dollar settlement, which I have approved. I understand he intends to match that figure out of his own funds, for a total of twenty thousand dollars on top of the retirement settlement. Those of you hired by the company will be started at the pay rate paid for new hires at your particular job levels. Unfortunately, this will result in a substantial pay cut for any man who is hired, which may be offset somewhat by our excellent benefit package. Your current health and life insurance will remain in effect for a ninety-day period. This will allow any of you who might be leaving time to make other arrangements. Those who stay will be covered under the company plan. I think this addresses the basic points of your question."

A.J. was a bit surprised. The severance package was awfully sweet and seemed to offer a healthy bonus to anyone with enough sense to simply walk away. In all probability, it would be getting a lot of use. He raised his hand again. Ellis kicked him under the table.

"What factors will you look at when deciding who will be employed?" Ellis kicked A.J. again, harder this time. He continued. "The mill has exceeded production goals five out of the last six years. Everyone in this room is a professional. What else could possibly matter?" Ellis didn't kick A.J. this time, and all eyes were on Ralph Hunter. Hunter's eyes were on A.J.

"You men certainly know how to make lumber, and plenty of it," Hunter began. "This will be taken into account. In addition, we have other requirements with respect to our supervisory personnel. But we will leave all of this in the able hands of Mr. Kramer. For now, we will adjourn. Some of you have shifts in progress, and a supervisor's first job is to supervise. So let's get at 'em." Hunter had tried to be one of the boys with his last statement, but he simply wasn't up to the task. A.J. hoped he would hire one of the real boys to be hale and hearty for him, because the need would occasionally arise and most or all of the group would need the work.

"Mr. Simpson, I wonder if you would mind meeting me in the personnel office?" asked Mr. Kramer, although it wasn't really a question at all. Ellis froze. Then he looked at A.J., who was a little surprised that the weeding process was beginning so soon.

"Welcome to the *Fortune 500*, Ellis," A.J. said softly. "Show them what you've got." He slugged his friend on the shoulder. Ellis left looking worried, his thoughts no doubt consumed by visions of nine hungry children without shoes watching their mama, Raynell, working her fingers to the bone taking in ironing. A.J. thought they should have at least offered him a blindfold and a cigarette. He hoped maybe they were starting with the ones they were keeping, but in his heart of hearts he knew it wasn't so.

"Mr. Longstreet, can I have a minute of your time?" Ralph Hunter asked, and again, it really wasn't a question at all. The room had cleared out. "There are some things we need to discuss." A.J. was certain that the hardball was about to begin. They were moving him up to the head of the line. It was a compliment, really, like shooting the rogue steer first so the rest of the herd would be easier to control.

"Mr. Longstreet," Ralph began, briskly flipping through the pages in front of him in a businesslike manner. "According to the information I have been provided, your shift has exceeded its production goals by substantial margins ever since you began your supervisory duties on night shift."

"Yes," A.J. commented.

"Additionally, your absentee rate is lower than industry average and none of your employees have ever suffered a serious injury." Hunter put his papers down and looked across the table at A.J. He leaned back and lit a cigarette. "How do you do it?" he asked.

"How many of the men who just left this room are going to be offered jobs?" A.J. countered. "I know I'm history, but what about the rest?" It was very quiet in the room.

"You will be offered a position, Mr. Longstreet," Ralph Hunter answered. A.J. couldn't believe it. There had to be a catch. Hunter continued. "Alabama Southern does not plan to offer any of the others salaried jobs. They will all be given the choice of leaving or filling hourly positions in the mills. Monetarily, those who move on will do quite well. Those who stay will be able to make a living. I believe I am correct in my understanding that they all promoted up from the ranks in the first place, as you did. We will fill the slots they vacate with excess supervisory staff from our other locations. All veterans, all more qualified." A.J. had to give Hunter credit. He hadn't blinked. He apparently had more than a little of the rough stuff under his belt, which was no doubt why the Lumber Executives had sent him on this mission. It was why Ralph got the ham hock in his beans.

"Well, you were honest," A.J. admitted. "The problem is, I can't think of a more qualified group. What are you looking for that they don't have? Why are you offering them all twenty thousand dollars to leave? They know how to make this mill run. They know the machines and the employees. Why don't you want them?" A.J. had made his pitch.

"We require that all members of management have a college degree," Ralph Hunter replied. "None of your co-workers has a degree, and three of them did not graduate high school. Additionally, we have historically had less than satisfactory results when we assimilated an existing supervisory staff. It just does not work out. As you pointed out, we are making leaving a very attractive option. We do try to be fair about these things. And any who stay will not be singled out. There will be no hit list, unless, of course, the job performance is not satisfactory, which is sometimes the case in demotion situations. To keep all of this in perspective, you need to remember that we could simply fire you all on the spot. No options, no money, no anything." A.J. knew he had a point.

"I have a college degree," A.J. replied, "and it isn't worth a damn down in the mill. It didn't get me the job, and it hasn't helped me keep it."

"We have our requirements," said Ralph Hunter. "And I disagree with your statement that your degree has not helped you. In spite of your antagonistic demeanor throughout this meeting—which I understand and sympathize with, incidentally, whether you believe it or not—I would like to offer you employment." The words hung there.

"If you're dumping everyone else," A.J. finally said, "I guess I'm gone, too. I can't be the only one who gets out alive. Get the checks ready." A.J. hated to have to make the decision, but he knew it was the right thing to do. He did not have what it took to make a side deal, and he simply did not like Ralph Hunter, even though, as Ralph had pointed out, they could have canned everyone outright. He hoped Maggie would understand.

"You misunderstand," Hunter said. "I'm not offering you your old job. I do think, however, that you may be the man we're looking for to fill a training position we're creating. We need someone who knows the facility and the people to work with our new supervisors and bring them up to speed. That is the job I am offering to you. It will be a temporary position, but it could last as long as a year, depending on how things go." A.J. wasn't quite sure he had heard correctly. From the moment he had walked in the door, he knew he was going to be fired. He knew his reputation as unsecured artillery had preceded him. He had thought the best he would be able to manage would be to exit with dignity. Then Ralph Hunter had offered up the ultimate insult. A.J. slid back his chair and stood. He looked over at John McCord.

"Did you know about this, John?" He stared at McCord, who appeared to be inspecting the wood grain on the tabletop.

"Mr. McCord and I discussed the idea earlier today," Ralph said. "He told me that you would decline. I believed you might accept. The possibility exists that opportunities might be found for you at other facilities if the transition period here goes smoothly."

"I told him that you would tell him to stick it," John McCord commented, still inspecting the furniture.

"You told him right," A.J. said, turning to Hunter. "Stick it, Ralph. I'm not interested, and I won't go back to working hourly in the mill. I'll make room for the new talent." A.J.'s mind had been in a small cloud, but now he was clear as a bell. It was time to move on. "When do I get my money?" he asked.

"Mr. Kramer will be handling the details of all the severance packages," Hunter said. "Until such time as he deals with your case, you are expected to continue your usual duties." Hunter cleared his throat and directed a stern look in A.J.'s direction. "The very generous exit settlements we are offering are contingent upon your best efforts until you go. Negative actions such as production sabotage, work slowdowns, or attempts to sway hourly opinion against Alabama Southern will result in termination without benefits."

John McCord grimaced. A.J. gazed coolly at Ralph.

"Ralph," A.J. began, "you've insulted me twice now, and we've barely met. You are at your limit." Hunter lowered his eyes. Strangely, A.J. wasn't too upset. There were other jobs. He had begun to savor the freedom that came with unsalvageable situations. He headed for the door, thinking it had been a mistake, after all, to leave the bat in the truck.

When he entered the mill he was met by Ellis Simpson and Harry Ford. Harry handed a cup of coffee to A.J. and they walked out onto the log deck to lean up on a railing and discuss their troubles. A.J. was surprised to see Ellis was through interviewing with Kramer. It appeared that quick and clean was the Alabama Southern way. Ellis spoke.

"I've worked at this sawmill for nineteen years, and do you want to hear what job Kramer offered me? Laborer, that's what! I am forty-seven years old. I can't go back to pumping a shovel ten hours a day for $6.90 an hour. I haven't been screwed this good since my wedding night."

Ellis did have a small safety net of sorts. Raynell had a separate income as owner, manager, and sole employee of Raynell's Klip and Kurl. She plied her trade out of a small salon built with McCord lumber acquired piecemeal over time. Raynell gave a bad haircut but did a brisk business nonetheless, particularly among older gentlemen, due to her seemingly unintentional habit of poking an ample breast into the eye of the haircutee at least twice per session. So the Simpson family wouldn't starve, but neither would they be spending many sleepless nights worrying about the best investment strategies for their surplus revenues.

"What about you, A.J.?" Harry asked. He had not yet had his interview and held a touch of hope. "What did they say to you?" Harry was a mediocre performer but a very nice guy. He was employed for the sole reason that John McCord liked him and did not have the heart to put him on the street. His title was special manager, and his duties included making coffee and saying "Yes, John."

124

A.J. knew that Harry was doomed even though he made great coffee. Hunter had plenty of college boys with more seniority to brew for him, men who would brew loyally.

"They offered me a job I couldn't take, just like they did Ellis." Harry looked dejected. A.J. merely shrugged. There was no way to soften the blow. "Boys, we're all screwed. They don't want us."

"So you're taking the money?" asked Ellis.

"I'm taking the money," A.J. replied as he threw his empty coffee cup onto a pile of bark. He hoped the action didn't constitute production sabotage. "My advice is keep your mouth shut, hang on long enough to get your check, and give them the finger on the way out the gate." He sighed. It was very strange, but he realized he was going to miss the place. He stuck his hands in his pockets and headed on in. He had at least one more shift to run.

I have pictures of your husband with two hookers from Memphis.

—Excerpt of posthumous letter from Eugene Purdue to Misty
Hunter, wife of Ralph Hunter, Vice President, Alabama Southern

A.J. SAT IN HIS TRUCK, PARKED UNDER THE HANGING-
tree at the foot of Eugene's Mountain. It was just before dawn on
the Saturday following his meeting with Ralph Hunter, a date that
would live in infamy. He couldn't explain why he was there, except
to say it was as good a place as any to be, and better than some. He
sighed and flipped his cigarette out the vent window. With any luck
at all it would start a forest fire and burn down several thousand
acres of pine trees destined to become Alabama Southern lumber.
He had been unemployed now for about five hours, and even though
he had known it was coming, he had not yet arrived at complete objectivity regarding the condition.

The shift following the meeting with the mortal incarnations of
Alabama Southern had passed without incident, although the mill
was abuzz with rumors, and the men were unsettled. A.J. decided to
call a meeting right after break to address the crew's concerns. He
arrived at the break room as the crew was filing out. Luther Barnette

had just won the Wednesday night pool, and everyone milled around outside for a few moments out of respect for Luther's abilities.

The second shift's Wednesday night flatulence contest was legendary, and a respectable sum had changed hands over the years based upon its results. The competition was divided into three categories—decibel, duration, and effect—although there was some overlap due to the inexact nature of the groupings. Side bets were common, arguments were frequent, and any contestant who could clear the canteen took home the pot. Many exotic dishes were consumed by the hopefuls during the hours preceding the festivities as the aspirants searched for a combination of edibles that would provide the extra edge. The man to beat was Luther Barnette, who suffered from a blood condition that required his daily ingestion of a prescription drug containing sulphur. He usually won with authority.

Once they were able to reenter the lunch room, A.J. called the meeting to order. "This will be short," he said when he gained their attention. "I'll tell you everything I know, which isn't much. John McCord has sold the mill to an outfit called Alabama Southern. They're a big company with a lot of mills, and as of now you all work for them. I'm sure there will be some meetings to explain your benefits and such, and since this is a union shop, I don't see how any of you can get hurt on the deal. They have to honor your contract for its duration. After that, it's up to you. As for me, I'm history. The new owners are bringing their own supervisors with them. I don't know when that will happen, but it'll be soon." There was some murmuring and stirring. A.J. had always tried to be a good boss and was popular with his employees.

"When the new boy gets here, he might not run so good," said

Luther Barnette. He had an ominous tone.

"He might run like a short pig in deep shit," agreed Luther's brother, Snake. He was a quiet man, and he had just doubled the number of words A.J. had ever heard him say at one stretch. There were grunts of approval and nods of assent throughout the room, as if they had all seen short pigs run and had liked what they had seen.

"It's always a sad thing to see someone crash and burn," observed Fred Wallace. He loaded a good dip of snuff while casting a look that conveyed questionable intent.

"Whoa," A.J. said, holding up his hands. "Don't even think about lying down on these people. You can't help me, and you'll only end up hurting yourselves. Contract or no contract, they'll fire you if they catch you screwing around. Just do your jobs, collect your pay, feed your families, and keep your mouths shut." A.J. looked at them and wondered if they would follow the good advice he had given. It didn't look promising.

"Sawmill's a dangerous place," offered the infamous Mayo Reese of Sand Valley fame. He had walked into the mill one evening seven years earlier and asked for a job. Any job. His wife was sick, his children needed shoes, and Outlaw Pete, King of Modular Living, was about to haul the double-wide back down to the land of E-Z Credit. A.J. had taken pity. Life had casually done to Mayo that which no mere mortal had been able to manage. It had beaten and humbled him. A.J. couldn't stand it. He had given Mayo his hand and a job, neither to his regret.

Mayo expounded on his subject. "A stack of lumber could fall on him, or he could get sucked up into the chipper." The conversation was taking an ugly turn.

"Mayo," A.J. said, "do *not* kill the new boss. Don't even hurt him. Hell, he may be a great guy. But even if he is a dick, I don't want to be hearing about any accidents. I'm serious."

Mayo shrugged his shoulders. A.J. could have it his way.

"A.J., I want to work for *you*," said Brickhead Crowe, one of A.J.'s favorite people anywhere. Brickhead's given name was Conley, and he and A.J. had known each other since boyhood. He was intellectually challenged, and his nickname stemmed from the undeniable fact that he was as dumb as a brick. His alternate nickname, Pickhead, further illustrated the point. He had acquired it by knocking himself unconscious with his own pickax.

"I want that, too," said A.J., smiling gently at the large, slow speaking man. "But we can't always have what we want. You just do as good a job for the new people as you've always done for me, and you'll be fine." A.J. hoped this would be the case, anyway. He had always made allowances for Conley. It was an unspoken agreement on A.J.'s shift that everyone kept an eye on him. To do otherwise was to invite the Longstreet wrath.

A.J. had started school with Conley and had been keeping tabs on him ever since. Conley's mother, Eurlene, conceived him late in her life, long after the best eggs were gone. It is the way of children that they will harry a weaker member of the herd, but it became common knowledge among the pack early on that this was not to be done to Conley in front of A.J. He held a soft spot in his heart for his less capable schoolmate and would not tolerate any abuse of the slow but sweet child.

As was often the way in those days, Conley was passed from grade to grade, even though he had not mastered the work. Thus, he was allowed to remain with his classmates, and A.J. was afforded the opportunity to watch out for him. A.J. helped him with his schoolwork and ran interference when the necessity arose. Later on, when Conley felt the need to demonstrate his prowess on the grid-iron, A.J. was there. The big boy was strong and could hit hard, but he had no clue when it came to memorizing plays. So A.J. showed him, play by play, what was expected. They would line up, and A.J. would point to an opponent and say *hit him, then pull left.* And Conley would hit and pull left. This arrangement became so formalized that Coach Crider came to hold A.J. responsible for Conley's performance. *Goddamn it, Longstreet,* Coach would yell, *Brickhead missed his man by a mile and a half. What the hell is wrong with you boys?* So A.J. would talk with Conley and explain the error, and they would go at it again.

Some of the hardest words ever exchanged by A.J. and Eugene were over Conley. They were all sitting down at the depot one night sharing two quarts of beer when the conversation turned to Cyndi Hawkins. She was an older girl of twenty-one who had a small child, and legend had it that she would share the occasional favor. This subject was of great interest to Conley. His hormones had finally caught up with him, and he believed Cyndi was the most beautiful woman in the world.

In his halting manner, he asked how he might make his intentions known to her. He wished to declare on her and needed for his friends to coach him. He directed this query mainly to Eugene, who was the acknowledged swain of the group. By this point in time, Eugene had gotten lucky four times. Actually, he had been *astoundingly* fortunate once and had paid for it the other three. A.J., on the other hand, had not fared so well. He had almost managed to dance the waltz once with Diane, but there had been technical difficulties. So Eugene was deferred to on the matter at hand.

"What you have to do, Brick, is be direct," he began. "You have to walk right up and ask 'em. What would it take to get some of that pussy? If they're interested, they'll tell you what it will take. If they're not interested, they'll let you know that, too." A.J. immediately objected to this advice.

"Conley, that's all wrong," he said, glaring at Eugene. "What you have to do is be nice. Be polite. Maybe buy her some flowers." Conley looked back and forth between his advisors. He was confused. A.J.'s method sounded promising, but there was no getting around Eugene's impressive track record.

"Brickhead's not wanting a girlfriend," said Eugene. "He's just wanting some of that thing. You're going to mess him up, A.J." Eugene was amused.

"No, a girlfriend would be okay," Conley responded seriously. He had seen some pictures of that other business in a magazine and found it all a little hard to believe. But he was trying to take it on faith.

"What would it take to get some of that pussy?" Eugene intoned. "You listen to me, and I guarantee she'll be crawling all over you." Conley held both sides of his head, which was his way when presented with a quandary. He could only process so much information and was definitely in overload. He began to walk toward his car, still holding his head. A.J. walked with him.

"Eugene is full of shit," he assured Conley. "Do what I told you to do, and you'll be fine. If it doesn't work out with Cyndi, don't give up. It will work out with someone." He patted Conley on his shoulder and sent him on his way.

Eugene was still chuckling when A.J. walked back up and slapped the beer bottle out of his hand. It crashed on the pavement, spilling warm, brown foam onto the road.

"How many times have I told you to leave him alone?" A.J. asked. They were nose to nose. The humor had left Eugene's eyes.

"Fuck you, A.J. I was just having some fun. You know he's not going to buy her flowers *or* ask her for any. Women are not for poor old Brickhead." A hard tone entered his voice. "You owe me a beer. And the next time you pull this kind of shit, I'm going to have to hurt you."

"Hurt me now," A.J. said, pushing his shoulder. "Come on, Eugene. What would it take to get some of that ass?" They eyed each other a moment. Then the interlude passed, and the slow process of de-escalation began.

"You're crazy," Eugene said as he brushed past A.J. on the way to the newly acquired Lover.

"Leave Conley alone," A.J. hollered at his back. "I don't care who else you screw with, but leave Conley alone."

The postscript to the evening's events proved one of the pieces of advice had been valid and one had not. After much deliberation, Conley determined that A.J.'s suggestions would suffice. Stylistically, he was the Typhoid Mary of romance, but his heart was in the right place. Thus it was that Cyndi was inclined to kindness when Conley walked up to her and shoved a bouquet of slightly bent flowers into her arms. She smiled as he stood there, holding his head with both hands while inquiring about her health. She had known him since their childhood and knew him to be a harmless, gentle soul, one of the few she had encountered.

Cyndi's lot in life up to that point had been to hoe the hard row. Her mother, Louise, was unparalleled in her ability to select marginal members of the male gender with whom to frolic, and the only positive result from her many unions was Cyndi. Cyndi's father, Earl Hawkins, left for parts unknown via the Merchant Marine soon after impregnating Louise. He was a sensitive man, and had he known about his young wife's condition he would have gone anyway, but he would have felt bad about doing it. Cyndi never knew him, and none of the misfits who took his place during her childhood made much of an impression on her, except to produce in her a general uneasiness about the male of the species. In retrospect, those were the good years, and they ended upon Louise's marriage to Skim Murdock.

Skim was a man for whom the veneers of civilization held no appeal. He came to town with the county fair during the fall of Cyndi's fourteenth year and elected to stay on when the fair slipped off a day early while Skim was passed out due to an excess of alcohol, cocaine, and two of the employees of the girlie show. During his tenure with the organization he had offended the sensibilities of an entire carnival, and they unanimously took their opportunity to cut and run when they saw it. When Louise and Cyndi arrived at the fairgrounds looking forward to a little fun, they found instead a large amount of garbage, a broken car from the Tilt-a-Whirl, and Skim, sitting on the ground eating a corn dog while wondering what in hell he was going to do now.

Louise cast her eyes upon this banished remnant of the rites of autumn and decided he was the finest man she had ever seen, which wasn't saying much, considering what all she had seen. As usual, her instinct about men had failed. Louise was a moral woman, and all of the many souls who had visited her personal valley of paradise had first had to acquire title to the tract. So she married Skim Murdock in short order and moved him into her happy home, a well-kept trailer house sitting just across the Southern Railway line.

Cyndi had the misfortune to be an early bloomer, and by the time the honeymoon was over, Skim began to notice that she had flowered quite nicely, indeed. Unbeknownst to Louise, who worked the second shift over at the glove mill, Skim began to make improper advances upon Cyndi. Thus it came to pass that Cyndi was forced to gain carnal experience at the hands of her newest stepfather. Louise was blissfully unaware of the family dynamic she had created, so Cyndi determined her best course was to run away. Late one night right after she turned fifteen, Cyndi made her break. She had only walked about forty feet, however, when her small plan evolved into a grand scheme that held permanent solutions.

In front of her, the drunken and immobile form of Skim Murdock was draped across the Southern Railway line. He had apparently decided to have a few drinks before coming home and had been thirstier than he thought. Cyndi looked at her watch and noted that the coal train was due. Time being a luxury granted the young, she sat down, reached into her rucksack for a Coke, and calmly sipped while she waited. She loved trains and suspected she would absolutely adore this one. It was quiet except for the crickets and the snores of Skim. In the distance she heard the thrum of her salvation.

As the train neared its target, the victim began to stir. He was feeling the vibrations through the steel ribbons. The engines came around the bend and bathed his form in bright light. The engineer saw the body on the tracks and applied the brakes as he began to blow the horns repeatedly. The lights and noise roused Skim from his stupor, and he saw his predicament. Then he saw Cyndi, who appeared to be taking a drink of Coke.

"Goddamn it, girl, help me," he roared at her as he attempted to gain his hands and knees. It has been noted that young girls do not always know their own minds, but Cyndi knew exactly what she wanted, and Skim knew it, too, as their eyes met for the final time. She reared back and chunked the Coke bottle at him, and he screamed when it hit his forehead. The scene was ghostly as the train slid past with horns blaring and sparks flying. Skim was frozen in the harsh glare, and then he was gone, given a boost down the highway to hell courtesy of Southern Railway, Jim Beam, Coca-Cola, and Cyndi.

The freight train finally stopped about a mile down the tracks. Most of Skim had reaped the whirlwind, but enough was found to bury, although pieces of an unlucky raccoon were irretrievably mixed in with him. Cyndi removed the Coke bottle from the small pile of remains before they were shoveled into the bucket. It was a keepsake marking the best time she had ever had with Skim. All in all, no one seemed to be much upset over the incident except Louise. Fortunately, she got over her loss fairly quickly with the help of a grave digger from Boaz who took a shine to her at Skim's funeral based mostly on how nice she looked in those tight, white jeans. Time heals most wounds, and love will find a way.

Cyndi turned wild and acquired the reputation for being bountiful with her indulgences, a relative rarity in a culture where milk was seldom dispensed without prior cow purchase. So she was popular, but her full dance card brought her no joy. She was punishing Louise, God, and herself, but neither of the first two seemed to take much notice.

Cyndi's salvation arrived in the form of a five-pound, seven-ounce baby girl whom she named Hope. She didn't know who the baby's father was, but it didn't matter, because they were all pretty much the same anyway. What counted was her determination that the child never know the trials Cyndi had known. So she gave up her wanton ways and set about the business of raising her daughter.

And this was the new-and-improved Cyndi for whom Conley had set his cap, but he was making no headway. Although she was always nice to him, she seemed immune to his charms. He consulted A.J., who advised him to be patient, because these things take time. So Conley devoted more effort and ingenuity to the endeavor. Cyndi would come home to a freshly mown yard, and there would be Conley, head in hands, staring at his shoes. Gifts began to appear on her porch, dime-store luxuries he believed to be grand, and he was always available to carry groceries, take out the trash, or wash the car. Cyndi knew he had a crush on her, and although she in no way encouraged him, she was patient. She did not want to hurt his feelings and felt he would soon grow tired of pitching his woo. She was incorrect, for she did not understand the depth of the feelings he had for her.

Eventually, Conley found it necessary to move on to plan B. On that fateful day, Cyndi came out of the glove mill and found him standing there, waiting.

"Hello, Conley," she said in a light tone. It was payday, and she was in a good mood. He mumbled a phrase, but the mill at her back was noisy. "I'm sorry, Conley, I couldn't hear. What did you say?" She looked at him. He was trembling and seemed to be in grave distress. Then he raised his head, and in the single most courageous moment of his life, he spoke what was on his mind.

"What would it take to get some of that pussy?" he asked quietly. Then he lowered his head and awaited his doom. He had tried A.J.'s methods with little success, and now he was hauling out the big guns.

Cyndi looked at the terrified form of Conley. She was taken aback, but not as much as she might have been, for she had once heard those words from another source: Eugene. Since his survival would have been virtually impossible if he had committed to her requirements, however, their love had gone unrequited. So Cyndi knew Conley's rough request had been the result of some extremely bad advice, and that he meant no harm.

Many thoughts crossed Cyndi's mind as she looked at Conley. He stood there quaking, and her heart went out to him. Because she had traveled the hard way, she was capable of great compassion. She saw before her a lonely man who had tried valiantly to win her affections. She, too, knew the bitter taste of loneliness, and she did not want to end up with a succession of rogues the way Louise had. Realistically, she knew her prospects were limited; small towns are not kind to women with checkered pasts. What she wanted was a lifelong companion, a partner to share her joys and sorrows, someone to love. She didn't think it was too much to ask.

And then she realized with a slight startle that standing in front of her was the most decent man she had ever known. The epiphany rolled over her like the coal train had run over Skim. Impulsively, she reached and raised his chin so that their eyes met.

"What it would take, Conley, is for you to marry me. Love me, love Hope, and never hurt us or leave us. Work hard, bring your check home every week, and build a home and a life with me." She had not intended to say any of this, not even remotely, but sometimes words operate of their own accord. His eyes said yes before his mouth did, but Conley always was a little slow of speech.

They married shortly thereafter, and Conley was as good as his word. He treated Cyndi like a queen and Hope like a princess, and he and Cyndi built a fine life. Cyndi, too, was as good as her word, and Conley was afforded plenty of opportunities for intimacy. Thus it was that presently along came Rita Sue, Tammy Faye, Brandy Starr, Sweet Melissa, and the twin boys, Starsky and Hutch.

A.J. snapped from his reverie and noted the sun climbing the sky. He looked at his watch. It was just after seven in the morning and he needed a cup of coffee and a friendly ear. John Robert was off on a hunting trip, and Maggie and the children were gone on a trip to visit Maggie's sister, Eudora Welty. She was entering the bonds of holy matrimony that very afternoon after a painfully long engagement to a history professor named Carlisle Davenport, of whom A.J. suspected a lack of intellectual rigor.

A.J. dropped the truck into gear and headed up Eugene's Mountain. The Purdues were notoriously early risers, and A.J. discounted the possibility of awakening Eugene. Thanks to the recent grading job, the trip to the cabin was quick.

The clearing appeared to be the scene of catastrophic events.

Eugene's Jeep was totally obliterated, and A.J. was forced to weave around large pieces of it. The Lover was up on its side and was missing some critical components. The hackberry tree was reduced to a splintered stump. Craters pocked the area. The door to the cabin opened, and out stepped Eugene wrapped in a blanket. Beside him limped Rufus, bandaged but still malicious. He made a start for A.J., but the sudden movement seemed to cause him pain. He abandoned the assault and sat down to nurse his wounds. Eugene absently patted him on the head.

"Don't worry, boy," he said to the dog. "You can attack A.J. twice next time." Eugene moved slowly, and his breathing was labored. He was favoring his right arm, and his eyes had dark circles tinged with yellow. He shuffled to his chair and sat. He was fully dressed and wrapped in a blanket, but still he shivered. On the cable spool was a large quantity of marijuana along with the usual collection of medications, spirits, and firearm supplies. In addition, there were three hand grenades piled carelessly in a bowl. A.J. knew what had destroyed the clearing. Eugene spoke.

"I didn't know if I'd see you today. I thought you might still be a little pissed." He shifted in his chair, wincing with the movement. He seemed to be searching for a comfortable spot that was always just one step ahead. He looked bad.

"I wasn't pissed," A.J. replied, taking a seat. "I had to go rinse out a few things and take care of some long overdue correspondence." He gestured to the carnage in the yard. "Someone run a little air strike in here? Slim finally figure out who got the bus?" Eugene picked up one of the grenades and handed it to A.J.

"These are great," he said. "That bit about pulling the pin with

140

your teeth is a crock of shit, though." He pointed at the remainder of one of his incisors. "Broke this one. Hurt so bad I dropped the damn grenade. By the time I found it, I was a little pressed for time, and I barely got it thrown out of here. Almost blew up poor old Rufus. He took some shrapnel, but I got it out." Rufus looked over at the mention of his name. A.J. felt a little bad for his canine foe. It must be difficult to be Eugene's dog.

"Where did you get them?" A.J. asked, hefting the lethal object. It was heavier than he thought it would be.

"Bird Egg brought them to me. He's been coming up a couple times a week with supplies, and he thought I would enjoy them."

Bird Egg was an institution, a man whose mission in life was to never draw another sober breath. He was a local boy who had gone off to help Douglas MacArthur stamp out the Asiatic Hordes, and he had returned from the Korean peninsula with strong aversions to bitter cold, sudden death, and heavily armed yellow people wearing tennis shoes. He was currently in charge of Eugene's beer joint and was the perfect man for the job. His duties included selling beer and liquor, playing cards, breaking up fights unless he was personally involved, and paying off Red Arnold, the ancient and venal county sheriff. He took no wages other than what he drank and ate, and he even left his substantial poker winnings in the general fund.

"Where did Bird Egg get hand grenades?" A.J. asked, handing the pineapple back to Eugene.

"I have an associate from Fort Benning who occasionally lays his hands on some interesting war surplus items."

"War surplus?" asked A.J. "You could get thirty years for receiving stolen government goods." Eugene rolled his eyes, and A.J.

realized his warning was foolish, given the circumstances.

"I'll take it," Eugene commented. He stood, pulled the pin, and hurled the grenade into the woods.

"Duck," he said. He hit the deck gently, as if he were in slow motion. A.J. was not nearly as graceful as he kissed the floorboards. When the explosive went off, the porch shook, and bits and pieces of the forest landed in the clearing. A.J. was slow getting up. His ears were ringing, and his body tingled from the force of the blast. Eugene was grinning from ear to ear. "I just love these things," he said. "Now you throw one. We can blow up your truck. I'll buy you another one."

"I like my truck."

"Your problem is that you don't know how to have fun," Eugene said as he settled himself back into his chair. He attempted to light a cigarette, but his hands were shaking badly and he couldn't manage. A.J. lit it for him.

"How is Bird Egg doing?" A.J. asked, changing the subject. He had not seen the old man in a while.

"He's been stabbed again," Eugene replied. "I found out about it yesterday. Red came up to tell me. He also told me that I'm closed down for a week." He gazed at one of the craters in the yard.

"That's no big deal," A.J. said. "He's always getting stabbed or shot. It's a tradition with him." It was true. Bird Egg had been winged often during his long, checkered time. He was opinionated and tended to incite strong emotions in others.

"This time it's a big deal. Termite Nichols stuck a *long* knife in him and nicked his liver." Termite was living proof that occasionally abortions are necessary. And prisons, should intervention not be possible in that crucial first trimester. "His liver hasn't had an easy life," Eugene continued, "and it damn sure didn't need a knife stuck in it. He's in bad shape." There was a long pause. Bird Egg wasn't much, but he was theirs.

A.J. felt a small wave of sadness lap at him. Too many constants were changing, belying the illusion of permanence. He hated change, and it seemed everything was in flux. The way things were going, Maggie would probably meet a handsome academic down at Eudora's wedding, one with patches on the elbows of his corduroy jacket who made quotation marks with his fingers. He would suggest he and Maggie "have coffee," and that would be the old burrito for A.J. Maybe he would get the kids on alternate weekends. Eugene spoke.

"Do you ever wish you could do something different? You know, that you could go back and do just one thing over, do it better maybe, or maybe not do it at all?"

"I wish I had gone to sea," A.J. replied without hesitation. "I wanted to see the world, and smell the salt air on the midnight watch, and ride out a hurricane, and find out if it's true what they say about Chinese girls." He shrugged. "But I didn't, and now the time is gone." John Robert had sailed four of the seven seas in his day, and it had been a wondrous time, although that part where the Japanese boys tried to crash their planes into his ship hadn't been so great. He instilled this love for the sea in his son, but one thing had led to another, and A.J. never made it up the gangplank.

"It's not true about Chinese girls," Eugene said, comforting his friend. "If I could do one thing over, I'd be better to Diane." He sighed. The enormity of his crimes was heavy upon his soul. Then

143

A.J. had an epiphany.

"Well, hell, Eugene. She's not dead. Let's hop in the truck and go find her."

"I don't know about that," Eugene said, sounding doubtful. He winced and grabbed his side, fumbled for some pills, and washed them down with a taste of bourbon. Then he fired up a pipeful of the marijuana and took two or three deep hits. "Helps with the nausea," he croaked, offering some to A.J., who declined. "I have some suppositories, but I'd rather smoke dope."

"Get up," A.J. said to Eugene. "We're going to town. Maybe get a cup of coffee. Maybe run into Diane. Hell, bring a gun. We might see Johnny Mack, and you could shoot him." That idea appeared to cheer Eugene considerably, and he made up his mind.

"All right, let's go," he said. "I haven't been down the mountain in a while. I need a change." He stood and dropped his blanket. Then he went inside, and when he came back he was carrying a shoe box under his arm. He had donned his Grateful Dead jacket. The skull on the back of the garment bore a strong resemblance to Eugene, and A.J. made a mental note that they needed to visit Doc Miller while they were in town. Eugene loaded several items of importance into his jacket pockets: pills, his pipe and some contents for it, a fresh pint bottle of Ancient Age. He lingered over the grenade bowl as if he could not decide, but finally shook his head and passed them up. A.J. wondered how it would have gone if the jacket pockets had been larger. They made slow progress across the clearing to the truck, and A.J. noticed how much Eugene appeared to have gone down during the past week. If he had not witnessed the decline for himself, he would not have believed it.

"You drive," Eugene said, climbing into the passenger side.

"Good idea," replied A.J. They headed down the road. A.J. missed as many bumps as he could in light of Eugene's frailty. Still, the trip was rugged, and Eugene braced against every jolt. When they finally gained the highway the ride eased considerably, and Eugene unscrewed the cap from the whiskey and took a tentative sip.

"You seem a little low yourself," he said, taking another taste before screwing the lid back on. "What about? If it's Rufus, don't worry. He's going to make it just fine."

"I got fired last night," A.J. replied. "I don't have a job." A.J. recounted the tale of his short tenure with Alabama Southern. Since he had survived a mere three days, it didn't take long to tell the story. Boy meets employer, boy pisses employer off, and boy gets shown the door. It was the same old story.

"Let me get this straight," Eugene said. "They showed up at two o'clock this morning right after your shift and fired you?"

"The personnel guy and someone I didn't know were waiting for me when I got to the office. Handed me my money, wished me a nice life, and took away my keys. I asked the other guy if he was my replacement, and he said he was. I gave him my paperwork and told him that there was the number to beat. Then I left." Actually, the new guy hadn't seemed a bad sort, and A.J. hoped Mayo didn't throw him into the chipper.

"That was a nice touch," commented Eugene. "Let the boy know he's in the bigs now. Tell you what. I've got a rifle back at the cabin I guarantee will take all of these fuckers out at one thousand yards. Got a tripod and a scope and everything. Even *you* couldn't miss. Let's go get it."

"As you pointed out last week," A.J. said, "I can hit what I'm aiming at."

"Pardon me for being indelicate, but on full automatic it's kind of like mowing the grass. We're talking fine work here. Ridge work." His voice failed, and a small shudder overtook him. He downed a couple of pills with the bourbon, and then sat quietly.

"Where do you want to go?" A.J. asked as they neared the outskirts of town. The town wasn't much, so neither were the outskirts. A decision would have to be made quickly.

"Take me to Diane's house. I want to talk to her a minute." A.J. looked at his watch.

"It's still a little early. Why don't we have a cup of coffee and give her a chance to wake up?"

"No, I was kind of hoping to see her in her nightgown once more before I die," Eugene said. "She always looked fine in her gown." His eyes were closed, and he was slumped down in the seat. His voice held a deep weariness. "I didn't think I ever wanted to see her again. But as soon as you mentioned going to town, I knew I wanted to talk to her."

So A.J. drove across town and pulled up by the side of Diane's home. He turned off the truck and waited for something to happen. When nothing did, he spoke.

"Eugene, we're here. What now?"

"How bad do I look to you? Be honest."

"You look pretty bad," A.J. said, telling the truth and hating its lack of mercy.

"That's what I figured. How about going in and telling her I need to see her? Kind of prepare her."

146

A.J. sighed. He had somehow known this was going to happen. He looked at his friend and saw the sadness in his eyes.

"Sure. I'll be right back." He walked up to the house and rapped. At first there was no answer, but after a subsequent knock, the door opened. There stood Diane, and Eugene was right. She looked fine in her nightgown.

"A.J., what are you doing here?" she asked with confusion on her face.

"I need to talk to you. I swear it won't take long. Can I come in?" She looked unhappy with the request. "This is important," he said. "Please." She considered for a moment. Then she shook her head before looking over her shoulder.

"The boys spent the night with their granddaddy," she said quietly. "I have company. Could you come back in about an hour? We can talk all morning then, if you want to." A.J. sighed. It was a good thing the porch was unobservable from the truck.

"I have Eugene in the truck," he said. "I'll be back in an hour." A look of wariness entered her eyes. "Diane, please. I wouldn't have brought him if I didn't think it was important."

"Okay. One hour. I'm trusting you on this, A.J." She closed the door, and A.J. made his way back to the truck. Eugene appeared to be asleep, but he opened his eyes when the truck door slammed.

"I couldn't get anyone to the door," A.J. lied. "She must be in the shower. We'll try back in an hour or so."

"I still have a key to this house," Eugene said. "She looks even finer in the shower than she does in her nightgown."

"Let's just come back later," A.J. said, U-turning on the spot so Eugene would not see the mystery visitor's car parked out front. A.J.

had recognized it and was having difficulty absorbing its implications. "If I saw Diane in the shower," he continued, "we would just have to fight again. It would look bad for me to whip a man in your condition. I'd do it, but it would look bad."

"I can whip you with one pancreas tied behind my back," Eugene responded. A.J. could tell he was tired and decided to swing by and see Doc Miller while they were waiting for Diane's appointment book to clear up. He did not burden Eugene with the information, but they were going to the doctor, and that was that. Eugene looked bad and sounded worse. Predictably, he bowed up as soon as they entered Doc's driveway.

"Hell, no," he said.

"You come in, or I'll bring him out. Pick it."

"Bastard," Eugene said, opening his door and getting out.

"Language," A.J. said as he walked him slowly to the steps. They progressed to Doc's door. Eugene stood there with his shoe box and grumbled while A.J. knocked. Presently, Doc answered. He was wearing a pair of pajama bottoms, a T-shirt, and a pair of worn slippers. He held a cup of coffee and the door as they filed in.

"Doc, you need to take a look at Eugene," A.J. said.

"They dress a little better down at Emory," chided Eugene as he eyed Doc's footwear.

"Well, go on down to Emory, or come on in the office," said Doc testily. "My eggs are getting cold."

Doc and Eugene went into the examining room, and A.J. sat down to wait. Minnie offered a cup of coffee, which he gratefully accepted. It had been a long night and was turning into a longer morning. To pass the time, he raised the lid of Eugene's shoe box, which had been entrusted into his care. It was full of twenty-dollar bills banded neatly into stacks. All told, the shoe box contained fifteen thousand dollars. A.J. whistled softly and closed the lid. After about twenty minutes, Eugene and Doc came out of the office. They were arguing.

"No, Doc, I won't do that. If it's my time, then it's my time."

"Damn it, Eugene. It doesn't have to be your time yet. We can buy you five, maybe six months." Doc sounded exasperated.

"*Fuck* five or six months," Eugene said intensely. "What good are five or six months?"

"Eugene, if you don't do what I say, you will die."

"Doc, if I *do* what you say, I'll die anyway. No offense, but I'll pass. How much do I owe you?"

"I don't want your money," Doc said. "I want you to use your head." He looked over at A.J. "You talk some sense into him."

"He won't listen to me," A.J. said. "Never has." Eugene reached for the shoe box and removed one of the stacks of twenties. He placed the cash on the table.

"I appreciate all you've done for me, but you can't save me, and I'm not spending my final days wired up like a stereo. I'm going my way, and now I'm going to the truck." Eugene walked out the door.

"What was that all about?" A.J. asked.

"Ethically speaking, I'm not supposed to discuss it with you, but what the hell. Along with about twenty other things that are going wrong, his liver is starting to fail. Or at least, that's what I think. He needs to be in a hospital for some tests and some treatment, and he needs to stop drinking. Hell, he smells like a distillery right now."

"He won't do either," said A.J. There was no use pretending.

"His time is short," Doc said, "and he won't lift a damn finger to prolong it." He pointed at the money on the table. "I don't want that."

"You know he likes to pay his way, Doc. Keep it. Treat the widows and orphans with it." A.J. was forming a question in his mind. "Do you know long he has?"

"I have no idea how long. We are no longer even nearly in the six-month neighborhood. In medical terms, he's circling the drain." Outside, they could hear the truck horn blow. Doc stepped back in his office and returned with a bottle of pills. "When his pain becomes severe, these will help. I ordered them especially for him." Doc graced A.J. with an appraising glance. "The dosage is a little tricky, especially when mixed with alcohol. As the pain gets worse, the medication has to be increased. A little too much, and he just doesn't wake up. Lethal but painless." There was a long silence, a pregnant pause rife with unspoken thoughts. The truck horn blew again.

"I've got to go,. Doc," A.J. said, pocketing the little pills that were guaranteed one way or another to end Eugene's pain. He wondered what was going on in Doc's mind, but he knew there would be no clarifications. He looked at Doc momentarily, and then walked to the truck. Eugene was petulant.

"The man just told me not to put on any long-playing records, so you stand around and shoot the shit with him for half the day. Great."

"Sorry about that." A.J. looked at his watch. They were in the launch window for the visit to Diane. He drove in the direction of

150

her house. On the way, they met the vehicle driven by Diane's companion of the previous evening. The two drivers traded glances and recognition. A.J. grunted. Life was peculiar at times.

They arrived at Diane's, and he pulled up close and parked. Eugene had preened during the drive and looked more presentable. A.J. wanted to wait in the truck, but Eugene had other ideas. He seemed desperate for an ally, and A.J. relented. Together they walked up on the porch, and A.J. knocked. Diane answered almost immediately. She was wearing blue jeans and a grey sweatshirt. Her hair was tousled. She gasped. A.J. recalled that she had not seen Eugene for a while.

"Eugene, what's happened to you? You look terrible!" Her hand went involuntarily to her mouth.

"I've been a little sick," he said. "Can we come in?" She held the door, and Eugene stepped through, holding his shoe box. A.J. looked at his watch.

"I've got something important to take care of," A.J. said. After being up all night, a cup of coffee was important. "I'll be back in an hour," he called over his shoulder as he cut a quick retreat. He had gotten Eugene to the water, but it was up to him to drink or drown.

A.J. drove down to the Thou Shall Not Covet Thy Neighbor's Spaghetti Buffet Drive-In for a cup of coffee. Most of the Saturday morning crowd was there, and word was already on the streets concerning A.J.'s realignment from employed to not. The general consensus was that A.J. had gotten the dirty end of the stick, but these things happen. There was further agreement that John Mc-Cord should be shot, but there were no volunteers and A.J. was too tired to go do it himself. Maybe later.

After an hour of pity and commiseration, he estimated he had left the Purdues alone long enough. A.J. thanked Hoghead, paid for his coffee, and exited the diner and drove slowly over to Diane's house. He could always drive on past if things were going well, and he wanted to be nearby should gunplay erupt.

When he arrived, he saw that they were sitting on the porch swing. They seemed at ease with one another, and A.J. started to leave when Eugene waved him up to the porch. As he stepped up, he saw that Diane was softly crying. The shoe box was nowhere to be seen. Eugene arose, then bent down and kissed her gently on the cheek. She stood and held him close for many heartbeats, and then slowly, almost reluctantly, she released him for all time. She turned, went inside, and quietly closed the door.

"Take me home," Eugene said. His voice was husky and immeasurably sad. The drive to the cabin was silent. When they arrived in the clearing, Eugene got out without a word and went up on the porch. Then he turned.

"Thank you for that," he said quietly. "I'd like to be alone now."

"Maybe I'd better hang around a little while," A.J. said, concerned over his friend's state of mind.

"Don't worry," replied Eugene distantly. "I won't blow my brains out. It's not time for that. Not yet. When are you coming back?"

"I'm unemployed. I can come more often. I'll see you tomorrow." A.J. drove down the road. His ears strained for the sound of the gunshot, but it did not come. Eugene was correct. It was not yet time for that.

Being dead is not that bad. There are a lot of people here I know.
In fact, most of them were your patients.
—Excerpt of posthumous letter from
Eugene Purdue to Doc Miller

A.J. ARRIVED HOME TO AN EMPTY FOLLY. MAGGIE
and the children were due that evening from Eudora's wedding in
Atlanta, and John Robert was expected whenever he showed up.
The house was quiet, a condition it did not seem comfortable with.
A.J. was tired. He had endured a tedious night followed by an end-
less morning. Eugene's parting with Diane had been heartbreaking
and difficult to behold. Their farewells had produced in him a sadness he could not shake. Plus, he was jobless, but he found that once
the initial shock had ebbed, he was not greatly concerned over this
new status. It was not the first time he had been without visible
means of support, and there was no guarantee it would be the last.

Ironically, A.J.'s last bout with unemployment had ended when
he hired on with John McCord after he and Maggie reappeared from
college. When they returned from the ivy halls, freshly scrubbed
and bursting with the wisdom of the ages, Maggie landed a job as
the school social worker for Cherokee County. She had shown the

good sense to obtain a degree in social work, and if she worked hard and kept her nose clean, she could one day expect to command a salary on par with that drawn by Mr. Gus, the custodian at the elementary school. A.J., on the other hand, was having a hard time peddling his B.S. in Psychology to anyone for any price. He came, in time, to attribute new meanings to the initials B.S. But for all of that, he was still secretly proud of becoming a man of letters, even though it was only two.

In the interim between graduation and the delivery of Emily Charlotte about a year later, hard reality set in upon Maggie and A.J. Maggie had her low-paying job down at the school, which would become no-paying upon her commencement of maternity leave. A.J. had many irons in the fire, but his efforts to secure a permanent situation were not bearing fruit. In retrospect, he realized he should have earned a degree with more career potential, such as archaeology or astronomy. But that was water under the bridge, simply another eddy in the currents of his life.

He briefly drove a dump truck for Johnny Mack Purdue but decided he wasn't cut out for the trade on the very day his brakes failed in a curve halfway down the Alabama side of Lookout Mountain. He was hauling twenty-five tons of gravel at the time, and the remainder of the trip down the grade was completed with authority. He resigned as soon as the truck rolled to a stop. Johnny Mack tried to rehire him, stating that anyone who could have survived that trip was a natural driver, and good boys were getting hard to find.

A.J. thanked his benefactor and sought other avenues. He worked two weeks down at the Jesus Is the Light of the Barbecue Plates Drive-In, but Hoghead was forced to apologetically let him go because he couldn't get the coffee right. He moved on to working with John Robert out at the farm, but this resembled charity because it was, and he did not stay long. He temporarily pursued carpentry until the morning he discovered gravity's impact on careless elevated carpenters. By this point, he was harboring thoughts of running Mr. Gus off the road so he could get his hands on that cushy janitor's job at the school. Finally—and with a strong sense of *déjà vu*—he went to work dragging slabs down at John McCord's sawmill. Ironically, he was almost passed over for his old job because now he was overqualified.

So A.J. knew what it was to be economically idle, and it gave him no pause in its current incarnation. Something would come up, and they would not starve in the meantime.

A sad rain fell, turning the air chill. A trace of coal smoke drifted up the valley. He donned his jacket and stepped onto the back porch for a smoke. The breeze tugged his collar. This was normally the kind of day he loved, but today it struck him as bleak. There was a hole in him that he was unequipped to fill, and he wished his family would come home. He needed their comforting presence the way the dying need the gods. He sat quietly in the porch rocker that had been Granmama's. His mind wandered back in time to her final day. His memories were like fine crystal etchings, the remembrances delicate and fragile.

The call from John Robert came early on a Sunday morning. Clara had suffered a stroke and was to be transported to the hospital in Chattanooga the moment the ambulance arrived. A.J. awoke Maggie and explained what was happening, then roared into the night. He was at Granmama's bedside in twenty minutes.

155

"I heard a noise like she was falling down," John Robert offered, his face grim. "When I came in here, she was on the floor. I called Doc right away. He says it doesn't look good." Doc was listening to her chest with his stethoscope, shaking his head and muttering. He looked up at A.J. and John Robert.

"This was a big stroke. If we get her to the hospital before she bottoms out, we might save her. After that, I don't know." The ambulance from the county service arrived, and Doc lashed the attendants like a mule team while they loaded their patient in record time. Slim arrived in the cruiser with blue lights flashing, and Miss Clara and entourage made for the bright lights of the big city.

By noon it was apparent the situation was deteriorating. She was still alive, but she was attached to most of the machinery in the intensive care ward and surrounded by many somber-faced members of the medical community. A.J., John Robert, and Doc paced the waiting room. Slim had tears in his eyes and kept referring to her in the past tense. *She was a saint. She was a damn saint*, he said repeatedly. A.J. could see that this tribute was wearing on John Robert's nerves, so he prevailed upon Slim to take Doc home. Then he and John Robert sat down to wait.

"How old is Granmama, John Robert?" A.J. asked. He was bad with dates and ages. "Is it eighty?"

"Eighty-one," John Robert said. "That Slim is a real idiot," he continued. The observation caught A.J. off guard. It was uncommon for John Robert to cast a disparaging remark, but it was an unusual day.

"Yeah, you're right about that," A.J. agreed. "But he sure does think a lot of Granmama."

Around four in the afternoon, A.J. called Maggie. "How is she?" Maggie asked. A.J. took a breath that sounded like a ragged tear in a piece of cloth.

"She's dying."

"I'm so sorry," Maggie said. "How is John Robert holding up?"

"He's smoking and staring a lot. You know how he is. He doesn't talk much."

"I know. Call me if there's any change. I love you."

"I love you, too," A.J. said. "I'll be home in the morning, or I'll call if I need to stay longer."

Around 6:00 that evening they were visited by the neurologist. Dr. Prine was a compact person whose eyes held weary compassion. She explained that Clara's stroke had been massive, and she was left with no brain function. Barring a miracle, she would not regain consciousness. A decision would eventually need to be made on the subject of life support. Dr. Prine left after expressing her sympathies and telling them she would see them the following day. For a long time after she had gone, no words were uttered by the pair. They were an island of silence in the sea of life. Then A.J. spoke.

"I don't know what to do."

"I do," came John Robert's reply. "We talked about this a long time ago. She always said she didn't want to be kept alive past her time. She even wrote it out on paper." He fell into a stare. Then he arose and walked outside, where he lit a cigarette. A.J. joined him.

"So you're going to tell them to let her go?" he asked. John Robert did not speak for an entire Pall Mall, and he was a slow smoker. Then he looked at his son and spoke.

"I can't do it. It would be like killing her myself." A.J. was overcome with pity for his father. He reached out and touched John Robert's shoulder. The world as they knew it was coming to an end.

"I'll take care of it, John Robert," he said. It was the last thing he wanted and the only thing to do. John Robert slowly nodded. The night passed in silence, and next morning A.J. conferred with Dr. Prine. Granmama's condition had worsened. He gave a sigh.

"It was my grandmother's wish, and it is my father's wish, that we remove life support when there is no sound medical reason for it to remain." The words hung in the air, limp as wash on the line.

"Is this your wish, as well?" His wishes probably did not matter, but it was considerate of Dr. Prine to inquire.

"My wish is that she hops up, and we go get in the truck and go home," A.J. sadly replied. "But that's not going to happen."

And so, late in the afternoon, the ventilator was removed and the life support was shut down. The candle that was Granmama began to burn toward its nub. Not long after, Clara Longstreet, mother of John Robert and grandmother of Arthur John, matriarch of the Longstreet clan, flickered out of this world and took her place beside the clumsy young husband who had waited patiently for her all those years. What Jehovah and a hay baler had put asunder, A.J. and Dr. Prine had now rejoined.

A.J. felt nothing. He supposed he was numb or maybe in shock. He and John Robert stepped out to the loading dock for a cigarette. A hearse was parked there, waiting to load some hapless soul for the long trip home. They both averted their eyes, as if they had seen something illicit. As they stood there, smoking and staring at the ground, A.J. attempted to make himself feel sad. But the effort was wasted, and no emotion would come to him. *I'm sorry, Granmama,* he thought. *I loved you, and I will cry for you when I can.*

Granmama had wanted her final arrangements to be done up in the old style and had left several pages of instructions written in her spidery hand. A.J. and John Robert read through these the day after her death while she was over at the Fun Home being prepared. The Fun Home was Raymond Poteet's Funeral Home, and not a great deal of fun had ever been had there. It had become the Fun Home as a result of the second poorest business decision of Raymond's career. He was a thrifty man, and in his early days as town mortician he discovered that the sign maker he had retained charged by the letter, so he instructed the rogue artisan to abbreviate the word *funeral* by using the letters f-u-n followed by an almost imperceptible period. The Fun Home was born.

Raymond's *worst* decision—arguably the poorest business move ever made by anyone, anywhere—occurred when he attempted to open a barbecue restaurant in a small building that adjoined the Fun Home. Sensibilities being what they are, not much barbecue was sold, and theories about the origin of the meat outlasted the establishment—named Heavenly Ribs—by many years.

Clara's instructions were clear. She wanted to lie in state and receive visitors in her own home. From the tone of her note, it was clear she expected large numbers, and she instructed A.J. to crawl up under the house and inspect the floor joists to be sure they were up to it. She had already arranged for an old-fashioned pine box, and when A.J. picked it up from Nub Williams, he had to admire its simplicity and quality. It was constructed of pine boards and configured in the archaic six-sided shape, like the coffins occupied by John Wesley Hardin and Count Dracula, to name but two.

"Nub, they don't make pine like this anymore," A.J. said to the carpenter, rubbing his hand down the side of the coffin, respecting the obvious excellence of the construction. There were so many coats of varnish on the vessel that it appeared to have depth.

"I come up on those boards years ago," came Nub's nine-fingered reply. Pride could be heard in his voice. He had done a good job and knew it. "I was savin' 'em for somethin' special. When me an' your granmama talked last year, I decided right then I knew what those planks were meant for." A.J. asked about the charge for the work. Nub looked hurt.

"I wouldn't let her pay me, and I don't want your money, neither. She was a fine woman, and there ain't no charge." A.J. thanked him and hauled Clara's coffin over to Raymond Poteet.

Clara had left no detail uncovered. She specified the nightgown she wished to wear into the void and the hairdo she wanted to sport when she went. She wanted to be put away next to her husband down in the grove by the lake. The songs she requested were "Amazing Grace" and "Swing Low, Sweet Chariot," both to be sung by Angel Purdue, whose voice was beautiful even if she was Catholic. The instructions went on and on.

"John Robert, have you seen this list of pallbearers?" A.J. asked.
"No."

"I'm going to need a court order and a backhoe to get four of them. The fifth is down at Raymond Poteet's right now, and not for the barbecue. The sixth is Doc Miller." They both grimaced.

"We'll make Doc an honorary pallbearer," said John Robert. "Do you think you can line some folks up to do the carrying?"

"Yeah, John Robert, I'm sure I can." So the horsepower for

Granmama's trip down that last mile was supplied by a collection of willing volunteers. A.J.'s only problem was in selecting only six out of the large number of applicants for the positions. Eugene was the first to raise his hand.

"I'd like to be in on the deal," he said. "She was a good old girl."

When it came time to lay the corpse, Raymond Poteet brought her out to the farm and arranged her in the parlor. She was up on two sawhorses, as requested, surrounded by flowers, favorite mementos, and pictures from her life.

"I haven't done one like this in twenty years," Raymond said, admiring his handiwork. He was decked out in his best funeral suit, somber, black, and respectful. He had arranged and rearranged until everything was just so. "This is a slice of history," he said to A.J. and John Robert. "There won't be any more like this, done in the old way." John Robert raised his eyebrow, and A.J. knew it was time to send Raymond back to the Fun Home. He ushered the undertaker out to the yard, and they stood by the long black Cadillac hearse. A.J. brought up the subject of payment.

"You've done a fine job, Raymond," A.J. said, shaking his hand. "Get the bill totaled and I'll be down in a couple of days to settle up." Not surprisingly, Raymond already had a figure in mind. He had indeed done a fine job, but business was business, and he wasn't an undertaker solely because he liked to be around dead people. But when he related the sum for the preparations, A.J. was confused. "That sounds a little low, Raymond," he said.

"I'm doing your granmama at cost," Raymond said simply. "She was a fine woman."

A.J. had to blink a tear. Raymond was a cheapskate from a

long line of excessively frugal people. As such, money was naturally very important to him. The only other person ever to receive
"at cost" service was his own mother, a fact verified by Charnell
Jackson, who had handled the estate. The honor of the gesture was
not wasted on A.J., and he suspected that even Granmama might
have approved, although she had not always been charitable when
it came to the subject of Raymond Poteet. She had once observed
that the only part of dying she really dreaded was that Raymond
Poteet would see her unclothed. That part, at least, was over, and
since she hadn't rolled over, maybe it hadn't been as bad as she had
thought it would be. A.J. thanked Raymond again and sent him on
his way. Then he went back inside to sit with John Robert, Maggie, Eugene, and with Granmama. Emily Charlotte was staying
with Carson McCullers, one of Maggie's sisters, and was due to be
dropped off when Carson came to pay her respects.

The preacher arrived, a young theologian by the name of
the Reverend Doctor Jensen McCarthy. A.J. liked the man who
had ministered to his granmama's spiritual needs for the last six
or seven years, even if he did appear to be around fourteen years
old. His deceased predecessor had been a crusty old so-and-so,
and A.J. had always figured his ascension had depended heavily
on whether God had been grading on the curve that day. But the
Reverend Doctor seemed sincere and honest, qualities that washed
a multitude of sins, even in a preacher. Still, A.J. was uneasy. He
supposed it was the close proximity of John Robert to anything
pertaining to the Almighty.

The Reverend McCarthy expressed his condolences and spoke
in complimentary tones on the subject of his departed parishioner.

The trouble began at the call to pray when he noticed all heads had bowed but John Robert's. A more seasoned veteran in local affairs would have let it pass, but the Reverend Doctor decided to gently lead John Robert to prayer. In his defense, he could not help himself. It was what they had taught him to do at preacher's school, and he truly felt it was his mission to help John Robert. A.J. was sitting with head bowed and eyes closed, so it was a surprise to him when Jensen McCarthy spoke.

"John Robert, at times like these it is a comfort to know the Lord," he said, his tone reasonable and compassionate. "Come. Pray with me." He held out his hand to the elder Longstreet. The room held no sound. A.J. looked at the Reverend Doctor with respect, amazed at the obvious level of commitment and belief shown by his actions. A.J. knew it would do him no good, but Jensen certainly seemed to have the courage of his convictions, a rarity worthy of note. After a long silence, John Robert spoke.

"Reverend, Mama thought a lot of you, and you seem to be a well-meaning man. It is not my place to interfere with what you need to do. In her instructions, she said you knew all the arrangements. I leave all that to you. Please take care of your business." John Robert rose and began to depart.

"You need to know God," said Jenson McCarthy quietly and sincerely to John Robert's retreating back.

"I know Him," came the reply. "I just don't care for His company." The screen door squeaked as John Robert left. After an uncomfortable silence, the Reverend Doctor turned to A.J. He looked pained and sad.

The remainder of the visit was anti-climatic. Reverend McCarthy

led them in prayer, and the invocation seemed to restore him somewhat, but he was still not quite himself. A.J. wanted to tell him to not
take it so hard, that it was impossible for a mere mortal to put John
Robert on his knees. But the opportunity did not present itself, and
A.J. did not press. They briefly discussed the arrangements for the
following day over a cup of coffee.

"A.J., I apologize," Jensen McCarthy said on his way out. "I
picked a poor time to try to convert an unbeliever. I owe an apology to John Robert." He spoke in a subdued tone. A.J. thought that
Jensen looked like he could use a couple of belts, but it was impolite
to offer. For that matter, he could have used a swallow himself.

"Don't worry about it, Reverend. We all know that John Robert has his ways, and Granmama knew it, too." A.J. paused. "You're
wrong about one thing, though. He's not an unbeliever." John Robert's hatred was sustained by his belief. A.J. was surprised the Reverend
Doctor had not understood. He seemed sharper than that.

"That went well," he said to Maggie after the preacher had gone.

"I thought so," she said, smiling ruefully.

"Next time you get married, maybe you ought to shoot for normal people."

"Maybe," she replied, coming over and holding him. They
were still for a while, holding one another while Granmama slept
the long sleep.

"This is too weird for me," said A.J. "Do you know I don't even feel
sad? I don't feel anything. I'm just as screwed up as John Robert."

"You're sad," she said with concern in her voice. "I can tell."
She held him a little longer.

The ritual that followed resembled an Irish wake, although the only Irish present were third and fourth generation, and no consumption of alcohol was evident except for the occasional nip Eugene secured in the yard. Friends and neighbors began to drop by to express their regard, and by dark it was standing room only. Food was brought by all of the female mourners, and the kitchen and dining room were filled to capacity with hams, fried chicken, potato salad, and an uncountable array of side dishes, pies, and cakes. Everyone commented on how good Granmama looked, which A.J. considered nonsense, because she was dead. But the observations were well meant, and there isn't all that much that could *be* said about a dead body. Granmama had covered the subject at length in her final instructions, and A.J. smiled when he remembered her words on the notebook paper:

I don't want the whole town to see me when I'm dead, but I don't suppose that it's decent to have a closed coffin unless there has been an accident or a fire. But you mark my words on this. I do not want Estelle Chastain throwing herself all over me and having a fit. *She tends to do that. You remember what she did at Bonnie Cotton's funeral. She got in there with Bonnie, and they had a time getting her out. What they should have done was just nail her up, since she always said she was so close to Bonnie, although Bonnie remembered it differently.*

So A.J. nodded and shook hands as the town filed past, but he kept a close eye on Estelle to make sure she behaved herself. She did, mostly, and A.J. was quick to escort her out for a medicinal dose of potato salad on the one occasion she seemed to be working herself into a state.

The public portion of the ceremony began to wind down around nine o'clock, and by ten or so the group had dwindled to

John Robert, A.J., Maggie with a sleeping Emily Charlotte on her lap, Charnell Jackson, Doc Miller, Eugene, and Slim Neal, who was grief-stricken. Eugene told A.J. that Slim had actually broken down earlier in the day while writing a speeding ticket and had let the scofflaw off with a tearful warning when he found himself too over-come to resume. This was not the Slim they had all come to know and love, and even John Robert was unable to bring himself to run the maudlin public official off.

"Well, she's in heaven now," offered Charnell Jackson, raising his glass in tribute. With the crowds gone, John Robert had allowed the bar to open. Granmama herself had enjoyed the occasional drop of wine.

"Surrounded by ten million birds who want to have a word with her," A.J. noted quietly with a smile. Eugene choked on his drink.

"*Thirsty* birds," Maggie said with a chuckle.

"Ten million thirsty birds with the attitude that they wouldn't eat a vegetable if you paid them," Eugene said, laughing quietly. John Robert had a broad smile, the first on his features in some time.

Granmama had been a Christian saint among the women of the world, but she would not tolerate a bird in her vegetable patch. Her solution to this perennial problem did not involve scarecrows, which were ineffective, or shotgun blasts in the air, which tended to separate the telephone wires from the house. Ever since A.J. could remember, she had fed the birds to keep them out of her garden. Every morning, Clara pinched off a wad of biscuit dough for her feathered friends and loaded it down with as much salt it would as-similate. Then she made little balls out of the mixture and scattered them around her garden. The unsuspecting winged felons would

166

hop up, cute as could be, and partake of these tidbits. An hour later they would be dead as a stone.

"Look, she's feeding the birds," Maggie had said during her first visit to the farm. "Your granmama is so nice."

"She's killing the birds," A.J. corrected her. "She's like the Joe Stalin of the bird world. She's killed more birds than Colonel Sanders."

"That's not funny," Maggie replied, taking Granmama's side. She looked so sweet out there with her straw hat and apron, slowly working her way to the left in an attempt to flank an especially cunning blackbird that was resistant to her wiles. *Coo, coo* could be heard wafting in the breeze, although A.J. had no idea why Granmama was trying to lure a blackbird by making pigeon noises.

"I swear it's true," he said to Maggie. "Every day I go down with a bucket and pick them up. This place is bird hell." So Granmama had been a tad judgmental with the avian population, but that was small potatoes when compared to the sins of the wretched world.

They toasted her quietly once again, and she in her pine box accepted their tribute with quiet repose. More stories emerged, testimonials to the life she had led and the woman she had been. Maggie shared the advice that had been offered upon her marriage to A.J.: *Now, honey, you'll have to put up with a certain amount of that business if you want to have children.* Much good-natured kidding was heaped upon A.J., and for a few moments the cat had his tongue. Doc Miller told of the time he suggested she take a tablespoon or two of wine at mealtimes to aid her digestion. This was sound medical advice, and often the old ways were the best. Clara took right to the idea, and before long she was consuming a bottle of wine per day, but always one tablespoon at a time.

"She enjoyed her tablespoon of wine," John Robert agreed, smiling slightly as he remembered the exact manner in which she poured her dosage.

"Damn, Doc," Eugene said. "It's a good thing you didn't put her on salty dough." Eugene had consumed uncounted tablespoon-fuls of good Canadian whiskey by this time, but his observation had nonetheless been presented with the greatest respect.

They moved out to the porch, and the narrations continued into the night, verbal monuments carved on the gentle Georgia breeze, a celebration in flesh and word of one of the good Lord's finer pieces of work. There was a sweet sadness underlying the vignettes, and a gentle humor. She had not been perfect, and she did not change the world, although in her small part of it she had been a force to contend with. Her legacy was right there on that porch, friends and family who remembered her well and who wished she had not gone, plain people gathered together to try to fill the empty space now left in their lives. Her harvest was the dozens of visitors earlier in the evening who had felt the need to express a fare-thee-well. Her eu-logy was the quiet murmur drifting from the porch in a generally starward direction, simple soliloquies in which no hard word could be discerned from people who would not let her face her last dawn aboveground alone.

The night passed, and the sky to the east shaded from black to blue. The quiet before the sunrise was broken by the chirping of birds as they got an early start on the daily business of survival. The early ones got the worms, and the rest would be left with the salty dough. The group on the porch began to move around and stretch. A.J. stepped out to the old pump by the well house and worked the cast-iron handle. The antique was there long past its necessity because Granmama had liked it. A.J. washed his face in the cool gush of water. Eugene joined him.

"Are you in the mood to dig a hole?" A.J. asked. Eugene had his head under the spout. He came up and shook his head like an old hound.

"Let's do it," he said. Granmama wanted her final resting place opened and closed by hand and had specified this requirement in terms that held no ambiguity. So while Eugene threw some digging tools into the truck, A.J. walked up to the house to see who wished to participate. Doc did, but he had checked with Minnie and had to go. There were still some out there he could save. Slim wanted the honor but was duty bound to go make a round. He promised to return shortly if no criminal activity detained him. Charnell also wanted to be of service, but Doc forbade it.

"You know what I've told you about your heart, Charnell," Doc said. "If you try to help dig this grave, we'll end up putting you in it." So Charnell agreed to help Maggie make some breakfast. The plan was formed to bring the gravediggers hot coffee and fresh biscuits presently. John Robert appeared on the porch. He was clean shaven and wore a fresh white shirt.

"Are you ready, John Robert?" A.J. asked.

"Ready."

"You're going to ruin that shirt."

"Expect so."

The burial party piled into A.J.'s truck and headed for the grove. John Robert marked off the grave while A.J. unloaded the tools—spades, a mattock, and an axe for the inevitable tree root. They set

169

to, one on the mattock and the others on the shovels, and before long they were shin deep. A truck pulled up, and they looked over, expecting to see Charnell and the biscuits. They saw him, and he had more than breakfast with him. In the cab were Slim and Bird Egg, and a group of Sequoyah's finest filled the cargo compartment: Hoghead, T.C. Clark, Brickhead, John McCord, and Jackie Purdue. The second shift took over the digging as A.J., John Robert, and Eugene took a coffee break. The work progressed swiftly, and the task was completed before the sun had climbed to the tops of the oaks. They adjourned back to the house, where Eugene and A.J. meticulously washed A.J.'s old truck, which would serve as Clara's caisson to the grove. She had possessed a soft spot for the vehicle, calling it a *good old pile of junk*, and A.J. thought she would prefer it to a hearse. All was ready for her *bon voyage*.

And so they sent her off. On a spring afternoon so blue and mild that it snatched the breath, Clara claimed her reward. Her mortal remains were placed carefully beside her husband, and the Reverend Doctor offered kind and comforting words. Angel sang so sweetly that surely even God above turned His vast attention toward high Georgia and looked with favor upon His gathered children. Then dozens of willing hands—men, women, and children—quickly replaced the dirt that had been earlier removed. It was done. Clara Longstreet weighed anchor and set sail, and neither she nor her equal would again grace the lives of her loved ones.

A.J. snapped out of his reverie with a start. He had not thought of Granmama's death in a long time. The misty rain had grown to a drizzle. The chill in the air had turned to cold. He did not know the time and could not swear to the day. A deep melancholy

170

descended upon him, a profound sadness, and he could not remember ever being as totally alone as he was in that instant. A tear slid down his cheek, then another. His throat closed, and his body shuddered as he tried to deny the emotion. His self-control crumbled and he began to cry.

"Well, shit," he said between clenched teeth. He was grateful that Maggie and the children were not present to witness the spectacle.

A.J. sat and cried in the cold rain. He cried until his eyes were dry and his voice was hoarse. He cried for Eugene. He cried for the millions of souls who never saw it coming. And he cried for Granmama. She had been cold in the clay for ten long years. Finally, A.J. had found his tears.

Whatever you do, don't marry someone like me again.
—Excerpt of posthumous letter from
Eugene Purdue to Diane, his ex-wife

A.J. WAS SITTING AT THE KITCHEN TABLE EATING
fried Spam when his family arrived home from Eudora's wedding.
Spam was a treat reserved for when Maggie was elsewhere, because
she could not tolerate the smell of the sautéed delicacy. A.J. had
never understood this point of view and finally came to the conclusion it was a gender phenomenon, something to do with the Y
chromosome. So he ate faster when he heard the van door slam in
the driveway. His one thought was to remove the evidence. The
can was already in the garbage, and he had rinsed the pan right
after sliding the greasy brown rectangles onto his plate. Long years
of illicit Spam eating had taught him to eradicate the trail. He
swallowed the last bite just as J.J. burst through the door, followed
by his two older sisters. Maggie brought up the rear looking somewhat the worse for wear.

"Daddy, Daddy!" J.J. shouted as he jumped in A.J.'s lap. "I won
the license plate game!" This was one of the cherished car games

of the Longstreet children. On long drives they would compete to see who could spot license plates from different states. A.J. found it odd that his son had won. The boy was vague on the rules and had once claimed a *Get Your Heart in Dixie or Get Your Ass Out* plate on the front of a Dodge pickup.

"He did not win," stated Harper Lee. "He counted Georgia licenses forty-two times. He cheats." There was disgust in her voice, as if her sibling were something she had discovered on the bottom of her shoe.

"I don't cheat!" J.J. hollered.

"How many states did you count?" Emily Charlotte asked, her voice reasonable and calm. A.J. wanted to warn J.J. that anything he said would be used against him.

"Seventy-seven," he replied. A.J. cringed. He was on his own.

"There are only fifty!" Emily slammed her point home. She brushed past on the way to her room.

"Are not!" came J.J.'s rebuttal. He jumped from his father's lap and followed his nemesis from the room.

"He is such a creep," said Harper Lee. "We should give him away." She took car games very seriously and was hard pressed to accept dishonesty in the ranks. They could hear the debate raging upstairs. She shook her head as she left the kitchen. A.J. arose and went to Maggie.

"Good trip?" he asked as he gave her a hug.

"Does it sound like it was a good trip?"

"They were just exploring their limits."

"I smell fried Spam," was her reply. She wrinkled her nose.

"Nope. No fried Spam here."

"There are two things a woman can smell on her husband," said Maggie. "One is a truck stop waitress. The other is fried Spam."

"I'm caught," he said, abashed. "Her name is Rochelle. She told me that if I left you, I could fry all the Spam I wanted."

"She'll tell you that *now*. Just wait until the first time you try it." She sat down at the table and began to rub her temples, as if the thought of Rochelle frying Spam was too much to bear. A.J. came up behind her and took over.

"How was the wedding?" he asked. It had been quiet long enough, and he was hungry for some conversation.

"It was fine. Eudora was beautiful, and Carlisle looked very handsome in his tuxedo." She was silent a moment as A.J. continued to coax the stress away with his fingers. "Your father-in-law had a few too many at the reception and started a little card game. Deuces and one-eyed jacks. Took about a thousand dollars off of Carlisle's father, who apparently fancies himself a gambler. My sister could have killed them both." A.J. did not doubt it. Eudora took a dim view of such behavior and was not shy about expressing her opinions. A.J. was surprised she hadn't confiscated the money and put the offenders to doing the odd job or two out in the yard.

"Did the children do okay?" A.J. asked. All the Longstreet children had taken part in the ceremony. J.J. had been the ring bearer, Harper Lee had been the flower girl, and Emily Charlotte had stood in attendance. They had all been excited about their participation except J.J., who had thrown a screaming fit when he first viewed his miniature grey tuxedo. *He'll never wear that*, A.J. had said, wondering why women insisted upon dressing little boys to look adorable. *He'll wear it*, had been Maggie's reply, and she was right. But it had been an act of will on her part, and she was a strong-willed woman.

"My daughters were angelic. Your son was not." She shook her head. "I swear they gave us the wrong baby." This was their old gag when J.J. became challenging, which was most of the time. The joke lay in the fact that they had not delivered him in a hospital at all.

He had been born during the worst blizzard in Sequoyah history, which surprised neither A.J. nor Maggie once they came to know him. Georgia is not snow country, and even the mountainous areas get only a light dusting two or three times each winter. But J.J. was born on the night of the Hundred Year Storm, when nearly thirty inches of powder were unceremoniously dumped on the mountain valley during a twelve-hour period. Temperatures hovered around zero, and howling winds from the west chased the wind chill to minus thirty. Trees began to snap and fall before nightfall, taking with them the electricity that warmed the valley and kept the darkness at bay. A.J. lit the lanterns and built a large fire before wading out into the storm to retrieve his neighbor, Estelle Chastain.

"I don't want to be snowed in with Estelle," he grumbled as Maggie directed him into his boots and coat. She handed him his scarf.

"Go get her, anyway," was the firm reply. No elderly neighbors were freezing to death on her watch. They settled Estelle into the Folly, and she and the children curled up in front of the fire. It was a scene straight out of the eighteenth century. Outside, the arctic winds lashed the Longstreet sanctuary. Inside, the children and Estelle drowsed by the hearth. A.J. was discovering that it was difficult to read by lantern light regardless of Honest Abe's luck with the practice. Maggie and John Robert were rocking quietly, staring at the fiery phantoms on the grate.

"This is kind of cozy," said John Robert. "Reminds me of the days before the TVA."

"Yeah, it could be a lot worse," agreed A.J., feeling at peace.

"My water just broke," said Maggie. She was eight months pregnant. At her regular visit two days earlier, the doctor had pronounced her fit as a fiddle and right on schedule. But be all that as it may, the snow had just hit the fan.

"You're not due yet!" said A.J., stating the obvious. Impending childbirth always pumped him right up.

"I can't help that," she said. "I've been having pains for about two hours. I thought that maybe it was back strain, but we're about to have a baby." A.J. thought she was awfully calm, given the circumstances.

"But you're not due yet!" he said.

"If you say that again, I will hurt you," Maggie said. She was up and pacing while holding her back. She always walked during early labor, and her communications tended to be unambiguous. John Robert jumped from his chair. It was no time for sitting. First he tried the phone, which was dead. Then he shoved past A.J. on his way to the door.

"I'll go warm up the truck," he said as he put on his coat and his old hat with the fur earflaps. A.J. stared at him for a moment before shaking his head.

"There is no way we can make it to the hospital in this storm," he said to his father. The wind howled loudly, as if agreeing with him. A.J.'s mind raced to come up with a plan. Estelle startled awake. When advised of the situation, she sprang to her feet and went to boil water on the gas stove. A.J. thought for another moment, and then he spoke.

"We need to try to get her to Doc Miller's place. It's not too far." He looked at Maggie, who had paused from her stroll around the living room to breathe through a pain. She was notorious for short, dramatic labors and showed every indication of moving right along with this one. "Maggie, I think we should try to take you over to Doc's. What do you think?"

"I think I would rather have this baby naked in a snowdrift than to have Estelle help deliver him. Let's go before she comes out with a knife to cut the pain." So A.J. went out to warm up the truck while John Robert helped her into her coat. Then they bundled her into her makeshift ambulance, and A.J. and Maggie set off into the storm. The truck bed was filled with a load of firewood cut the previous day, and A.J. was glad for the extra weight. Even so, he had to let most of the air out of the back tires before the vehicle would gain traction. As they pulled away, he saw in his mirror the forlorn sight of John Robert waving. Standing by him was a disappointed Estelle, steaming teakettle in one hand and butcher knife in the other.

The trip to Doc's was surreal. The landscape was chiseled in snow and ice. Green lightning flashed, but there was no thunder. Trees were glazed and bent to the ground. A.J. heard the crack of a power pole as the ice brought it low. The Longstreets lived only three miles from town, but it took thirty minutes to cover this distance. They were off the road as much as on, and the truck added several dents and scrapes to its already impressive display. They were traveling backward when they entered the outskirts of town, with A.J. cursing softly as he tried to gain control. Luckily, the post office stopped their momentum. Maggie groaned involuntarily before pointing out in unkind terms he could expect to be short lived if he bounced her like that again.

"How are you doing?" A.J. asked as he attempted to get the truck off of Federal property. The tires spun and caught. His headache felt as if someone had driven a splitting wedge between his eyes.

"Better than you, looks like," she panted as another pain hit. She dealt with the contraction, braced and rigid, and then continued. "We seem to have hit the post office just now."

"We're taxpayers. In reality, it is *our* post office. We can hit it if we want to."

"We need to be hitting Doc's house soon," she replied.

They came to Doc's long downhill drive almost as soon as she spoke. A.J. nosed it in and hoped for the best. They gained speed as they approached the carport and drifted counterclockwise with all four wheels locked. He wondered how he was going to stop but needn't have worried. The good Lord was keeping an eye on the Longstreets that woolly night and sent a sign in the form of a beautifully restored Sedan Deville. The truck was perpendicular to the fins on the back of Doc's old Cadillac when the two objects collided. A.J.'s door collapsed inward and knocked him over into Maggie's lap. His new position seemed to add to her duress, so he quickly clambered out her door, where he promptly slipped and fell on the ice. When Doc emerged, he was greeted by the sight of A.J.'s truck impaled on the substantial fins of his Cadillac. Maggie was in the truck, trying not to push, and A.J. was on the ground, nursing a cracked rib from the truck door and a broken wrist from the hard concrete.

"What the hell . . . ?" Doc began.

"Maggie's having her baby," A.J. informed him. Doc stepped back inside. He returned with a flashlight and a box of ice-cream salt. Doc scattered the salt, stepped gingerly to the truck, and made a brief examination of Maggie.

"The baby's coming breech. Help me get her inside." To Maggie he said, "Don't push."

"Easy for you to say," she growled between gritted teeth. A.J. and Doc trundled her into the house and onto the spare bed, and thirty minutes later after much deft maneuvering by Doc and a great deal of waterfront cussing by Maggie, the Longstreets were parents again. A.J. and Minnie had assisted, with Minnie doing the skilled work while A.J. filled the position of tote-and-fetch boy. Maggie's eyes shone in the lamplight as her fine baby boy was laid at her breast. A.J. and Doc shook hands, and it was difficult to tell who was prouder, the new father or the old physician, hopelessly out of date but still able to deliver a baby breech during a snowstorm in the dark.

"All these new boys would have been doing C-sections, getting excited and hollering *stat*. Whatever the hell that means," Doc growled as he sipped the coffee Minnie had brewed on the gas grill. It had a slightly smoky taste.

"You did good, Doc," A.J. said.

Maggie had worked hard, and it was late. Eventually, she drowsed. While she slept, Doc splinted A.J.'s wrist and taped his ribs. Then A.J. sat in a chair by the bed. After a time, Maggie stirred and awakened. She saw him and smiled.

"I dreamed you were gone," she said sleepily.

"I was here the whole time," he responded, taking her hand. Thus, the youngest member of the Longstreet clan came into the world on a blizzard's coattails, and his difficult entrance set the tone for the life that was to follow.

"I swear he planned it," Maggie said, back in the kitchen recounting the high points of Eudora's wedding. "The minister had just finished saying that any objectors should speak now or forever hold their peace. The church was quiet. Then J.J. tugged on my dress and announced he had to pee. 'Right now, Mama,' was the way he put it. I thought Emily Charlotte was going to die on the spot."

"Well, we told him to always let us know," A.J. offered. J.J. had been tough to train. "I bet Carlisle loved the bathroom break."

"He raised an eyebrow, but everyone was laughing by that time."

"Well, the main thing is that Eudora has finally reeled Carlisle in," A.J. said. "Now she can be truly fulfilled as a woman." He grunted when Maggie kicked him under the table.

"Watch it," she said. "I'm still in the mood to hit something."

"Apparently," he responded, rubbing his shin. "Husband beating is a serious deal. With the right lawyer, I could clean you out."

"Save your money. I don't have anything but the children, and you can have them."

"Just forget it." A.J. got up and poured them both coffee. "Let's go to the porch."

They sat in silence in the big rockers on the porch and enjoyed the twilight. The evening was serene. The slightest of breezes was blowing, bearing the hint of meat cooking on a grill. Estelle was burning yet another steak on her high-botch-ee.

"I missed you," said Maggie. "Did you have fun being a bachelor while we were gone?"

"It was one party after another. I vacuumed about two truckloads of blond stewardess-hair out of the carpet right before you got here. By the way, if you happen to find a pair of red panties somewhere in the house, they're mine."

"Red has always been your color," she replied. "But I think you're lying. I think you worked, went and saw Eugene, ate some fried Spam, and missed me." She reached and took his hand. "But if you are messing around with a blond stewardess, you had better get in the habit of calling her a flight attendant, Plow Boy."

"There are too many rules these days," he responded forlornly. "Actually, you hit it pretty close, but you left out the part where I got fired." She momentarily assimilated this data.

"Well, it's not like we didn't know it was coming," she said finally. "Did you get the severance pay?"

"I got part of it. I still need to look up John McCord."

"That's it, then. I'm glad you're out of there. I've never liked that place, and I've always believed you could do better. You rest for a few weeks. Then we'll get busy finding you something else." She sounded upbeat as she squeezed his hand.

"You know, I might not find something right off," he cautioned. He did not want to dampen her optimism, but facts were facts.

"You have nearly a year's pay in your pocket, counting what John McCord owes you," she said. "You'll find something before it runs out. I think you should start that remodeling business you've been talking about. There are enough old houses in bad shape in these mountains to keep you busy until you're ninety."

THE FRONT PORCH PROPHET

It was true. History was ignorant and had a mean streak, so it tended to repeat. Sequoyah and the surrounding areas had been rediscovered by the great-grandchildren of the elite who had once had their summer homes in the mountains. Young professionals had been snatching up property left and right, and the right local boy who could fix up an old house could certainly capitalize on the situation. He and Maggie had already turned down two fairly substantial offers on the Folly, tendered by individuals who wanted to live in a restored home without actually having to restore it. A.J was fairly tolerant of this new breed of Sequoyites, all things considered, even though he had almost been hit once by a rogue Volvo, and in spite of the fact he no longer knew the names of everyone having Saturday morning coffee down at The Lord Is My Shepherd; I Shall Not Want Thick and Frosty Milkshakes Drive-In.

"Maybe," he said, in response to the remodeling proposal. "We'll see." They finished their coffee in comfortable silence. As the night descended, a mist stole across the high valley and crept onto the porch. Maggie shuddered.

"Goose walk over your grave?" A.J. asked.

"It's going to get cold early this year," she responded.

"I think it might," A.J. said. "It's about time for it anyway. Halloween's next week." This was one of his favorite holidays, and he enjoyed immensely the ritual of dressing up to take the children out. Some of his more notable disguises were Richard Nixon, George Armstrong Custer the Day After, and a Rambler American, which was a great costume although a bit on the heavy side. This year he was planning to go as Nikita Khrushchev and was already beating podium-shaped objects with his shoe.

"Don't remind me," Maggie said. "I've got costumes to arrange."

"What are we going to be this year?" he asked.

"I've got you to thank for this," she said. "Most kids want to be ghosts or witches. Maybe a mime. But not my children. Nothing normal for them. Emily wants to go as Topo Gigio, Harper Lee wants to go as a fish, and J.J. wants to go black-and-white."

"I don't get that one."

"You ought to get it," she replied. "You started it when you told him the world used to be black and white. He said you even proved it."

A.J. remembered. He and the children had been watching an old Basil Rathbone movie when J.J. asked why there was no color.

"The world used to be black and white," he said to the children. "But aliens landed and zapped us with a color ray."

"Uh-uh!" Harper Lee said.

"No way!" J.J. chimed.

"Daddy!" Emily added.

"I can prove it," A.J. replied. He retrieved his videotape of *The Wizard of Oz* and plugged it in. The children watched open-mouthed as the film turned to Technicolor upon Dorothy's arrival in Oz. "They were making this movie when the aliens landed," he explained. "You can see right when we got zapped." The young Longstreets were used to their father's leg-pulling, and over the years he had made many an unfounded claim. But this time, it was different. They had seen the bona fides for themselves. There could be no doubt of the veracity of the claim. They believed.

"How hard can it be?" A.J. asked Maggie, referring to J.J.'s request. "Put him in black pants and a white shirt. A fish is going to be much harder."

"Big talk, Nikita," she responded. "He wants to look like he's in a black-and-white movie. You know, that shades-of-grey, grainy look."

"I have confidence in your ability," A.J. smiled. "Maybe you can find him some size-four spats down at the Pic-N-Save."

"Maybe you can quit filling their heads with garbage and make my life easier."

"What do you want? An easy life or children who can think creatively?"

"Keep it up, and I'll beat on you with my shoe," Maggie said.

"Now, that's more like it. Hold up while I go splash on a little Hai Karate." He possessed what he believed to be the last bottle of the exotic fragrance extant.

"No, that's all right. The fried Spam was bad enough."

"I never admitted that," he reminded her.

"You didn't have to," she reminded him back.

They lapsed into a contented repose and watched as the stars roused themselves for another night's work. A.J. was glad to have Maggie back. Without her he was adrift in a world full of reefs. He no longer really understood where he left off and she began. She was the best person he had ever known, and he preferred her company above all others.

"How is Eugene?" she asked.

"He's slipping fast," came A.J.'s reply. He described the visit. She listened without comment, although her eyes mirrored sadness when he recounted the tale of Eugene's reunion with Diane.

"I'm glad you made him come to town. I hope he and Diane made their peace."

"They did," he said. "He was low when I left him, but he asked me to go. He said he wanted to be alone."

"Poor man," she said simply. There was nothing else to say. Eugene had been a lucky man all of his life. Now his luck flowed away like water pouring from a hole in a bucket onto the sand in July. "You said Diane had company when you first arrived," Maggie continued. "Who's her new boyfriend?"

"I didn't say a word about a boyfriend," A.J. responded.

"But you said—"

"I said she had a friend. I did not use the word *boy*," he replied.

"I'm missing you on this," Maggie said, confused.

"I discovered Diane in a post-coital glow after having spent the evening with Truth Hannassey." Truth had been among the first wave of new-and-improved Sequoyites. She had stumbled upon the little town a few years back and had fallen in love with its charm, beauty, and potential for financial gain. She had bought and restored a fine old home and from that base had proceeded to have her way with Cherokee County.

A.J.'s first meeting with Truth had been under unusual circumstances, and he would be the first to admit they had gotten off on the wrong foot. He felt the misstep was her fault, but the fact of the matter was that they had taken an instant dislike for each other, as if they had hated one another for many lifetimes.

A.J. had a habit of sleeping on the screened side porch during the warmer months and was doing just that one morning after a hard night at the sawmill when he was awakened by a loud pounding. Maggie was at work, the two girls were at school, and J.J. was fishing with John Robert. Still half-asleep, he arose, unhooked the screen, and stood eye to eye with Truth Hannassey. She was dressed in a nicely tailored business suit, and he was in his boxer shorts.

"Good morning," she said, offering her hand. "I hope I didn't wake you up. My name is Truth Hannassey." He took her hand.

"A.J. Longstreet," he mumbled, fighting to alertness. He figured she must be lost, broken down, or beset by other emergencies compelling enough to cause her to awaken sleeping strangers.

"I would like to talk to you about buying this house," she continued briskly. He felt at a slight disadvantage in his drawers, confused and a little unnerved, but he was raised to be polite to strangers and to women, and his visitor was both.

"I'm sorry," he said, stifling a yawn. "It's not for sale." He smiled, nodded, and began to turn away.

"Maybe you should hear my offer," came her reply. A.J. stopped in mid-turn, rotated back, and took her gaze. Her tone wasn't unfriendly. More like pushy. A.J. hated pushy.

"Ma'am, I don't mean to offend, but it doesn't matter what your offer is," he said, taking one more cut at the ball. Some people just couldn't take no for an answer. "I don't want to sell my house. I do, however, want to go back to sleep. Please excuse me if I don't show you out, but as you can see, I'm not wearing any pants." He turned once more, intending to go find some peace.

"I notice that you're wearing a wedding ring. Maybe you should talk over my offer with your wife." A.J. *again* about-faced and stood boxer shorts to business suit with Truth Hannassey.

"Lady, go away. If you want to talk to my wife, come back at one a.m. and drag her out in her panties. Wear a raincoat, because I guarantee she'll turn the garden hose on you. But for now, go away and let me sleep." He pointed in the direction of the highway. There was a strange dynamic at play. Truth's hardball stare had never left him. Finally, she flashed a smile.

"Your fly is open," she said as she turned to leave.

"That's not for sale, either," came his reply.

"Not interested," she hollered over her shoulder as she sauntered across the yard. He stood there, hairy-legged and bare-chested, and wondered what in hell that had been all about.

When Maggie arrived home, A.J. discussed the encounter with her and discovered that Truth had bought several properties around the county. Maggie had acquired this knowledge while lunching with Ms. Hannassey, who had tracked Maggie down after her chat with A.J. She had apparently been unwilling to take his word on the subject of selling the Folly. This knowledge did little to enhance his regard for her, and according to Maggie, the feeling was mutual. The word on the streets was that Truth was a wealthy real estate genius who had no use for the male of the species, living or dead.

"Well, neither do I," A.J. said, stating their common ground, amazed that Truth had hunted Maggie up. He was a small town boy and liked it that way, a hayseed by conscious choice and not just dumb luck, and he had encountered very few beings similar to Truth on his travels through the maze. Indeed, he felt he could have gone much longer without the privilege. "At least you got to wear your pants while you were talking," he noted.

"No wonder you didn't get along with her," Maggie said. "She's very intense. Definitely not your cup of tea."

"So, did you sell the house?" A.J. asked.

"No, but it was tempting. She offered two hundred thousand

dollars."

"Damn. I would have put on my pants for that." Maybe he had been hasty.

"She also offered me a job," Maggie continued. "She said she liked my style, but my taste in men sucked. She wanted me to be a liaison between her and the locals. She felt that I could open a few doors." Maggie was smiling.

"Please tell me you turned her down," he said. He just couldn't envision having the boss, Truth Hannassey, over for dinner. It was too much to bear, trousers or no.

"It was a very good offer," she said. He grimaced as if he had stepped on something jagged and rusty. "But I turned it down. The money would have been nice, but I don't think I'm right for the work. I guess I'm pretty satisfied with what I do and what I have." He quietly exhaled the breath he had been holding. "I'll tell you one thing, though," she continued. "I really like her. I think we're going to be good friends." He coughed. The whims of fate were as cruel as November wind.

Eugene, too, had made the acquaintance of Truth. She had walked into the beer joint and offered Eugene a very respectable sum of money for his mountain, on top of which she wished to build a subdivision. Eugene liked his mountain and had no need for more money, so he had declined the offer. There was, however, a complication. Eugene had become smitten with her.

"Man, you just know she has some fine pussy on her," Eugene drooled.

"Eugene, she's a lesbian," A.J. told him. "She doesn't like boys. She likes girls."

"Give me thirty minutes with her, and I guarantee you I'll have her straightened out," he said, lust heavy in his voice. He had a bad case of it.

"I don't think it works that way," A.J. replied. "Anyway, you're married. You don't get to play with the big-city girls."

"Well, you just mark this down," Eugene had vowed. "It's her destiny to enjoy a little Purdue bliss." Thus was it written. Thus was it eventually done.

"Diane and Truth Hannassey together?" Maggie asked, incredulous. "I'm having a little trouble swallowing that one." It was an accepted fact that Truth had a roving eye, but most of her companionship to date had been imported, due to the size of the local gene pool and its basically conservative demographic.

"Me, too," A.J. agreed. "But there it was. I'm glad Eugene didn't catch on. It would kill him to know he has driven Diane away from men completely." He paused before continuing. "I think he was hoping for a reconciliation, and maybe one more for the road."

"Sounds like that's not going to happen," Maggie said, distracted. "I'm sorry, but I'm still getting used to the concept. Are you sure it was Truth?"

"I swear it. I saw her."

"Relationship-wise, Truth is probably a bigger disaster than Eugene. I hope Diane keeps her eyes open."

"I think she ought to trip the light fantastic with Eugene one more time," A.J. said.

"Why should she?" asked Maggie. "All that's over between them. She doesn't love him anymore. Why should she sleep with him?"

"Charity. Sympathy. Decency. I don't know, but she ought to do it," A.J. said. "You would give me one more tumble, wouldn't you?"

"Yes, I would. But you haven't been an absolute shit for the last twenty years. It is through works, not faith, that dispossessed husbands earn one more for the road. Besides, I thought you had a pride problem when it came to charity sex."

"I do, but I'm not obsessive about it." He smiled.

"I might find myself in a charitable mood later," she allowed. "But first we have some children to feed."

"Great," he said. "I've been kind of steamed up since I saw Diane in her gown." He earned an elbow in the ribs for the revelation.

They arose, and together they set to the evening chores. A.J. cooked supper while Maggie oversaw the bathing of their offspring. Later, the children were put down, each with a kiss and a story. Later still, in the glow of the moonlight as it filtered through the windowpanes, Maggie and A.J. drifted off in the easy embrace of two people unquestionably in love.

CHAPTER 10

What would it take to get some of that pussy?
—Excerpt of posthumous letter from
Eugene Purdue to Truth Hannassey

A.J. AWOKE EARLY THE NEXT MORNING. HIS EVENING of intimacy with Maggie had done much to improve his mood. She had the ability to make him feel like he was a part of the world rather than just a mildly interested observer, and he felt renewed. He slipped out of bed carefully, so as not to awaken her, although she stirred and reached for him. He sat on the side of the bed and took her hand, and she murmured an almost inaudible sound as she settled back into slumber. He gently stroked her hair while she slept. He often watched her in repose; it instilled in him a sense of serenity.

She loved to sleep late, although the opportunity to do so did not often present itself. A.J., on the other hand, slept very little, never longer than five or six hours. He had received this trait from John Robert, and there was nothing much he could do about it. It was a factor set at conception, like hair color or political affiliation. Pigs can't fly because pork is heavy, snakes crawl on their bellies because they have no feet, and A.J. was up before the sun because his eyes would not stay closed.

"If I had known you never sleep," Maggie had observed not long after their marriage, "I might have had second thoughts." It was three o'clock in the morning, and her new husband had inadvertently awakened her while making a sandwich.

After their initial introductions in that cotton mill so many years ago, it was some time before A.J. made Maggie his own. There were difficulties to overcome before he could press his suit, the first of these being geography. Maggie was from the Alabama side of Lookout Mountain, and this cartographical anomaly coupled with his banishment to Dogtown made it nearly impossible to simply run into her. So he was forced to casually hang around the parking lot of the cotton mill at midnight to even get a glimpse. Luckily, stalking had not yet been invented, and diligent pursuit was still somewhat smiled upon as long as it didn't involve firearms, state lines, or lengths of rope. So A.J. coincidentally bumped into Maggie at every opportunity, always keeping up the pretense of happenstance even though he was fooling no one. Maggie evolved the habit of smiling when she saw him, unless the meeting was excessively serendipitous.

The second obstacle in the path to matrimony was Roger Cork, called Killer by his friends and Pootie by his detractors, A.J. chief among their legion. The origin of the Killer moniker seemed to be a very poor impression of Jerry Lee Lewis singing "Whole Lotta Shakin'" complete with plenty of *oh, baby's* and some spirited but bad piano playing with his nether regions. The more customary nomenclature, Pootie, stemmed from an unfortunate set of circumstances involving thirteen Krystal cheeseburgers—also known as gut bombs—a six-pack of hot Pabst Blue Ribbon beer, and the questionable wisdom of riding the Zipper at the county fair after ingesting all of that. The chemical reaction brought about by this combination was a tribute to digestive systems worldwide. The ride was cut short at the insistence of the other revelers, one of whom threatened to kill both the operator and Pootie if matters did not immediately improve. Because he was an amusement professional, the carny complied, but by then Roger Cork's new nickname had stuck like gum to a desk bottom.

A.J. did not care for Pootie for two reasons. First, he had been one of the unlucky occupants of that Zipper car. In later years he regretted his rash words to the operator, but he never once felt bad about offering to put Pootie out of his misery. Indeed, his fellow thrill-seekers were urging him to action and offering suggestions as to the best way to get the job done. Many of the recommendations were quite creative, although one of the proposals was most likely impossible, given the laws of physics and the actual size of Zipper cars.

The second reason for A.J.'s animosity toward Pootie had to do with timing. To put it simply, when A.J. came to call, he discovered that young master Cork had beaten him to the punch.

"Would you like to go out Friday?" A.J. asked Maggie one night in the parking lot of the cotton mill. "I've got tickets to the Doobie Brothers." He had been sleeping in his car when she noticed and awakened him.

"I'm sorry," she replied, smiling. "I've promised Roger Cork I'd go out with him." This was hard news for A.J., but he took it well.

"My advice is, don't go to the Krystal," he said. "I'd skip the fair, too." He determined from her bewildered expression that she was unaware of Pootie's seamier side.

So A.J. was faced with the need for an alternate plan of action. Sadly, he was not a divergent thinker, and he could envision no better strategy than to park on the other side of the mill parking lot. So that was what he did, although he didn't harbor much hope the plan would bear fruit. Fortunately, there are unfathomable forces at work in the universe. Love would find a way. The following night, he was sitting in his Impala on the other side of the parking lot when his car door jerked open.

"Get out, Longstreet," a voice boomed. A.J. recognized it, and he smiled. He took a sip of beer. Then he opened his eyes and looked up at Pootie, standing tall and indignant. He was blocking A.J.'s potential view of Maggie.

"Pootie," he said, stretching the first syllable. "How about a beer?" A.J. was trying to be sociable, but his nemesis was as rigid as a walnut timber and as flexible as cold-rolled steel. He loomed in his muscle shirt with his fists clenched tight and his gut sucked tighter. A.J. yawned for effect and lit a cigarette. Then he removed himself from the interior of the Hog Farm and slouched against the car with his hands in his pockets. He eyed his foe.

Pootie was pretty, and he was rich on top of that. In A.J.'s limited experience, when the two qualities were combined it was not an absolute guarantee that the individual possessing them would be a shit head, but historically the correlation had been strong, and A.J. was in no mood to allow for individual exceptions. He didn't like pretty boys, and he didn't like rich boys, and if Pootie had been neither, he would have found something else.

"I hear you've been trying to mess with my girl," Pootie said, foregoing the soup and getting right to the main course. He looked and behaved much like his father, Jack Cork, whose money had made no one happy, especially Jack.

"You can hear most anything around these parts, Poot," A.J. observed, looking over his companion's shoulder and noticing the carload of associates he had brought along.

"I'm not playing with you, you fucking hippie. If I catch you around her again, I'll be on you like white on rice."

"Get ready," A.J. informed him. "You'll be catching me around her in about five minutes." A vein throbbed on Pootie's forehead, and A.J. hoped he hadn't been eating any Krystals lately. There was movement in the Mustang, and the three running buddies eased out and arranged themselves. A.J. reached in the open window of the Hog Farm and retrieved the Louisville Slugger. He smacked it against the side of his venerable Chevrolet, adding a dent to the collection while indicating his resolve to the worthies standing opposite. One of them flinched. Pootie's eyes narrowed to a squint.

"I've heard about you and that bat," he said. "Chicken shit."

"Oh, great," A.J. said, his eyes not leaving Pootie. "You bring three guys to do your talking for you, and I'm a chicken shit."

They stood at impasse, and it may have gone bad but for the intervention of the Gods of Romance, one of whom chose that moment to stretch, spit out his cosmic toothpick, and address the situation in the parking lot below. He was a union god, apparently, and had finished his smoke break before springing to action, but late is better than not at all.

So up drove Maggie. Pootie and company stood in the harsh glare of her Torino's headlights, gesturing wildly. Opposite them stood A.J., with the tip of his bat resting on Pootie's chest. She stopped the car about a foot from the boys and got out.

"What are we doing?" she asked quietly. By silent agreement, Pootie's compadres shuffled over to the Mustang, looking like a low-budget edition of the Keystone Cops. Pootie stood his ground but would not look at Maggie. A.J. looked at her, but his bat remained planted on Pootie's sternum. Maggie removed her hands from her hips and folded her arms. This pose had the unintended effect of accentuating her bust line, and A.J. got weak in the knees. He swallowed and spoke.

"We're just talking," he said. Although he had not started this, he knew he was in trouble. He was raised to take his medicine, but he hoped it wouldn't be too bitter.

"Just talking," Pootie agreed. He, too, knew he was in a predicament, and he was not the most astute rich boy to ever climb out of a Mustang.

"About?" she directed her query at A.J., who didn't know if it was a good sign he was now spokesman for the group.

"Well, I'll tell you," he began, throwing caution to the wind. "Pootie here seems to think I'm trying to steal his woman—that would be *you*—and he wanted to discourage me. I was about to explain to him that you are way too fine for his sorry likes, and that I intend to do whatever it takes to make you mine." Pootie did not appreciate the "sorry likes" part and started for A.J., but A.J. shoved him back with the Slugger.

A.J. had a tendency to second-guess himself, but not this time. He had not planned to speak, but he would not recant a single word if he had a year to rewrite the discourse. The declarations drifted in the air like cotton fiber. Finally, Maggie spoke.

"I am nobody's girl," Maggie said. "Roger," she continued, "I think it would be better if we didn't go out again." A.J. brightened. It seemed to be rolling his way. "A.J.," she continued, "when I need someone to make me his, I'll let you know. Until then, take your bat and go play baseball. And quit bothering me every night while I'm trying to go to work." It had been rolling his way, all right, and it had flattened him when it arrived. Having spoken her piece, Maggie turned and walked toward the mill. A.J. watched as she crossed the parking lot, his heart fractured. He looked over at Pootie, who was staring at him with hatred.

"I'll be seeing you around," Pootie promised as he backed away from the bat.

"We'll get some Krystals and drink some beers," came A.J.'s reply. He was saddened by his setback, and climbed into the Hog Farm with the firm intention of having a smoke and a think. Pootie left several dollars' worth of tread on the asphalt when he roared away.

A.J. came to the conclusion he was confused on the subject of women. He did not know where he was going wrong with Maggie. He had twice demonstrated his willingness to fight for her honor, and she wasn't impressed. He had shown his undying devotion to her by making a nuisance of himself, and she didn't seem enchanted by the gesture. He had declared his intentions and had been told to go away. He just didn't get it.

A.J. deliberated as the night waned. He considered getting good and drunk, but that avenue seemed low. He supposed he could make the grand gesture and do away with himself, but the plan seemed limiting. He tarried on the idea of finding Pootie and beating him up. He knew it would make him feel better, but he didn't want to lose his parking spot, so he grudgingly let the notion fade. When the whistle that marked shift change blew, he was toying with the idea of buying a new Mustang and drafting three riding companions, because at least Pootie had been allowed the privilege of a couple of dates before getting the heave-ho, whereas A.J. had been forced to take his heave-hos straight up. They were a little dry that way, a trifle laborious to swallow.

The night crew began to file out of the mill, and with them came Maggie. A.J. got out of his car and leaned up against the dent he had made the previous evening, as if attempting to hide the evidence. She paused when she saw him, a diminutive half step of indecision. He felt a trickle of sweat trace his spine. His mouth was as parched as baked sand.

"I thought I told you to quit hanging around," she said to him when she came up. She spoke in a no-nonsense tone, but behind the message lingered a lack of absolute resolve, as if she had found a bit of charity for the pitiable wreck before her. He was looking at her shoes.

"Well, what you said was to quit being here at night," he said lamely. He was a drowning man holding a broken spar, hoping to get off on a technicality. "This is morning." A small point, admittedly. She leaned next to him on the Hog Farm.

"Listen to me," she said. "You seem like a nice guy, and I know your heart is in the right place." Her voice was relaxed and sensible. "The problem is, I think you're looking for something that I'm not. I don't want a steady boyfriend. We could go out once in a while, maybe, but you've got to let me have a little room. Okay?"

"Would you like to go get some breakfast?" he asked. She did not respond for what seemed a lifetime. Then she sighed and spoke.

"Okay," she said. "Just breakfast. I'm sort of hungry anyway. But this is not a date, understand?"

"Absolutely," he replied, holding the door for her. When she climbed in, he continued. "Maybe after we eat we could go for a swim at the quarry."

Having overcome geography and Pootie, A.J. still had one more river to cross, and that wide river was Emmett Callahan. As the courtship progressed, it became apparent Emmett was less than enthralled by the long-haired boy in the ragged Chevy who was spending more and more time at the Callahan household. He was protective of his daughters, and A.J. was frankly not what he had in mind. In later years, A.J. would come to understand the point of view, but at the time it had made for a tough swim.

Emmett's campaign of discouragement was not subtle, but it was creative. One evening while A.J. was catching a few winks in the back of the Hog Farm—parked in Maggie's driveway after a late date—Emmett had the old Impala towed. Another time, A.J. noticed a lively odor and upon investigation found several sacks of Callahan garbage in the trunk of his car. Once, Emmett performed a citizen's arrest on A.J. and held him until the Alabama equivalent of Slim arrived to haul him off. Admittedly, A.J. was soused, but the incident did little to enhance their relationship.

But A.J. toughed it out and slowly honed Emmett's rough edges. Nothing worth having was easy to obtain, and such was the case with Maggie Callahan. In later years as her sisters all married, A.J. would listen to his brothers-in-law lament about Emmett and he would smile. He had taken the brunt, had taken the drawknife and slowly shaved the bark off the gnarled hickory that was Emmett Callahan, and all who came after were standing on his shoulders.

On the night A.J. proposed, he and Maggie were sitting on the broken dam that held back Lake Echota. The dam was at an isolated site and had been built during the Great Depression by a diverse group of young people with poor prospects who became dam builders because there was nothing else for them to do. A.J.'s granmama and her husband had met and married while working on the project. Their initials were discretely written in the concrete, a lasting memorial to true love, Portland cement, and the WPA.

"What's wrong, A.J.?" Maggie asked. "You've been quiet all day." The west end of the dam was in ruin, and the water roared through the breach. They sat in the causeway on the east side, trailing their toes in the green, cool water. The day had been a pearl, and the only mar on it was the sunburn Maggie had acquired in an area where the sun does not normally shine. Hopefully, she would not have to explain it to her mama.

"We need to talk about something," he blurted out. The words were abrupt, not at all what he had in mind. He stood and looked out over the dam, silently pledging to throw himself into the cataract if he screwed this up. He knew a spot where the rusted rebar would be bound to impale him.

"Tell me what it is," said Maggie with concern in her voice. She arose and stood next to him.

"I need for you to marry me," was his reply. A soft breeze brushed the surface of the lake. He studied the far shore. His fist was in the pocket of his denim cutoffs, clenched around an engagement ring. He intended to fling it far if she declined to wed.

A.J. risked a quick peek out of the corner of his eye at Maggie. She was looking at him and smiling. She took his hand and squeezed it gently, and he removed the ring from his pocket and placed it on her finger. Her eyes widened a touch in surprise, but she was still smiling.

"Pretty sure of yourself, weren't you, Farm Boy?" she asked. The ring was too large, so she slipped it on her thumb for safekeeping.

"You haven't said yes," he pointed out.

"Yes," she responded.

Thus their paths merged, and from that point on they traveled the same road. They spent the remainder of the summer and autumn preparing for their leap of love and faith, and they pledged their troth on a cold January day in a simple wedding attended by family and friends. John Robert was the best man, and Maggie's maids of honor were her many sisters. The reception was catered by Granmama, who made the fanciest dishes she knew: cocktail wieners in barbecue sauce, cheese balls, and little cucumber sandwiches. The cake was made by Maggie's sister, Eudora Welty, and it was magnificent even if the layers did bear the vaguest resemblance to coffee cans, which is what she had used for pans. Emmett Callahan gave his daughter away and in deference to the solemnity of the ceremony only glared momentarily at A.J. The rings were exchanged, the veil lifted, and the kiss given and received. And then it was done. The two became as one in the eyes of God and the governor of Georgia. They became the current incarnation of a devotion that spanned the long ages of the world, a fidelity destined to last until the end.

Now, years later, A.J. softly kissed his sleeping wife. He dressed quietly and went downstairs. He poured a cup of coffee brewed by John Robert. Then he stepped on the porch to greet his father. The elder Longstreet was busy cleaning the fish he had brought home the previous evening. They had spent the night in a bucket of water and now were taking the final step to becoming full-fledged members of the food chain.

"Morning, John Robert," A.J. said, settling down in his rocker. He knew that John Robert had been up for some time; he was an early riser even by A.J.'s standards. Back when he was employed, A.J. would arrive home from the sawmill around four in the morning, and invariably he would be greeted by his father, who would be busying around on some small project or other while waiting patiently for the sluggards of the world to arise.

"Thought you were going to stay in bed all day," John Robert replied. The sun had not yet risen. His razor sharp knife flashed with quick, sure movements.

"I'm getting lazy since I became unemployed," A.J. said, taking a sip of coffee. It was painfully strong.

"I heard about that yesterday in town," John Robert grunted. He finished filleting the last fish and laid the grayish-white squares of bass in the pan along with the others. They would make a fine supper that evening, served fried alongside cabbage slaw, salty fried potatoes, and hush puppies made of sweet yellow cornmeal. Admittedly, the fare would be better for the soul than for the heart, but no one lived forever. "They didn't waste any time," John Robert continued, rinsing his hands in the bucket.

"No, they didn't," A.J. agreed, taking another sip of coffee.

204

"They are very efficient people." He felt a coffee ground on his tongue and spit the offending particle over the porch rail. John Robert made coffee in the old way, by boiling a handful of grounds in a pot that had been timeworn when Granmama was still a slip of a girl. The resulting brew was not for the faint of heart.

There was no enmity in A.J.'s voice, and he wished no harm to the people from Alabama Southern. Not much, anyway. Maybe the odd broken leg or unfaithful wife, just to smooth out any unlevel spots in their bloodsucking, tree-sawing karmas.

John Robert picked up his pan of fish and headed into the kitchen. The screen door squeaked a second time as A.J. followed him in. The elder Longstreet rinsed the fish at the sink, then put them in the refrigerator to chill. He poured himself a cup of coffee and sat at the table.

In the harsh fluorescent light, he looked his age. This was a recent phenomenon; he had aged well until this year, the heart attack notwithstanding. Now he looked like an old man, and it was hard for A.J. to get comfortable with the idea.

"Have you given any thought to what you're going to do now?" John Robert asked, looking at his son.

"I thought I might borrow Slim's big shotgun and go kill them all in their beds," A.J. replied.

"Will you be back by supper, or do you want me to make you a plate?" John Robert inquired, surprising A.J. Most of his attempts at kidding with his father were met with deadpan looks and stony silences.

"I'll be back in time," A.J. said with a broad grin.

"Want some breakfast?"

"No, I don't think so." A.J.'s years of shift work had left his eating schedule in ruin, and he tended to eat at different times than most people. He looked at the clock on the wall and noted it was time to be moving along. He had awakened this morning wishing he had not promised Eugene a visit. He was ashamed of this reluctance and strengthened his resolve, but he hoped to get the visit completed early in the day. He stood and stretched.

"I'm going up to see Eugene for a while," he told his father. "I should be back around lunch. Maggie's worn out, so let her sleep. She can go to church twice next week."

"How is Eugene doing?" asked John Robert.

"I don't think he has very long."

"Tell him I'm thinking about him," John Robert said in a somber tone. "Tell him if I can help him, to just let me know."

"I'll tell him." A.J. left the house and climbed into his truck. It was balky in the cool morning, but he coaxed it to life after a few false starts and made the short drive to town. As he drove through Sequoyah, he noticed several vehicles parked outside of the Follow Me, and I Shall Make You Fishers of Pecan Pie Drive-In. One of them was John McCord's truck. A.J. liked his loose ends tidied, so he entered and sat at the counter next to his former boss.

"A.J.," John said, sounding truly happy to see his former employee. "Hoghead, bring some coffee and collision mats for A.J." Hoghead appeared wearing a coat and tie and whistling what may have been "Will the Circle Be Unbroken," but with his whistling skills it was hard to be certain. Sunday morning coffee and collision mats comprised Hoghead's ministry. He opened early and provided them free of charge so that all comers would be fed and alert when they got to church. Around ten o'clock he would close up and go down to the Rapture Preparation Holiness Temple to get his weekly dose of rapture preparation.

"How is it going down at the mill?" John McCord inquired.

"Couldn't really say," responded A.J. "I lasted two days longer than you did, but I think your check was probably larger." There was an uncomfortable silence that A.J. did nothing to mellow. He figured John needed to squirm. It would build character.

Finally, McCord broke the silence with a grunt. His movements were slow as he reached into the breast pocket of his jacket and re-trieved his checkbook. As A.J. and Hoghead looked on, John McCord wrote out his portion of A.J.'s severance package. Hoghead whistled low. John stood up, leaving the check on the lunch counter.

"You know, A.J., I don't owe you a damn thing," he said with tension in his voice.

"You don't now," A.J. responded as he picked up his money. They faced each other. Then John turned and left.

"I think he feels bad about it," observed Hoghead.

"We can hope," said A.J. He finished his coffee and asked Hog-head if he would pour a large one for Eugene. Hog poured two and provided a sackful of collision mats, as well. A.J. thanked him and headed for the truck.

He drove slowly as he left town, enjoying the coolness of the morning as it blew in the vent window. He occupied his mind with the thoughts of the picnic he intended to take later in the day with Maggie and the children. As he drove, he passed the spot where Slim had arrested Patty Hearst years earlier, and he smiled.

That was the summer Patty Hearst had decided for some bizarre reason that robbing banks was intrinsically better work than being a millionaire heiress. The resulting nationwide girl hunt took on a circus air, and Slim Neal succumbed to the frenzy along with many of his law enforcement brethren. Patty Hearst loomed large on his mind, and the obsession led him to erroneous conclusions on the day he observed a road-worn young woman hanging about the outskirts of town. It was true the lass bore some resemblance to the fugitive in question, in that she possessed two breasts and lacked a penis, but other than that, the similarities were scant. Slim was never one to let facts deter a good investigation, however, so he scooped her up and ran her in. When the FBI agents arrived, they discerned fairly quickly that the woman Slim had in the slammer was not the infamous Hearst. Slim was impressed with the swift work of the Feds and wanted to know in detail how they had made such short work of the affair. Was it fingerprints? Were dental records used? Had they contacted Interpol?

"Patty Hearst is a white girl," said Agent Simser, the more talkative of the two. Then the FBI boys loaded Shereea into their car and gave her a ride to the nearest Greyhound terminal.

A.J. was still smiling when he turned off the highway. As he bumped along the ruts, he could smell the fresh fragrance of pine in the early morning air. When he reached the hanging-tree, he turned left and headed up Eugene's road. He kept an eye peeled for Rufus, who could strike at any time. But the trip to the clearing was without incident, leaving him to wonder what was going on. He could not see Eugene, and the canine from hell should have long since attacked. He blew the horn. Then he got out slowly with his bat at the ready. The coffee and collision mats could wait for the all clear.

Eugene appeared at the door, wrapped in a blanket. He stepped out and sat on the porch. His hair was uncombed, and the dark circles under his eyes were clearly visible from the yard. It was evident he had endured a bad night. He peered in A.J.'s direction, and a smile crossed his face.

"Rufus! Sit!" he shouted. A.J. whirled, and there was the dog. He had infiltrated to within five feet and would have had Longstreet hash for breakfast if Eugene had not intervened. Rufus glared, and A.J. could swear he saw triumph in the canine's evil eyes.

"Old Eugene won't always be around to save you," Eugene patiently explained. He was enjoying the episode a great deal. A.J. was shaken. Rufus had nearly won the prize, and the prize was having difficulty with the concept. "You're going to have to tighten up, if you want to live to be old," he observed, lighting a cigarette.

"Words cannot express how much I hate your dog."

"*Hate* is a strong word," said Eugene. "You merely have different priorities. He wants to eat your ass, and you want to save it. Anyway, he's your dog. I gave him to you." Eugene took a drag from his cigarette and broke into a coughing fit. His frame was racked with the effort, and he appeared weak and pale.

"Maybe you should switch to filter tip," A.J. said with concern.

"Maybe you should kiss my ass," Eugene croaked, trying to catch his breath. His hands shook, and he seemed to be in pain. He twisted the lid off of a small bottle and tossed back the contents. He took a deep breath and closed his eyes.

"Are you okay?" A.J. asked.

"Stupid question," observed Eugene.

"Yeah, I guess. How about some coffee?"

"I'd like a cup." A.J. got the coffee and doughnuts and brought them to the porch. He stepped inside for some sugar, which he poured freely into both cups. Eugene took a big slug and sighed in appreciation.

"I like my coffee like I like my women," he ventured, waiting for A.J. the straight man.

"You like your coffee to cost forty dollars? You like your coffee to have big breasts?" A.J. leaned over and looked into Eugene's cup, as if checking.

"Nobody likes a wise guy," said Eugene.

"Have a doughnut," said A.J., handing the sack to Eugene. They took the remainder of their coffee break in silence. The coffee and the collision mats seemed to revive Eugene. He looked better and seemed more at ease. Hoghead's coffee tasted like medicine, and A.J. had always suspected it had medicinal value. He made a mental note to tell Hog that Eugene had enjoyed the breakfast. It was the kind of news the old cook liked to hear.

"Anybody interesting in town this morning?" Eugene asked as he finished his coffee. A.J. handed over his own cup.

"I saw John McCord down at the drive-in."

"Did you hit him in the kneecaps with your bat?"

"No. We had a cup of free coffee and he paid me off." He showed the check to Eugene.

"If you don't tell Maggie May about that," Eugene noted, nodding at the draft, "you can have some good times."

"Just one festivity after another," A.J. agreed. "Girls, girls, girls."

"Never mind. I can tell your heart's not in it. You'd end up showing the girls pictures of Maggie May and the kids."

"I do have some nice shots," A.J. remarked, reaching for his billfold.

"I've seen them," Eugene said, holding up his hands. "Real nice shots." He shook his head. "You're hopeless. Don't you ever get the urge?"

"I think you've got the urge now," A.J. said, sidestepping the question. "Maybe we can find someone to help you out with that."

"What I'd like is to take care of one last urge with Diane," Eugene said. He turned and asked, "What do you think my chances are?"

"I really couldn't say," said A.J.

"Come on. Don't give me that. What do you think?" There was an earnest urgency in his voice that tugged at A.J.'s heart.

"I don't think it is such a hot idea. Why don't I run you up to Chattanooga? We can find you some girls to urge with, as many as you want." In previous lives this plan would have held great appeal for Eugene. A.J. had noticed, however, that standing with one foot in the grave and the other in a daub of axle grease had clarified Eugene's thinking.

"No, my Chattanooga days are over," he said with a trace of melancholy. "Why don't you think it's a good idea to see Diane again? We got along real well yesterday."

A.J. didn't know what to do. On one hand, he felt it would be cruel to let Eugene harbor false hope. On the other hand, illusory anticipation is better than none at all, particularly among the hopeless. A.J. was mulling the best road to travel when Eugene spoke again.

"Shit. I know what this is," he said, hitting his head with the heel of his hand. "She's seeing someone, right?" A.J. was inscrutable. "Right?" Eugene insisted.

"I think maybe she is," said A.J. slowly. He wanted to be out of this discussion.

"Who is it?" Eugene asked. There was defeat in his voice. He seemed to sag almost imperceptibly, as if a slight diminution of the life force had occurred, a quickening of the sand through the hourglass.

"I don't know who it is," A.J. said.

"You lie."

"Okay, I know. But it won't do a damn bit of good to tell you. Diane divorced you, and she can see whoever she wants to. So can you. That's the way it works." Eugene seemed to consider this argument, to hold it to the light as if checking for flaws. Then he spoke.

"I'm just curious," he said petulantly.

"Bull. You're just wondering who to go shoot, and you're not getting anything from me." He knew Eugene and his willful ways. And as much as he disliked Truth Hannassey, she didn't deserve being shot. Not fatally, anyway.

"Just tell me if I know who it is," Eugene obsessed. The subject held morbid fascination for him.

"You know the person," A.J. said. "Now, let it go." They fell silent. It seemed that the limited possibilities of the conversation had been exhausted. A.J. was glad to be moving to higher ground.

"Did you ever sleep with Diane?" Eugene asked. A.J. looked at him.

"Where the hell did that come from?" he asked. Eugene was slumped in the chair with his eyes closed. He presented a pitiful picture, unkempt and seedy.

"I don't know," Eugene said. "It just sort of popped out. I am curious, though. Did you?"

"Sleep? No, no sleeping," A.J. said enigmatically. The question really peeved him.

"You know what I mean," Eugene said. His eyes were still closed, and there was scant emotion in his tone.

"Yeah, I know exactly what you mean. What I'm having trouble with is that you even asked me something like that." The fact that he was only technically innocent of a premarital interlude with her was beside the point.

"Diane talks in her sleep," Eugene stated, almost slurring the words. "One night I woke up, and she was talking to you. Apparently, you were doing a good job." He fell silent. A.J. felt guilty, and the feeling of culpability was about the stupidest thing he had ever heard of.

"It was a dream, Eugene," he said. "Her dream, not mine. I wasn't really there."

"I know. I just always felt bad that she was dreaming of you. She had a habit of comparing me to you anyway. *I wish you would spend more time with your children, like A.J. does with his*, she would say. Or, *A.J. always treats Maggie nice.* You're a tough yardstick to be measured against." A.J. was embarrassed for the both of them.

"You know, I'm just as screwed up as everyone else," he said.

"Oh, *I* know what a sack of shit you are," Eugene said. "It's the women who are confused."

"Just so we're clear on that point," A.J. said emphatically. They fell into silence. The dissonance produced by Diane's fantasy melted away.

Presently, Eugene started to snore. A.J. attempted to rouse him but had no success, so he stepped inside and brought out a pillow. He arranged Eugene and left him to nap, then went back in the house.

Eugene's housekeeping skills were poor, and the cabin was a shambles. A.J. decided to remedy the situation. He had time to kill, anyway, since he did not want to leave without saying good-bye. So he set to with a vengeance, and the cabin slowly became habitable again.

Later, he was resting on the porch when Eugene awoke. A small bonfire burned in the yard, fueled by the detritus from the cabin. The scent of pine oil lingered in the air, mixed with the meaty aroma of the stew A.J. was simmering. He was worn out. Cleaning the cabin had been a big job, and he had been forced to employ untraditional methods. First he had shoveled the floors. Then he had dragged the hose in through the back window and washed the place out. It was during the final phase of the project he discovered the letters. He had been straightening the chaos on Eugene's desk—several planks laid across sawhorses—when he stumbled across a cache of correspondence. Presumably, Eugene was in the process of writing a note to nearly everyone he knew. Some of the letters were finished, sealed, and ready to mail. Others appeared to be works in progress.

He had been about to move on to the kitchen when he noticed an envelope addressed to himself. It was unsealed and contained several sheets of paper. His curiosity was aroused, and he wondered what was contained within. Uncharacteristically, he removed the contents and began to read.

Dear A.J.,

I always thought it was cool when people in the movies got letters from dead people, so I decided to send a few myself. If Ogden doesn't screw it up, you will get this the day after I kick off. And since you're reading, I must be gone. Hopefully, it didn't hurt too much. Hopefully, you didn't let me linger. I don't have any doubt that you killed me. I hated to ask, and I know you really didn't want to, but I needed the help, and I was too much of a chicken shit to do it myself. You were the only natural born killer I knew, the only one who could cut through the bullshit and get it done.

A.J. stopped and sat down. He felt sick at Eugene's portrayal of him as an executioner. Almost involuntarily, his eyes strayed back to the testament before him.

There are some things I want to tell you that I couldn't say while I was alive. Well, I guess I could have said them, but I didn't. When we were in seventh grade, I stole twenty dollars from you. You probably don't even remember it, but it has been on my mind for a long time. I didn't need the money. I just didn't want you to have it. I thought you had it better than me. I'm sorry.

A.J. let his eyes drift to the Sequoyah Police Station sign on the wall. He remembered the twenty dollars. He had hauled hay for two long days to earn it and had always assumed that he had lost it. It had seemed to be a large amount at the time, which was why he supposed it had stuck in his mind. Eugene's posthumous confession saddened him. He read on.

A few years ago, I made a pass at Maggie May. It was the twenty-dollar deal again. Things weren't going so well with Diane, and it pissed me off that you had such a great marriage. You don't need to

215

worry, though. That girl can cut a nut when the mood is on her, and you can believe it when I tell you that she shut me right down. I apologize to you, and I apologize to her. It was a shitty thing to do.

He dropped the letter like a hot rivet, then rose and shuffled into the kitchen. Without thinking, he began to peel potatoes. Then he washed and peeled some carrots that were past their prime but salvageable. He needed an onion, but there wasn't one in residence. As he cut up the deer roast he had dislodged from the freezer, his mind moved back to the letter. Eugene made a pass at Maggie? He didn't want it to be true, but why would a dead guy lie about something like that? And why had Maggie kept it to herself all this time? He dumped all the ingredients into a pot and placed it on the burner. Then he wandered slowly back to the desk. He was developing a dislike for letters from beyond the grave.

There is something else I need to tell you. I wasn't going to, and I don't know if it will do any good for you to know, but here goes anyway. You and I are brothers. Jackie told me. It beats me how he knew, but when I asked Angel, she admitted it. She said John Robert was the best man she ever knew, and she sort of wished out loud that things had been different, that he had been available. But she knew he wasn't, even though your mama was gone. I must be getting in touch with my feminine side now that I'm dead, because I think the whole deal is kind of sad. John Robert was so in love with your mama that he wouldn't try to steal Angel away from Johnny Mack. It didn't even occur to him to try, and she was a babe back in the old days, even if I do say so myself. And Angel was so in love with John Robert that she respected his wishes

216

and backed off. She told me I was her bonus, and that she never once regretted having me, that I helped her endure the pain of being alive. So at least I was good for something. I'm not telling you this to screw up your head, and I don't want you to be beating up on John Robert. Being a living damn saint is hard work, so cut him a little slack. He doesn't know about me, and that's the way Angel wanted it. So swallow down your little-brother-of-Jesus act and let it pass. I'm telling you this because I am proud that you are my older brother, and I wanted you to know it. You are better than I was. Of course, I had a better time than you did, but you never were much on having fun anyway. There is a box buried under the tree I killed. It is full of money that I really shouldn't have, so don't flash it around too much. Make sure Diane and the boys get taken care of, and Angel. The beer joint is yours. If you don't want it, close it. But my advice is, don't be a damn fool. If I learned anything in life, it was that people will pay good money to sin. Bootlegging will make you rich. Just don't forget to give the Law a little taste from time to time. The deed to the mountain is also in the box. I don't care what you do with it as long as Johnny Mack doesn't get it. I trust your judgment. Thank you for whacking me. I was afraid of the pain, and I knew I could count on you to get me out of trouble. You always were your brother's keeper, but we just didn't know it. Like it says in Proverbs, "There is a friend that sticketh closer than a brother." Damn. Bible quotes. I must be hedging my bets. Tell Johnny Mack I went out singing Psalms. It will make his day.

Your Brother, Eugene

P.S.—Cremate me in the cabin. Make it a big fire. Don't let Raymond Poteet get ahold of me. That boy ain't right. Rufus likes a Chicken McNugget from time to time.

A.J. folded the letter neatly and placed it back in its receptacle. Then he went to the kitchen and stirred his stew. Granmama had always told him that curiosity would kill the cat, but this was extreme. He had a brother. He didn't doubt a word of it. It felt true. He stepped out to the porch and sat down, and he was sitting there rocking quietly when his brother awoke.

"I must have dozed off," Eugene said. He sat up straighter and fumbled with his pill bottles before swallowing an assortment of medications. "My yard seems to be on fire," he noted.

"Yeah, while you were asleep, I decided to burn all your stuff." Eugene looked bad. He appeared frail and drawn. A.J. wanted to talk to him, to tell him that he knew, to share brotherhood with him. He started to speak, but all that came out was, "Let's get some food in you and put you to bed." Eugene didn't object, so A.J. helped him up and took him in.

"Damn," Eugene said, looking around the cabin. "I'll never be able to find anything now."

"Bitch, bitch, bitch," said A.J. "Here, eat some of this." He dished up a small bowl of the stew and served it to Eugene, who ate a few bites, mostly broth.

"This is good," he mumbled. "Maggie May better watch out, or some tender young thing will snatch you right up." He put down his spoon and sagged in his chair. A.J. walked him over to the john. Then he supported him to the bed. "Took too much of the good stuff," Eugene slurred. He crawled in and immediately fell asleep. A.J. covered him up and put a glass of water and all of the medications on the bedside table. He put the stew in the refrigerator and walked outside. Rufus eyed him closely. He pointed toward the open door.

"Go in there and keep an eye on him. I'll be back tomorrow." For whatever reason, the big dog went into the cabin. A.J. closed the door, picked up his bat, and walked off the porch to his truck. He had done what he could for his brother on this day, and tomorrow would bring what it brought.

Angel will find a better deal. Again.
—Excerpt of posthumous letter from
Eugene Purdue to Johnny Mack

THE FOLLOWING WEEK WAS PECULIAR, EVEN BY THE
liberal standard that A.J. had come to accept. His daily schedule
had always revolved around his occupation. The removal of this
cornerstone via sudden termination had left him with time on his
hands, and idle extremities are the Devil's workshop. So he decided
to be more proactive during Eugene's final days. He had known
all along that eventually Eugene's condition would deteriorate to a
point where it would be inadvisable to leave him alone. It seemed
the time had arrived.

It was late Sunday night, and they were sitting at the kitchen
table. John Robert and the children were in bed, and Maggie had
just been informed of her new status as Eugene's sister-in-law.

"I wasn't expecting that," she had said dubiously.

"Neither was I," A.J. had agreed.

He had not yet warmed up to the idea of John Robert, philan-
dering knave. On the rational level, he knew his father was merely

a human being like everyone else. His hang-point was more vis-ceral, and complete acceptance would take time. Maggie, too, experienced cognitive disharmony over the concept. After a little double-clutching, however, she caught another gear and proceeded to the subject of Eugene's health.

"Will he come down so he can be taken care of?" Maggie asked.

"No," A.J. replied. "He intends to die up on his mountain. That's his business, I guess. I just feel bad about leaving him in a drug-induced coma with the dog in charge."

"No, that doesn't seem right," Maggie agreed. She was in her cotton nightgown, looking better than she had any business look-ing after all their years in tandem. She continued. "I believe it has fallen to you to help look after him. This may even be the reason for you losing your job." She always sought the ultimate meaning of the universe, the Big Plan. "Think about it," she said. "Out of no-where, you hear from Eugene, and he's dying. Then you lose your job. *Then* you find out he's your brother." She shrugged.

"It does seem a little neat, but I don't know," A.J. said. His per-sonal belief system tended toward the Random Cruelty school, but what she said did exhibit a nice sense of order. And he did feel re-sponsible for Eugene. "So, what should I do? Move up there? Come see you when it's over?" He was unenthusiastic about the idea.

"Absolutely not," she replied. "There are other people in this besides you. Angel. Jackie. Diane. Even Johnny Mack. If the time has come for someone to be with him all the time, then I think you need to talk to his family about taking turns. If nothing else, you could hire some help. He has plenty of money, and he can't take it with him." As was often the case, Maggie's grasp of the situation

222

was superior to A.J.'s. He began considering the problems associated with full-time care for Eugene.

On Monday morning, he left the Folly with the full intention of bringing the remainder of the Purdues into the loop, but his plans were delayed when Truth Hannassey decided for some aberrant reason to kill Estelle Chastain's dog, Plug, by dropping a Nationally Historic Porch on him. The offending entryway fell off the front of the Nationally Historic House that Truth was relocating by helicopter from property she intended to develop. She had retained a company out of Charlotte that rented helicopters piloted by wild-eyed worthies who had gained their credentials under fire in tropical latitudes.

When A.J. stepped into the yard, he could hear the whop-whop-whop of the blades beating the air as the helicopter strained across the sky. He could see the conveyance in the distance, the house dangling beneath. It was more of a small cabin, but even so, the helicopter appeared to be toiling mightily in an attempt to remain aloft. A.J. could see that the porch was sagging as the house slowly revolved on its cable. Then it drooped a bit more. Finally, it simply separated from the house and plunged Plugward. Gravity was running true to form, and the notable veranda crossed the distance between *up* and *down* in short order.

Plug had not been an attractive animal even before he broke the porch's fall. He was a homely little hound, named after the proverbial fireplug because he was squat and leaky. He was also cranky, loud, and obnoxious, but Estelle loved him, and love is not always neat or explainable. When the Historic Porch landed on Plug, it flattened him right into the next universe, a bad but quick way to get there. A.J. saw the entire incident from thirty yards away, and he arrived at the tragedy in a bare moment. He was too late to save the dog or the porch, but he had a ringside seat for the aftermath.

Estelle had spent most of her life as a widow, and during her time alone she became eccentric and set in her ways. Her husband, Parm, had died for no apparent reason years previously after first surviving the Hun. He just went to bed one night and neglected to wake up the following morning. A.J. held the theory that he had simply lost the desire to continue and had willed his breathing to cease.

"The man survived everything the Axis could throw at him," he once observed to Maggie. "Lived through bombs, tanks, and prison camp, but Estelle did him in."

"Hush," Maggie had replied.

So Estelle's years alone had been abundant and prolonged. Somewhere along the way, she began to obsess on the idea of being robbed and raped by some itinerant or other, hopefully one resembling Tyrone Power. To protect herself from this eventual certainty, she armed herself with a variety of large shotguns. These were loaded, ready for mayhem, and propped at strategic locations throughout the Chastain household. Estelle believed she would be overcome when the moment ultimately arrived, but honor dictated that she put up a decent struggle before the sanctity of her private areas was disturbed.

She was standing that morning next to the largest of these shotguns when she gazed out her screen door and noticed a porch on her dog. Perhaps she believed that this was the prelude to rape— foreplay in the rough-and-ready style. Or maybe she concluded the evil Hun had once again arisen, threatening democracy and dogs everywhere. For whatever reason, she grabbed the shotgun, ran outdoors, aimed in a generally *up* direction, and let fly. Normally, Estelle couldn't hit the water if she fell out of the boat. But the pattern flew tight and true and struck the helicopter.

When the blast impacted the big helicopter, Vernon L. "Wormy" Locklear relied on the quick instincts that had saved his bacon on numerous occasions over in Nam. His reflexes did not seem in the least diminished by the pint of Old Granddad he had consumed that morning, and he jinked to the right and dove when he came under fire. He had historically enjoyed great success with this maneuver, but he found that attempting the strategy with a house in tow brought complications. Specifically, the dive, once commenced, was impossible to pull out of. The helicopter was overloaded to begin with, and the necessary horsepower was not available. Wormy would have been lost but for one stroke of luck; his brother-in-law, Meathead, had rigged the load. Meathead's nickname was not the result of an idle whim, and what he didn't know about slinging a house for transport by air was considerable. So it was not particularly surprising when the house, for want of more technical terminology, fell off the rope and alighted in the road north of town.

And that was where Slim entered the picture. He was on routine patrol just north of town when a log cabin came to earth on the highway right in front of him. The dwelling split in two upon its sudden contact with the asphalt, and he put the cruiser into the living room before he could get stopped. He clambered out of his car with sidearm drawn, ready to inflict punishment upon the scofflaw who had gotten the drop on him. Wormy, however, had bigger fish than Slim to fry. The loss of the house had gained him very little in terms of control. The helicopter lurched toward starboard, putting it on a collision course with the ridge north of town. It clawed at the sky, fishtailing back and forth as it disappeared behind the ridge. A.J. listened for the crash, but the sound never came. He hoped the pilot had regained altitude.

Back at the dog killing, Estelle came out to the landing zone after reloading Old Betsy. She viewed the wreckage with composure at first, but her calm dissolved into rage and misery when she spotted Plug's paw sticking out from under the Historic Pile of Lumber that was once a porch.

"I'll kill them!" she wailed, waving her shotgun like a divining rod. She was not specific as to the identity of *them*, but it was A.J.'s opinion that *they* would be wise to lay low.

"I think you may already have," replied A.J., recalling the erratic deportment of the helicopter as it descended behind the ridge. He eased the shotgun from her grasp.

"Do you think it hurt?" she asked as she viewed the remains, referring to the dog, presumably, and not the helicopter. She squatted down and touched the paw.

"I guarantee you that he didn't feel a thing," A.J. kindly replied. "When my time comes, I hope a porch falls on *me*." He was not good with this kind of thing.

"I can't believe you said that," Maggie whispered in his ear when she came up. She gave him an urgent jab in the ribs with her elbow. Then she moved over to Estelle and gave her a hug. Estelle sobbed quietly as Maggie led her to the Folly for a cup of tea and a little sympathy.

"Don't worry," he hollered after them. "I'll take care of this."

226

He reviewed the problem for a moment and then went for his truck and some tools. His plan was to haul it all—lock, stock, porch, and dog—to the landfill for a decent burial. He had just gotten the tailgate lowered when Truth Hannassey rolled up in her Mercedes convertible.

"What is that porch doing there?" she demanded. The implication appeared to be that A.J. was in some way responsible, that he had willed the porch to earth.

"It seems to be holding down that dog," he said, pointing at the rubble. "If you'd like, I can hook a chain to it and haul it over to the house." He gestured at the roadway. Truth looked in that direction and blanched. She had been so intent on the side issue of the porch that she had overlooked the main event in the highway.

"Oh, shit," she said.

"I think your helicopter went down behind the ridge," he volunteered helpfully, hiking his thumb in the direction of the whirlybird's last known location. "You probably want to report that to the police." He again pointed at the house. "You'll find him up in your house. He plowed into it when it landed in front of him." He paused, and then continued. "He gets touchy, sometimes. Don't come up on his blind side." Truth sizzled. She was so enraged he thought he might be in danger of being whacked. Then she seemed to regain her composure a little, and after taking two deep breaths she motored toward the highway to check on her real estate investments. A.J. climbed into his truck and drove toward the last observed position of the helicopter. Neither the Historic Porch nor Plug would be going anywhere, and it had occurred to him that *someone* ought to be looking after the downed transport.

A.J. found the helicopter sitting in the middle of the county road on the other side of the ridge. The landing gear looked bent, and so did the pilot. He was crouched in the open doorway, steadying his nerves with Old Granddad. The aroma of hydraulic fluid pervaded the scene.

"I hate it when this shit happens," the man confided in A.J. "Call me Wormy."

"I wouldn't think it happened that often," A.J. observed, his untrained eye checking for signs of trouble, such as fuel pouring out of a rupture or flames dancing within.

"This is my fifth time," Wormy quipped. He tossed the empty pint bottle into the woods.

"House moving must be a rough business," A.J. concluded. After further discussion, it turned out that the other four times had been over the Mekong Delta, random occurrences orchestrated by dedicated employees of that wily rascal, Ho Chi Minh.

"I sort of thought I was through being shot down," Wormy said ruefully, as if he were ashamed. "You don't know who got me, do you?" It was an odd question, but it seemed important to the downed flyer, a pride issue, perhaps, or something to do with insurance. The man was looking at A.J. with anxiety etched on his features.

"Crazy guy who lives across the ridge," A.J. lied. He could not say why. "Ex-Marine. Shoots stuff down all the time." It was not a convincing fabrication, but Wormy had been softened up by near death and plenty of alcohol and was not a tough crowd. He nodded, as if he knew several guys just like that. Good boys, but a little hasty on the trigger.

"Real badass, huh?" he asked with a grin. He apparently liked being taken out by the best. A.J.'s hunch was correct. It would have been cruel to inform the pilot he had been aced by a little old lady in a fit of revenge over a squashed pooch. He had undergone enough already. They decided that the helicopter would be fine where it was. It required repair to make it airworthy, and Wormy needed to check with his boss now that the load had become kindling.

"You think somebody'll hit it, sitting there?" Wormy asked as they climbed into the truck. A.J. perused the landing site. The machine was sitting on a straight stretch of road and was far enough off the shoulder to allow vehicles to pass one at a time.

"I only know one person who would be in any danger of hitting it," A. J. replied. "And she's tied up right now with a dog problem." He fired up the truck, and they headed for a phone.

"Dog too mean?" asked Wormy conversationally. He was fishing around unsuccessfully for something to smoke. A.J. removed a pack from over the visor and tucked it into Wormy's pocket.

"Dog too flat," he responded. Wormy nodded his head as if he understood just how much trouble a flat dog could be.

A.J. drove to the broken cabin and arrived just in time to witness the culmination of a misunderstanding between Truth and Slim. The problem revolved around two issues, the first being the house in the road and the second being the car in the house. Neither made Slim happy, and he could not seem to convey the extent of his unhappiness to Truth. Admittedly, it may have been his presentation, which was limited to stammering with rage while waving a loaded gun. Still, A.J. could see what Slim wanted as soon as he drove up.

He got out of the truck and sauntered over to the point of impact. He made plenty of noise as he came near; he didn't want to end up dead just because the skittish gendarme was having a mood. He squatted and looked up under the cruiser, then hollered to Wormy to bring the log chain from the back of the pickup. They attached one end to A.J.'s truck and the other to Slim's patrol car, and they had the cruiser extracted from its historic garage in no time. A.J. unhooked the chain from both vehicles and tossed it into the back of the truck. Slim was still waving his pistol and mouthing soundless words, but he seemed to be recovering from the conniption.

"There, Slim," A.J. said pleasantly. "You can have your car back. I don't know what we're going to do about this house, though. Maybe Johnny Mack can push it out of the way with his dozer." It sounded like an expedient plan, but it upset Truth.

"You can't just push my house out of the way with a bulldozer!" She folded her arms. "This is a National Historic Dwelling!" A.J., Slim, and Wormy all looked at the remains of the house.

"It's in pretty bad shape," A.J. said.

"You don't know what you're talking about!" She turned to Wormy, who was exhibiting the post-disaster flush of someone proud to be requiring oxygen. "Rig it back up, get your helicopter, and let's get back to work! I'm paying good money for nothing right now." Wormy smiled disarmingly and gave her a full-body shrug.

"I'd be happy to, but no can do," he replied. "My helicopter is out of action since the crazy guy shot it down."

"What crazy guy?" asked Slim.

"Never mind," A.J. interjected.

The committee by the log pile adjourned with no clear consensus. Truth exited the scene after first being cited by Slim on a zoning violation for owning a structure too close to the right-of-way.

THE FRONT PORCH PROPHET

Wormy received a ticket for illegal parking before riding to the jail to borrow the phone and check in. He was terminated by his superior, a former Army colonel called Maniac Monroe. This was a term of endearment imposed on him by the relatively small number of survivors of his various commands. Colonel Maniac had no patience with extenuating circumstances, bad luck, or the quiet of peacetime. He believed that heads and excrement should both roll downhill, away from colonels and others in charge.

Back at the flattening, A.J. began to disentangle animal from vegetable and mineral. He was about through when he heard a shrill whistle coming from the Folly. In addition to being stellar women named after famous authors, the Callahan girls all excelled at the fine art of whistling for effect, and Maggie was the most proficient of the lot. When she placed her two pinkies on her lower lip and blew, the resulting sound demanded respect.

A.J. answered his summons. He entered the kitchen and saw Estelle drinking tea at the table. She had gathered her dignity and was handling her bereavement well. He watched as she poured about a tablespoonful of tea into one of the exquisite Nortake cups that Maggie brought out on solemn occasions. A.J. called them the Death Cups. Then Estelle poured about a slug and a half of brandy in with her spot of tea. She tossed the mixture back in one quick flick, shuddered, and began preparing the next installment. A.J. eased up close to his wife.

"Why don't you just heat up the brandy bottle and put the tea away?" he whispered. He received another bump in the ribs to remind him to be nice. Estelle gulped another one down before speaking.

"A.J., I can't go with you to bury Plug," she said with a quaver.

"I just couldn't stand it."

"Don't worry," he replied. "I'll take care of him. I'll put him in deep, so a possum can't get to him." A.J. could not help it. He was well meaning but blithering when it came to bereaved women. This time, thankfully, it did not seem to matter.

"I think we should bury him next to Parm," Estelle said. She blinked a tear.

"Well, sure, Estelle. Whatever you want," A.J. said. He did not think Parm would care. Over the years, Estelle had augmented his gravesite with a goodly number of extras—the funerary equivalent of cruise control and stereo—and A.J. felt sure the deceased had become inured to additions to his eternal home, a place A.J. called The Parm Shrine.

At the head of the mound was a statue of a Parm-like figure locked in mortal combat with a Hun-like creature, and neither appeared happy over their timeless embrace. At Parm's feet was an eternal flame. It wasn't actually perpetual—there were no gas lines out at the cemetery—but it was a reasonable facsimile made by A.J. out of the guts of a camp stove. Estelle lit it each year on Armistice Day, the Fourth of July, and the anniversary of Parm's relocation to a better place. In A.J.'s opinion, a dead guy with his feet in a camp stove who had a Hun standing on his head ought not object to having a flat dog snugged in next to him. It was actually sort of the next logical step.

There was, however, a small problem; it was against the law to bury the animals with the people in Sequoyah. A.J. did not have it in him to break Estelle's heart, so he would simply have to work it out.

"Everything I love goes away," Estelle sobbed and nipped at her tea.

"We love you, Estelle," Maggie said, patting her shoulder. "We love you, and we're not going away." Estelle nodded and sniffed, gratitude etched on her features. A.J. left. He had a dog burial to fake. He went to Estelle's yard and finished loading the truck.

"Let's go, Plug," he said as they left.

His first stop was at the landfill, where he unloaded most of the porch and all of the dog. He buried poor old Plug on a slight rise overlooking some appliances. Then he tapped a little cross into the ground, a monument made of sticks and duct tape erected in memory of the best friend Estelle had left in this world.

"You were a hound," he eulogized. "But you deserved better than this."

He got back in the truck. His next destination was the cemetery. On his way, he stopped at Billy's for some gasoline. Wormy was there, killing time and drinking a Coke. A.J. was surprised when Wormy threw his duffel bag into the truck.

"Where are we going?" he asked.

"The graveyard," A.J. replied. Wormy gave a thumbs-up. A.J. kind of liked the downed aviator, and he figured that Wormy would love what was coming up next. They arrived at the burial ground and drove up close to The Parm Shrine. Then they got out.

"Bring the shovel," A.J. instructed as he grabbed the Plug-sized piece of porch he had saved. He needed to displace one Plug's worth of dirt for the mound to look right. They walked over to the area of interment. A.J. began to dig a hole next to Parm's grave. Wormy was busy inspecting the statuary.

"Is one of these guys buried here?" he asked, pointing at the sculptures.

"The one who looks like he's saying *Oh*," A.J. replied. He was down about a foot and wanted to go another.

"So who's the other one, the one who looks like he's about to puke?"

"That's his mortal enemy."

"This is cool," Wormy stated. "I want one of these when I go. Maybe a helicopter." He took the shovel from A.J. and began his turn. "How deep do we want to bury this wood?" he asked.

"Just a little more," A.J. said. Wormy took out a few more shovelfuls. Then he stepped out of the hole and stood, silent and respectful. He had no clue what was going on, but he knew that he was participating in a solemn rite of some sort.

"Parm, I'm sorry about this," A.J. said as he dropped the wood into the hole. "It's what Estelle wants, and you know how she can be." The breeze rustled through the fallen leaves, as if Parm were sighing in agreement.

"Is Parm the guy saying *Oh*?" Wormy asked as they filled the grave.

"He is," said A.J., shaping the mound.

"Is that his stick we're burying?" Wormy asked, attempting to pull together the many pieces to this puzzle.

"It's his wife's dog," A.J. said, dusting off his pants. Wormy nodded, as if it all made sense, now that he knew it was the wife's dog being committed to the ground.

"Was Parm a warrior?" Wormy asked.

"He was arguably the bravest man who ever lived," A.J. replied, picking up his shovel and heading for the truck. Wormy stood silent and cast a salute. It was his tribute to a fallen brother-in-arms, there at The Parm Shrine, adjacent to The Tomb of the Unknown Porch.

"Where are you staying?" A.J. asked conversationally as they drove away. "I'll drop you off." Wormy was still a bit overcome and could not immediately reply. After a moment, he regained control.

"Not staying anywhere," he responded. "Not doing anything." He related the details of his loss of employment. While A.J. listened, his mind began to form a plan. Wormy seemed like a decent sort. He needed a job and a place to stay. A.J. needed some help. Eugene needed full-time attendance. What would be wrong with Wormy?

"How about riding to see a friend of mine?" A.J. asked casually. He would see how they got on.

"Great," Wormy responded. "Let's go see your buddy. Uh, I hate to go empty-handed, and I could use a drink, myself. Is there somewhere around here we could buy a taste?"

"I can arrange that," A.J. said. They drove out to the county line and pulled up behind Eugene's beer joint. It was still closed due to the stiletto in Bird Egg's liver, but A.J. had a key. He opened the back door and invited Wormy in.

The beer joint's effect on the pilot was profound. He wandered with his mouth slightly agape, touching various containers of alcoholic beverage. He sat silently at the blond dinette table and fingered the poker chips and the playing cards. He observed the many photos taped to the walls, pictures of young women burgeoning forth, looking come-hither at Wormy.

"This is a good place," he observed. "Whose is it?"

"Mine," A.J. responded. Technically, it wasn't true, but it would be gospel soon enough. "Get what you want and put it in the truck. It's on the house." Wormy selected a case of beer and a half gallon of bourbon. A.J. picked up a jug for Eugene in case he was running low.

It was midday when A.J. and his passenger arrived at the foot of the mountain and began the journey up to the clearing. As he wheeled up the road, A.J. looked for signs of Rufus but saw no trace. When he rounded the last curve and entered the straightaway to the cabin, however, there sat the hound in the middle of the road. His paws were firmly planted, and his eyes were on A.J. This behavior represented a fair example of an old dog and a new trick.

"Bear in the road," noted Wormy. He had fallen naturally into the role of spotter for the expedition. A.J. halted about ten feet from Rufus. He didn't want to hit him—except maybe a couple of times with the bat—but the animal showed no intention of moving. He blew the horn, but there was no response. He hung his head out the window.

"Move, Rufus!" he yelled. Wormy raised his eyebrows. He seemed surprised that A.J. knew the bear. Then an extraordinary sequence of events occurred.

Rufus stood and looked over his shoulder at the road up to the cabin. Then he looked back at A.J. He barked once and headed up the track. A.J. slowly followed the dog.

"That's a dog, not a bear," Wormy corrected.

"That's the one you want to be dropping porches on," A.J. confirmed. "It'll probably take two."

When they reached the clearing, Eugene was not to be seen. Rufus crossed to the porch and stood patiently. A.J. parked and

236

slid the Louisville Slugger from behind the seat. If Rufus was lay-
ing a trap, he was prepared. Wormy slid out the other door and
landed lightly on the balls of his feet. He was tense as he scanned
the perimeter. Old habits and old soldiers died hard.

"Don't try anything you'll regret," A.J. said to the dog as he
crossed the clearing. Rufus barked and looked at the door. Wormy
was running a flanking movement from the right.

"Yeah, you're Rex the Wonder Dog," A.J. said. "But one wrong
move and you'll be out at the landfill next to Plug." He eased up
the steps to the porch. The dog barked one last time before entering
the open doorway. A.J. followed, wary but concerned. His sense of
foreboding was acute. Wormy materialized beside him.

The scene in the cabin was not as bad as he was expecting, but
it was mean enough. Eugene lay on the unmade bed. His eyes were
open, and he seemed semiconscious. He turned his head and cast
an unfocused gaze on A.J. The breath rattled in his chest. A.J.
moved in close. The smell of bourbon was heavy.

"I dreamed I went to the circus in my Maidenform bra," Eugene croaked, sharing the wisdom of the ages with his visitors. He
was drunk, high, and mortally ill. Everything was not going to be
all right.

"That happens to me all the time," A.J. responded absently
while mulling his next move. Wormy nodded as if he, too, occasionally ran down to the big top in a frilly undergarment, perhaps an
underwire for additional support. A.J.'s eyes roamed the room and
alighted on the shower. He believed in the potency of a hot shower,
and he stepped to the stall in the corner of the room and turned on
the spigots. Once the steam began to build, he crossed to the bed

and gently shook Eugene. Wormy stood at the ready.

"Wake up," A.J. said. "It's time to take a shower." Eugene startled, his eyes wild. Then he seemed to grasp the situation, but his gaze lingered on Wormy.

"We'll have to get to know each other a little better before we start showering together," he growled. A.J. and Wormy helped him to his feet and dragged him across the room. They peeled his clothing.

"I'm afraid you won't respect me in the morning," Eugene complained as he was eased into the stall.

"I don't respect you now," A.J. intoned, delivering the universal response on cue. Eugene slumped in the shower and let the hot water work its magic.

"Is he sick?" Wormy whispered.

"He is sick," A.J. confirmed. He dug around in Eugene's footlocker and came out with a pair of sweatpants and a sweatshirt. He laid the clothing over a chair and straightened the bed. Wormy rambled in the kitchen, muttering as he searched the cabinets. He turned to A.J. and spoke.

"What he needs is some coffee. I've got some in my pack." A.J. nodded. A cup of coffee would be a good idea for everyone. Wormy walked out to the truck. He was followed by Rufus, and A.J. was glad they seemed to be getting along. From the shower came snatches of an old Elvis tune. A.J. pounded on the side of the stall.

"Uh, humma humma," Eugene said as he stepped out. "Elvis has left the shower." He was still as high as a ball-game hot dog. A.J. could not find a clean towel so Eugene dripped dry while singing sacred songs from Memphis.

"I'm freezing my dick off here," Eugene complained.

"I wondered where it had gone," A.J. replied conversationally as he handed Eugene his clothing.

"Hey, hey, hey. Don't you worry about old Henry," Eugene said as he propped on A.J.'s shoulder and pulled on his pants. He slipped on his shirt and continued. "If you'd bring some women up here, you'd be seeing him snap to attention."

"I've been trying to line you something up," he said. "Your face is on billboards all the way to Atlanta. I've had a few inquiries, but they all want more money than you have." He handed Eugene a pair of running shoes.

"Shit. They'd be paying me!" Eugene hollered as he walked out to the porch. In the yard, Wormy was squatted in front of a camp-fire patiently waiting for the coffeepot to boil. Eugene sat in his chair and lit up a cigarette. A.J. sat next to him.

"What's the story with Daniel Boone there?" Eugene asked.

"Just a guy I brought along to make the coffee," A.J. responded.

"He sure is cute," Eugene observed. Wormy poked his fire with a stick. Rufus the loyal coffee-hound sat by him, guarding him from danger.

"I'm glad you like him," A.J. said. "I got him for you."

"You want to run that one by me again?"

"It's simple," A.J. said. "You need someone around to give you a hand. Wormy needs a place to stay. I need a little peace of mind when I'm not here. You ought to give me money for coming up with this idea."

"Wormy?" Eugene asked. "Fucking Wormy? I know about nine guys named Wormy. They all look like him." Eugene was try-ing to be a tough sell, so A.J. brought out the big guns.

"He killed Estelle Chastain's dog with a porch today."

"Get out of here," came Eugene's skeptical reply.

"Swear to God," A.J. replied. "Then he dropped a whole house on Slim's police car." Eugene cocked his head sideways and gave Wormy a long look.

"Well," he said grudgingly. "The boy may have a little potential. Slim make it out alive?"

"Yeah, he got out," A.J. admitted.

"These things happen," mused Eugene with mild disappointment in his voice. "I guess the important thing is that he made the attempt." Out in the yard, Wormy looked up and smiled.

"The coffee is ready," he said. A.J. arose and scratched up a measuring cup, a mug with no handle, and a small soup bowl. They savored the hot drink in silence. Wormy broke the quiet before it became oppressive.

"Did the crazy guy blow up your cars?" he asked Eugene, pointing at the carnage on the other side of the yard.

"What crazy guy?" Eugene replied.

"Never mind," said A.J., holding the bridge of his nose. It had been a long day, outlandish and fraught with peril. His head was tired, and he wanted to go home. Wormy arose, walked out to the truck, and returned with both half gallons of bourbon. He broke the seal on one and turned it up in a long, slow swig. When he finished, he sucked the air in through his teeth and wiped his lips with the back of his hand.

"Does anyone mind if I have a little nip?" he asked as a courtesy.

"I like a man with manners," Eugene observed, tipping the other jug for his own extended guzzle. A.J. could tell that Eugene was warming up to Wormy. The pair started to talk.

A.J. eased out of his chair and moved inside. He found pencil and paper and made a list of supplies that needed to be trucked in. He could hear laughter and easy talk coming from outside. The boys were hitting it off and slugging it down. He returned to the porch and viewed his handiwork. There were apples in their cheeks and twinkles in their eyes. Eugene lifted his bottle and offered a toast.

"To Saint fucking A.J., the founder of the feast," Eugene proposed. He was two drams to the right of sober and generous in word and thought. They drank.

"To all the boys who died in the attempt," Wormy said solemnly, and they quaffed again. It looked to A.J. like it was going to be a long evening.

"To the women I'm not going to get around to," offered Eugene with a trace of melancholy.

"To how my eyes will be looking in the morning," intoned Wormy. He seemed to be planning on staying.

"To how everyone's eyes will be looking in the morning," came Eugene's reply.

"How will your eyes look in the morning?" asked A.J.

"Like two cigarette burns in a blanket," said Wormy.

"Like two piss holes in the snow," said Eugene.

"Like two road maps of Georgia," said Wormy.

A.J. figured it was one metaphor past high time to leave, so he slipped off the porch. They were doing fine and wouldn't miss him. He started the truck, and the boys didn't even turn to see him go. As he bounced down the mountain, A.J. thought that the matchmaking was a success. At least for a while, Eugene was not alone. It was not a perfect solution, but it wasn't bad as a temporary expedient. Wormy seemed to be the proverbial rolling stone, but maybe he would gather some moss before moving on.

He headed to town. When he neared the city limit, he turned up the county road that led to Jackie Purdue's place. He rounded a long, slow curve and came to the straightaway that held Wormy's crippled ship. Slim stood in the road. With him was a stern-looking man in military garb. He reminded A.J. of a coiled spring. A.J. pulled up and rolled down his window.

"Slim, could you move your car?" he asked, pointing at the slightly dented cruiser blocking the way.

"Sure, I—" Slim began to respond, but the man with him cleared his throat and impatiently tapped his leg.

"Is that a swagger stick?" A.J. asked, smiling. He had never seen one in person and was enchanted. From Wormy's description, A.J. realized he was in the presence of Maniac Monroe.

"Um. This officer informs me that you may know what has become of my pilot." Maniac tapped while he talked, his tone indicating he was comfortable in his role as a leader of men.

"You must be Colonel Monroe," A.J. said. Maniac stood as stiff as a starched Georgia pine. "Wormy told me all about you." A.J. offered his hand.

"Um. Yes," responded Maniac. "Do you know where I might find Captain Locklear? I need to speak to him about moving this helicopter." A.J. could sense the situation was not as shipshape as the colonel would have liked.

"The last I saw of Wormy, he was too drunk to fly. And he was under the impression that he was unemployed. He is talking to someone about another situation as we speak." A.J. didn't want to rain on Maniac's parade, but he had dibs on Wormy.

"Can you take me to him?" Colonel Monroe asked.

"Not today," A.J. responded, but not unkindly. "It's late, he's sloshed, and I have something to do. I'll take you to see him tomorrow. Meet me at the diner in town about ten in the morning, and we'll ride on up." Maniac nodded. It would have to do.

A.J. finished the drive to Jackie's house. Jackie was in his long handles, drinking coffee on the porch.

"A.J." said Jackie. He nodded his head.

"Jackie, how have you been?"

"Been working, eating, and sleeping," he responded. "And haven't been getting much sleep, at that. I swear they're trying to kill me." He smiled ruefully. The box plant was well known for long hours of overtime.

"If I had your money, I'd throw my money away," A.J. responded. Jackie worked all the overtime he could lay his hands on and put aside the fruits for rainy days. By all accounts, it could rain for years, and he would be just fine. He lived the single life. Having seen his parents' marriage up close, it had seemed to him that there were worse things than being an old bachelor.

So A.J. the unemployed husband sat with Jackie the overemployed bachelor and talked of many things under the sun. They talked about Alabama Southern, and about the rumor that they were purchasing the box plant.

"I may end up drinking coffee with you down at the drive-in," Jackie observed.

"No, you're not management. They'll love you," was A.J.'s

reply. Then they spoke of the brutal murder of Estelle Chastain's dog. The news was novel to Jackie, and he hid a smile as he heard the details.

"I never liked that dog much, but Estelle is okay, except when she's showing me her cleavage," he commented, referring to her many attempts to reel him in. She had set her cap for him years ago, but her bait was simply not up to par.

"Plug has gone to a better place, and Estelle needs you now more than ever," A.J. kidded. Then they discussed the weather, the price of gas down at Billy's, and the new salad bar offered by Hoghead at the drive-in. Finally, A.J. ran out of anything else to talk about and broached the situation up on the mountain.

He outlined Eugene's condition. He related his discussions with Johnny Mack. He described the sad discourse between Eugene and Diane. He shared his opinion that Eugene was sliding fast and in need of constant attendance. Then he finished by explaining the installation of Wormy until better arrangements could be made.

"Johnny Mack knows about this?" Jackie finally asked.

"Everything but Wormy," A.J. said.

"I talked to him yesterday," Jackie continued. "And to Angel. He didn't tell me any of this. And she seemed happy, so I guess he hasn't told her either." Jackie seemed embarrassed.

"You need to go make her unhappy, Jackie," A.J. said. It was the hard truth, flinty and cold.

That night back at the Folly, A.J. discussed his accomplishments with Maggie. He was satisfied with the day's labors, but Maggie voiced concern.

"You left a drunken, dog-killing, unemployed helicopter pilot named Wormy in charge?" she asked, putting the worst possible slant on the arrangement.

"It beats leaving him with the dog," A.J. said defensively.

The next day was busy. A.J. began his chores by taking Estelle out to the Parm Shrine so she could pay her respects to the chunk of wood A.J. had committed to eternity. Estelle was overcome at the sight of the small, raw mound.

"You did a fine job, A.J.," she boo-hooed as he endured a hug. He thought of Plug out at the landfill next to an Amana.

"Yes, ma'am," he replied.

After taking Estelle home, A.J. drove down to the We Shall Gather by the Salad Bar Drive-In to wait for Maniac Monroe. When he walked in, a couple of his old sawmill employees hailed him.

"How is life in the sawmill?" A.J. asked.

"They have lost their minds," said Duke Favors. He pointed his fork at A.J. "They've raised the production quota, and they have a bunch of new boys wandering around with clipboards looking for *waste*."

He shook his head in absolute disgust as he bit into a piece of bacon. "If they were really interested in waste, they'd start by shit-canning *those* guys."

"Tell him about the paper towels, Duke," urged Brickhead Crowe.

"Oh, man," said the Duke. "Somebody on the day shift wadded a bunch of paper towels in one of the johns. When they flushed it, it flooded the bathroom. So they got some of those damn air blowers that hang on the wall. You know, the ones where the fourth step is to wipe your hands on your pants. Our new supervisor—and this guy is a real treat, by the way—told us he guessed we wouldn't be stopping up the toilets anymore. Real shitty about it, too." Duke chased a bite of egg around his plate with his toast.

"Tell him the rest," Brickhead said with glee.

"Somebody—and I swear to God I don't know who, but I'd buy him a beer if I did—ripped those blowers off the damn wall and tossed *them* in the shitters. It was beautiful." Duke and Brickhead were laughing, and A.J. was glad to see that they were in good spirits. It seemed there was trouble brewing at Alabama Southern. He stood when Maniac Monroe came in.

"Conley, you need to be hanging way back when the shit hits the fan," he said to Brickhead Crowe. "Do you understand me?" Conley nodded. A.J. looked at him to be sure he understood. "I mean *way* back. Are you with me on this?" The big man nodded again. A.J. turned to Duke, whose ways he knew quite well.

"Duke, they'll fire you if they catch you, and probably press charges, too," he advised.

"What?" Duke asked, the paragon of innocence. He held up his hands, as if to show he had nothing up his sleeves.

"Duke, this is me, not some wet-behind-the-ears new boy. These people will not play with you. I'm telling you." Duke was still holding his innocent pose as A.J. left with Maniac. A.J. chuckled when he and Colonel Monroe got into the truck. The hand-dryers-in-the-johns deal was pretty good.

The trip to Eugene's was silent. They arrived at the clearing and saw Wormy squatted in the yard, cooking a bird on a spit. An open can of beer was to the left of him and Rufus was to the right. Eugene sat on the porch, strumming at an acoustic guitar. A.J.

headed to the porch to confer with Eugene. Maniac stopped at the bird-roast to speak with his former pilot.

"We should have become rock stars," Eugene offered. "I remember we used to talk about it all the time." He seemed wistful. "I wonder why we never did it."

"We never did it because we sucked," A.J. replied simply. It was the truth, and no use dancing around the fact. When they were boys, he and Eugene and three other lads had formed a rock-and-roll band with the unlikely name of Skyye. To their musically challenged minds, the extra *ye* at the end of the perfectly sufficient *Sky* constituted class, and considering the quality of their song stylings, they needed all the help they could get.

"We didn't suck all that bad," Eugene said defensively.

"We sucked so bad we're lucky we didn't implode," A.J. commented. He reached for the guitar, and Eugene surrendered it without a fight. A.J. began to tune the instrument.

"Well, okay, we mostly sucked," Eugene conceded grudgingly. "But Jimmy didn't suck. He was great."

"You're right," A.J. agreed. "*He* could have been a star." They were referring to Jimmy Weems, former lead guitar player for Skyye, onetime inhabitant of Sequoyah, and bygone participant in life. He could make music flow from almost any instrument, could pick out a song after hearing it once, and could play a guitar upside down and backward just like Jimi Hendrix. But he was luckless, and somewhere along the way he was stricken with crippling arthritis in both hands. By the time he turned twenty-one, his fingers were so bent and deformed he could no longer button his shirt, never mind skitter up the neck fast and sweet. Music was his life, and when the music died, so did Jimmy. He was gone when his mama found him, dead of an overdose of painkillers washed down with cherry vodka.

A.J. and Eugene fell silent for a moment, saddened by the memory of their friend. They watched Wormy and Maniac out in the yard where they carried on a lively conversation. Rufus sat beside Wormy and kept a weather eye on Colonel Monroe. Eugene pointed his finger in Maniac's direction.

"Who's he?" he asked.

"That's Wormy's ex-boss. He's come to try to hire him back. He needs him to fly the helicopter out of the road."

"He can't have him," Eugene said. "He works for me now."

"I didn't know you were hiring, or I would have hit you up myself," A.J. said. "What are his duties?"

"He gets drunk with me and cooks birds in the yard."

"I saw the bird," A.J. said, handing the guitar back to Eugene. "It looked like Wormy hit it with the helicopter. My advice is to go with some of the Spam I brought you." Eugene was even a bigger fan of Spam than A.J. was. He was the only person A.J. knew who had actually baked one, just like the optimistic picture on the can.

They chatted awhile, and A.J. related the tale of Duke and the hand dryers. Eugene was appreciative of the symbolism.

"That Duke is a pistol ball," he observed.

"Oh, that Duke," agreed A.J. When Duke had been his responsibility, A.J. had not thought him so droll. Wormy appeared before them, looking sheepish.

"The colonel wants me to fly the helicopter out of the road," he said. "I told him I would take it as far as Chattanooga. Then I'm coming back here." Having spoken his piece, Wormy went back to his bird.

"You gotta admire loyalty and a sense of duty," Eugene said.

"That Wormy is a jewel," A.J. agreed.

"I think I'm going to fly with him. I've never been on a helicopter, and I'm running out of chances."

"Bad idea," said A.J. "The reason they need Wormy is because there's probably no one else crazy enough to do it. The helicopter is bent in some places it shouldn't be. I don't think it's going to fly too well. It may even crash."

"Now you're talking," Eugene said. He clapped his hands and rubbed them together briskly. A.J. shook his head. He walked to the truck and unloaded some supplies as Eugene sauntered out to the barbecue pit to secure his travel arrangements.

In exchange for six-hundred forty dollars, Eugene was allowed to make the trip. The odd sum represented all the cash Eugene had on hand, and he had to sign a document that released Maniac from all liability for everything, everywhere, for a period of time stretching specifically from the Big Bang to the Second Coming. It was agreed that the operation would take place the following morning. Until then, a mechanic would go over the crippled ship with a fine-tooth comb. Maniac would follow Eugene and Wormy to Chattanooga in another helicopter, and if they were alive after the landing he would bring them back to Eugene's cabin.

"Wormy, you don't have to do this," A.J. said as Colonel Monroe walked to the truck. "You don't owe that man anything."

"It's hard to explain," Wormy replied. "I put it in the road, and it's up to me to fly it out." He sounded apologetic. A.J. slugged him

249

lightly on the shoulder. Rufus growled.

"Take care of yourself up there," A.J. said. "And for God's sake, don't fly over my house." Wormy nodded sagely.

"Because of the crazy guy, right?" he said.

"What damn crazy guy?" Eugene asked.

"Never mind," said A.J. He turned his attention to Eugene. "If you happen to get your killing tomorrow, is there anything you want me to take care of?" He knew the arrangements thanks to the purloined letter, but he didn't know them with authorization.

"There are a lot of things I want you to do," said Eugene lightly. "Charnell Jackson has the scoop. Get with him." A.J. turned to leave. "Look at it this way," Eugene said to his retreating back. "If I get it tomorrow, it takes you off the hook. I won't need that favor we talked about."

"What favor?" Wormy asked.

"Never mind," said Eugene, reaching for some squab.

A.J. did not attend the big fly-out the following day, but he did keep his family home.

"Why don't we have to go to school today?" Emily Charlotte asked.

"So a house won't fall on you," came A.J.'s reply.

"Like it did on Plug?" asked Harper Lee.

"Like it did on Plug," A.J. confirmed.

"Boy, that dog had a big penis," J.J. observed.

"I am always amazed at what passes for conversation around this house," Maggie said.

A.J.'s precautions were not necessary. Wormy's number was not yet up, and the helicopter did not crash, although the landing gear

THE FRONT PORCH PROPHET

fell off over Dalton, which made for an interesting landing in Chattanooga. The touch down was so dicey, in fact, that Wormy was not inclined to fly home after reaching *terra firma*. He had survived two crash landings in two days on top of several other previous occurrences, and he decided on the spot that his flying days were over.

"My mama didn't raise no fool," was his comment. So Eugene and Wormy caught a cab over to Car-O-Rama, and after some hard bargaining they became the proud owners of a 1988 Dodge Caravan with "Mom's Taxi" emblazoned on the bumper sticker in front.

A.J. heard the full story the following day as he walked around Mom's Taxi. He could understand Wormy's decision to remain on the ground, but he was having difficulty with the choice of vehicles.

"Was this the only one they had left?" he asked. That would explain it.

"Don't start," Eugene said. "Wormy liked the bumper sticker." Oddly, at that moment they heard a vehicle bouncing up the road. Visitors other than A.J. were uncommon.

"Sounds like you have company coming," A.J. noted.

"Is my hair all right?" Eugene asked. As he spoke, Jackie Purdue's vehicle came into view. Sitting beside him in the cab was Angel.

"Your family has come to call," A.J. said.

"Shit," Eugene said under his breath. "I'm not ready for this."

"No, but Angel is," A.J. said. He greeted Jackie, hugged Angel, and left. This was family business, and he wasn't family. Not officially anyway.

I shouldn't even mention this, but I'm sentimental.
Jackie really wants to jump your bones.
—Excerpt of posthumous letter from
Eugene Purdue to Estelle Chastain

THE THANKSGIVING SEASON HAD ALWAYS SEEMED
accelerated to A.J., a time of quickened and scarce days. This year,
however, he did not have a job to pilfer his hours, so he took advantage and began his preparations early. His festive demeanor
became contagious, and John Robert soon caught turkey fever. Between them, they left no detail uncovered, no stone unturned in
their quest for the perfect celebration.

The guest list was discussed and refined, and they finally agreed
to just invite everyone they knew. They spent a full day compiling
the menu, and another day combing the countryside for the turkey,
ham, and standing rib roast. Side dishes, casseroles, and desserts
were delegated to members of the guest roster based upon their
specialties. The exception was Estelle Chastain, whose forte was
cornmeal boiled in molasses. She called the resulting gruel Indian
pudding, and it was vile.

"What is this?" A.J. had asked Maggie some years back after

his first and last mouthful of the substance.

"Estelle calls it Indian pudding," Maggie said. "She says it is an authentic Pilgrim dish." Her spoonful had stopped in midair pending the outcome of his taste.

"I think she must have used canned Indians," A.J. said between gulps of cider. The flavor was insistent and would not leave him.

"Well, it is hard to get fresh ones this time of year," was Maggie's reply as she carefully laid a slice of bread over her portion. Since that time, Estelle had always been assigned a dessert.

Once the bill of fare was in order, A.J. and John Robert set their sights on the banquet hall. The Folly was scrubbed, waxed, and buffed. Curtains were washed, starched, and ironed. Windows were cleaned inside and out. Woodwork was oiled, and Granmama's silver was polished. By a week before the event, the house was perfect.

"It's going to be great!" A.J. told Maggie.

"You're obsessing," she noted, not unkindly.

"What makes you say that?" he asked defensively.

"I saw those little chef's hats you bought to go on the ends of the turkey legs," she replied. "I also found the family's Pilgrim costumes—which I, incidentally, refuse to wear—hidden in the sewing room."

"Oh."

"It looks to me like everything is prepared," she continued. "You and John Robert have done a wonderful job. Take the day off. Go see Eugene. You haven't been up there in a couple of days. Check on him, and renew his invitation for dinner. Ask Wormy to come, too."

"Well, I don't know," he began. "I have some baking to do, and—"

"I'll do the baking," Maggie interrupted. "Eudora and Carlisle will be in from Atlanta later today, and she'll want to help. Now go. Pick up some wine." She pecked his cheek and shoved him out the kitchen door.

He took a slow drive through town before heading up to Eugene's. In truth, there was very little left to do, and he was glad for the day off. Obsession is hard work and can only be performed at full speed for short periods of time. It was early in the day, and he stopped at the Judge Not That Ye Be Not Breakfast Anytime Drive-In for a bite. He sat down at the empty counter hearing the clatter in the kitchen as Hoghead prepared the lunch special. A.J. hoped it was chili-mac.

"What's for lunch?" he hollered. Through the round window in the swinging door, he could see Hog slam down a large baking pan.

"A.J., how are you doing?" Hoghead asked breathlessly as he whisked through the door. "I didn't hear you come in. We're having turkey pie." Turkey pie. A.J. didn't really care for the turkey pie at the drive-in. He had viewed its preparation on one occasion and couldn't get past the fact that the turkey had come in a large can marked Turkey, One.

"How about a cheeseburger?" A.J. asked.

"Comin' right up," Hoghead huffed. A.J. watched as the old cook worked the grill. He was a maestro at the short order, his moves graceful yet economical. The preparation of food was Hoghead's dance, his Sistine Ceiling. In a little more than no time at all, the steaming plate was before A.J. Hog scooped out a bowl of turkey pie for himself and sat down next to his customer. They ate their first few bites in a shared, comfortable silence.

"Are you still bringing your Swedish meatballs?" A.J. asked. He had requested the restaurateur to bring his famous appetizer to the Thanksgiving feast. Hoghead claimed to have obtained the recipe from a genuine Swedish girl while on shore leave in Hong Kong back in '53. No one knew why a Swedish meatball chef was with Hoghead in Hong Kong in 1953, but the tidbits were tasty, and A.J. thought it best not to pry.

"They are soaking in the sauce while we speak," Hoghead said proudly. He blew on a spoonful of the turkey pie. A.J. figured the hotter the better, in case the Turkey, One, had been in the can too long. Idly, he wondered if there were any cans in the back marked Meatballs, Swedish. He hoped not, but seldom was anything as it seemed. He finished his burger and was sipping his coffee when the bell at the front door tinkled. In walked Truth Hannassey. She clipped across the diner and sat on the stool next to A.J. Then she looked at him and smiled. Hoghead jumped up and cleared his plate.

"Yes, ma'am. What can I get you?" he asked.

"Oh, I don't know," she replied pleasantly. "What's good?"

"Try the turkey pie," A.J. advised her. "It's one of Hoghead's specialties." Hoghead beamed. He loved to hear his efforts applauded.

"Turkey pie sounds good. And maybe a glass of tea?" Hoghead set to. "I need to talk to you," she said to A.J. "Would you mind if we sat at a booth? My skirt is a little short for this stool." A.J. had, in spite of himself, noticed that it was. The glance had been instinctive, an involuntary reaction involving the optical nerve that runs from the eyes to the penis without making any stops at the brain.

"Sure, we can move," A.J. replied. His curiosity was piqued.

256

She was being awfully nice. They moved to a booth and sat down opposite each other. She folded her hands and made eye contact.

"I have purchased the old Finn Hall on the Alabama side of the mountain," she said. He was familiar with the property. It was a huge and stately old wreck—opulent in its day—that had been quietly rotting away on the side of Lookout Mountain for many years. It was built before the turn of the century by a group of Finnish people who had made fortunes in the lumber industry of the period. Thus it was named the Finn Hall, and it was where they all gathered together to socialize. As a group of people they did quite well, due to the combination of big, cheap logs to harvest and big, cheap Alabamians to harvest them with.

"I know the Finn Hall," he said. The mantle in his parlor had come from there on a liberal lend-lease deal involving a crowbar, his truck, and a dark night. "It was the fanciest building ever nailed up around here, that's for sure."

"It will be that way again," she said, and he could hear the excitement in her voice. "I am going to turn it into another Biltmore Estates. It will be beautiful." She looked at him, and he knew he was seeing a piece of her dream. But he still didn't know what she wanted. Hoghead whisked up with a platter laden with turkey pie, cranberry sauce, glazed yams, and hot yeast rolls. A piece of garnish completed the presentation. He had reached down deep.

"Well, good luck with it," A.J. said, referring to the Finn Hall and not the turkey pie. "As long as you've got the money and the time, you can make it magnificent."

"I've got the money," she assured him. She took a petite bite of turkey pie. "What I would like to know is, do you have the time?"

257

The question surprised A.J. He watched as she buttered a roll. Strangely, the idea of working on the Finn Hall held some appeal for him. He had actually once sketched out some plans for the old hall, some ideas he would like to try. He knew in his heart he could make that building his masterpiece. But he had some concerns with regard to the woman across the table. He and Truth had a little history behind them, some battered baggage sitting by the tracks.

"You want me to restore the Finn Hall?"

"Yes," she replied simply. She was really warming up to the plate before her.

"Why me?" he asked, a reasonable question given their record. "You must know all sorts of high-powered construction types. And you and I have not always seen eye to eye."

"This is not construction," she stated emphatically. "This is art. I have seen what you did with your house. Maggie showed me all of your before-and-after pictures. I want that same eye for detail and careful workmanship on this job."

"Did Maggie suggest we talk about this?" he asked.

"No, she didn't," Truth responded. "She liked it when she heard it, but it was my idea. She told me you've considered going into this type of work before. You're the one I want." She finished her pitch and her lunch, and she sat there silently, sipping her tea. He was in a quandary. He wanted to do it, but he wasn't sure about working for Truth. And money had not been discussed, but that could come later if he decided to do the job.

"Let me think about it a couple of days," he said. He wanted to talk to Maggie and see what she really thought. Also, he thought he might ride out to the Finn Hall. It had been a while since his last

258

look, and that peek had been after nightfall.

"That's fair," she said, holding out her hand for a shake. "We can talk more about it Thursday." She stood, left a generous tip, and walked to the counter to settle her check. A.J. was lingering back at Thursday. Was she coming Thursday? Maggie must have invited her. As he tuned back in, he heard Truth finishing a statement.

". . . fine. I'll pick it up Wednesday afternoon." She smiled at them both when she walked to the door. They watched as she strode up the sidewalk.

"She is nice," Hoghead observed, counting his tip. He appreciated women who ate his food and gave him money. "All the young bucks around here must be fast asleep." He had that old *if I were twenty years younger* look on his face.

"It's complicated," A.J. told him. "Don't torment yourself." Truth was no Swedish meatball cook from Hong Kong, and A.J. did not want to see Hoghead get hurt.

"She loved my turkey pie, and for a little girl, she could eat, too." This was high acclaim from Hoghead. "She ordered a big pan to bring with her to your house on Thursday."

"No kidding," A.J. responded. "Well, it doesn't get much better than that." He paid his bill, made his *adieus*, and headed for Eugene's via the beer joint.

He studied on the Finn Hall idea until his arrival at the beer joint, newly reopened and staffed by a slowly convalescing Bird Egg. He had overcome the long knife stuck in his liver by Termite Nichols, but he still weakened easily and could not carry heavy loads, so Eugene had provided Wormy as an assistant. The bootlegger-in-training spent two or three hours a day with Bird Egg, loading the coolers and hauling the garbage. The two were birds of a feather. Both had been to Asian wars of their country's choice and had survived, and every day since had been bonus time. A.J. pulled in and saw Mom's Taxi, which meant Wormy was in residence. He parked and entered.

"A.J.!" Bird Egg exclaimed. "How in the goddamn hell have you been, boy?" The exertion of the greeting sent Bird Egg into a coughing fit.

"I've been fine, Bird Egg. You're looking pretty good for an old guy with a hole in his liver." He was lying. Bird Egg looked like aged Kansas roadkill.

"Shit," the old man commented as he lit another Pall Mall. "It'll take more'n Termite Nichols to put me under." He was racked by another coughing fit.

Not much more, A.J. thought, saying, "That's the ticket, Bird." Wormy came in from the back carrying a couple of cases of beer. He saw A.J. and smiled.

Wormy had been a godsend. He enjoyed living up on the mountain and drinking the day away with his young ward, Eugene. But in addition to that duty, he took care of Eugene. He made sure that his patient had hot food and clean clothes. He saw that Eugene had medicine and booze, cigarettes and weapons of destruction. He kept the cabin clean and the yard neat. He helped out at the beer joint some, but he would not leave his charge for long.

"Wormy, you're working too hard," A.J. said. "I think you must be trying to take Bird Egg's job away from him." Bird was snoring on the sofa. Wormy removed the burning cigarette from the old man's lips.

"No, I don't want his job," Wormy said seriously as he looked with concern in the comatose rogue's direction. He didn't want Bird Egg to get the wrong idea, to think he was gunning for him. Fortunately, Bird Egg was not paying strict attention to the conversation.

"Well, I see what you mean," A.J. said. "Too much pressure." Bird Egg rolled over in his stupor.

"Exactly. Who needs it?" Wormy asked.

"Right," A.J. confirmed. He moved to the wine closet and rummaged around for selections sealed with corks rather than twist tops, obvious evidence of finer vintages. He put these in a box and placed them on the card table. Then he dug out the spiral notebook that served as the ledger and charged the wine to his tab. He felt better about it that way. The beer joint wasn't his yet.

"I'm heading up to see Eugene," he told Wormy as he picked up the box. "Is anyone up there with him?"

"Angel was still visiting when I left this morning," Wormy replied. "She came real early today." It was the rare day she did not come to see her baby son. Jackie provided the horsepower for her visits, so he saw Eugene as often as she did. Counting A.J. and Wormy, Eugene was attended most of the time, which was what A.J. had set out to accomplish. Predictably, Johnny Mack had not made the trek. A.J. held hope that he would find it in his heart to attempt a reconciliation before the end.

"You going to hang around down here long?" he asked.

"I'll be along as soon as he finishes his nap," Wormy said. He followed A.J. out to the truck.

"Bird Egg is looking pretty bad," A.J. commented as he climbed into the cab.

"I know dead guys in better shape," Wormy agreed. "I guess he's just too mean to die." A.J. had to agree that the old man was gritty. But too mean to die or not, it looked like the checkmark had already been placed by Bird's name. Maybe the Reaper had gotten stuck in traffic or stopped off for a short stack and a cup of coffee, but directly he would come to call. A.J. waved as he backed out. Wormy nodded as he began to police the area around the beer joint.

A.J. drove up the mountain. When he pulled into the clearing, he viewed Eugene asleep in his La-Z-Boy recliner. The chair and its occupant were out in the open in front of a bonfire. Eugene preferred the outdoors, and the arrangement had been Wormy's solution when it became too cold for Eugene to sit without heat on the porch. Four sturdy poles were implanted around the perimeter of the seating area so a tarp could be strung in case of rain. A cord of seasoned oak was split and stacked to the west of the area, providing handy fuel and a break from the prevailing winds. The venerable cable spool had been dragged from the porch and sat next to the La-Z-Boy, rounding out the ensemble. A.J. dismounted and walked over. He poked up the fire and tossed on a few more logs. There was more than a nip in the air, and the heat felt good. Rufus was snoozing next to his master. He stirred, cast a baleful eye, and growled with low menace. A.J. held up a piece of the split oak.

"Think of this as a baseball bat with bark on it," he advised the dog. Rufus blinked and resumed his nap. Wormy had been a calming influence on the old canine, and most times he was content to merely glare and rumble.

The last month had not been kind to Eugene. The dark circles under his eyes looked like twin shiners, as if he had unwisely made rude remarks to burly boys in a bar named Smitty's. The contrast with the yellowish tinge of his skin was stark. He had passed gaunt and was now skeletal. He slept a great deal, but it was difficult to say whether this was because of his condition or due to his treatment. He was on the downhill slalom, gaining momentum exponentially while barely dodging the trees. A.J.'s heart told him that it would not be long. He left his brother sleeping and walked on to the cabin. He intended to brew some coffee, thinking that Eugene might like a cup when he awoke. He opened the door, and there stood Angel. She looked as if she had been crying, and she gasped and put her hand over her heart when she saw him.

"A.J.!" she said. "I didn't hear you come up. You startled me." She sat down on the tall stool next to the stove. A small pot of vegetable soup was bubbling, and he could smell cornbread baking.

"I'm sorry, Angel," he said apologetically. "I figured you were gone, or I would have made more noise. Jackie didn't forget you, did he?" He put the coffee on to boil.

"No, he came. But Eugene was having a bad morning. Jackie helped me get him comfortable, and then I sent him on to work. He said he would be glad to stay, but you know how much it upsets him to miss a day. He was working the short shift today, and ought to be back soon."

They sat briefly silent while Angel stirred the soup. She looked over at A.J., and he could see that the tears were flowing. There was a quiet dignity to her sadness. They were on the hard way now, no mistake, and there was little he could do to comfort her. She stood and stared out the kitchen window at her son.

"I wish he would come in," she said. "It's cold out there." She smiled a blue smile. "He always was a little stubborn. Sort of like his daddy." A.J. decided to leave that one right where it was. Perhaps he would discuss Eugene's paternity on a day less mournful and joyless.

"Headstrong," he agreed. He stood by her and looked out the window. Presently, Eugene stirred. "Looks like he's waking up," A.J. said. "I'll go see if he wants some of that soup, or maybe some coffee." He walked out into the yard and dragged up a chair. Eugene looked over as his brother sat, and he offered a whisper of wisdom.

"Here's your chance," he said. "Rufus is asleep."

"I'll pass," A.J. replied. "If I can't take him out face to face, it wouldn't be right to sneak up from behind." He nudged Rufus with his toe, and the big dog snarled ominously in his sleep.

"You are a noble man," Eugene observed before knocking back a fair slug of bourbon followed by a small sip of one of his medicines. He coughed a moment before regaining control. "Rufus, on the other hand, is not. His preference is for you to never see it coming. Remember that." A.J. nodded his appreciation for the advice, although he had not been unclear on the subject to begin with. Eugene shrunk deeper into his coat and grew motionless. Finally, just as A.J. decided he had dropped back off, Eugene spoke.

"Do you have any cigarettes?" he asked. There was a bleakness in his voice, a timbre of defeat. It gave A.J. a chill. "Angel seems to have hidden mine again." A.J. lit one for Eugene and tossed the rest of the pack on the cable spool.

"Well, they are bad for you," he offered lamely. "And she is your mama."

"I know," Eugene said. They were quiet for a while. "What

264

time did Angel and Jackie leave?" he asked. He seemed to be feeling particularly bad at the moment.

"I don't know when Jackie left," A.J. answered. "Angel is inside. She's making you some soup." Eugene considered this information for a moment while enjoying his borrowed cigarette. He smoked it to the nub, flipped it in the fire, and lit another.

"Angel is of the opinion that soup will cure my cancer. Every time I turn around, she's bringing me some soup and hiding my fucking smokes." Eugene's voice was quiet, yet his words were harsh. A.J. didn't know what to say. Angel's soup wasn't that bad, and he could always slip Eugene another carton of the Surgeon General's bane.

"Well, she wants to help you," he said. "But she doesn't know what to do."

"Like I don't fucking know that," Eugene snarled. He seemed to coil, as if about to strike. "But there's not a goddamn thing that she can do. In the meantime, I don't have time to be hunting up a damn cigarette." A.J. knew that his brother was right. There was nothing anyone could do. Nothing at all. "I don't want to die," Eugene said. His voice caught, and he grew quiet.

A.J. was in a bind. He wanted to ease Eugene's anguish and bolster his troubled spirit, but he had no tools adequate to the task. He was not trained to handle raw emotion from hopeless souls. But the fat was in the fire. Eugene was going to die, and there would be no quarter. He reached over and took Eugene's hand. It was a totally uncharacteristic action, but it was all he could think of. At first there was no reaction, but after a moment he felt a slight returning pressure. And so they sat in silence for a long, stony time, secret brothers staring into the blaze, each with his own thoughts.

After an interval, A.J. heard a vehicle making its way up the road and Jackie's vehicle rolled into view. Eugene removed his hand and placed it in his coat pocket. Jackie parked next to A.J.'s truck and joined the boys at the fire.

"Man, it's cold," he said. He blew into his hands.

"There's some coffee in the cabin," A.J. offered.

"And soup," Eugene said distantly, although his voice had lost its steel edge.

"I think I'll get us all a coffee," Jackie said. "Coffee, Gene?" he asked his brother. Eugene nodded absently.

"That Jackie will just talk your leg off," Eugene said after Jackie had entered the cabin. "Blah, blah, blah, blah, blah." He had joshed Jackie for years on his lack of vocal acumen. He washed down a little more medicine with a lot more bourbon before lighting another smoke. He took a deep drag and closed his eyes. When they reopened, they had a softer look, glazed and watery around the edges.

"The thing about morphine is this," he expounded. "It's great." He looked over at A.J. "Just absolutely, fucking great. If I had known it, I would have been a junkie years ago." They heard the door shut, and Jackie made his way over to them with three steaming Styrofoam cups.

"Here's the Joe, boys," he said, handing out the fragrant vessels. They all sipped appreciatively for a moment.

"Sure is cold out here," Eugene offered in Jackie's direction. He was as high as government spending, feeling good enough to pick at his oldest brother.

"Man," Jackie agreed, oblivious to his brother's wiles. He finished his coffee. "Mama's tired," he said to Eugene. "She says she wants to stay, but I'm going to take her home." He looked at A.J. "Are you going to be around awhile?"

"Absolutely." A.J. thought she needed to go home, as well. She was not a young woman, and all of those years she had lived with Johnny Mack had each counted for more, like dog years. Jackie pitched his cup on the fire and went to get his mother. Eugene and A.J. watched as the cup melted away.

"Jackie is not an environmentally sound man," Eugene noted, as if it saddened him that his own brother was part of the problem and not the solution.

"Not like me and you, for sure," A.J. agreed, and threw his cup on the pyre. Eugene's followed.

"Maybe later we can spray some deodorant into the air," Eugene suggested. Jackie and Angel made their way to the fire. She was carrying a tray.

"Eat your soup and then we'll talk," A.J. said quietly when they walked up. Angel placed the meal on the cable spool.

"Eugene, I made you some soup," she said. "I want you to have some of it before it gets cold."

"Yes, ma'am," he replied. She looked over at A.J.

"Make sure he eats," she advised. He could hear the concern in her voice.

"Yes, ma'am," he echoed. She looked frail in the cold light of afternoon, tottery and infirm. She bent down and kissed Eugene on the cheek.

"I will see you tomorrow," she told him. Then Jackie took her arm and led her to the Bronco. A.J. and Eugene watched as they left the clearing, then A.J. uncovered the soup and handed the bowl to Eugene.

"Here. Eat a bite and I'm off the hook." Eugene complied. Then he surprised A.J. by taking two more spoonfuls before putting the broth down. He looked around on the cable spool for a moment. Then he sighed and shook his head.

"She took my cigarettes again," Eugene said with resignation in his voice. A.J. looked, and sure enough, they were absent.

"She's good," he said as he walked to his truck and removed the carton he had brought.

"She's driving me crazy," Eugene said.

"It could be worse," A.J. pointed out. "Estelle Chastain could be your mother."

"There's no call for that kind of talk," Eugene said, shuddering. "I need a drink," he concluded, reaching for the remnants of the sour mash on the cable spool. He drained the bottle. "I hope you brought more," he croaked.

"I did," A.J. assured him. "But I'm considering putting your whiskey and cigarettes up until you learn moderation." Eugene cast him a look that would soften lead.

"I have to put up with that kind of shit from Angel," he said. "You, I can kill."

"You seem to have your old good humor back," A.J. noted.

"I slept too long, and my feelgood wore off," came the simple reply. He directed unfocused eyes at A.J. "A man in my condition does not need for his feelgood to wear off." A.J. had to take that one on faith but did not mistrust a word of it. He nodded.

"Maggie told me to ask you again to come to dinner Thursday," he said. "So I'm asking. Why don't you have Wormy bring you down?" This marked the third time he had asked, but Eugene was extremely resistant to the idea, stating that he didn't have a hell of a lot to be thankful for.

"Do you think Diane will come?" Eugene asked, throwing a slow curve in A.J.'s direction. It caught the corner for a strike.

"Yeah, I think she will," A.J. answered. What he didn't mention was that she would likely be in the company of Truth Hannassey. The two had become a couple and were seldom separated. He still couldn't believe that Maggie had asked Truth to come. He made a mental note to stop by the beer joint and invite Bird Egg in retaliation.

"I'd like to see her," Eugene lamented. "And the boys, too."

"Well, then, it's a date," A.J. said. He would just have to talk to Diane and Truth and get them to work with him on this. "We'll eat, drink, and be merry. It will be good for you."

"Let me see what Wormy says," Eugene hedged.

"He wants to come," A.J. said. "He told me that he has never been to a real Thanksgiving feast. Give him a break." Eugene sighed.

"I'm looking pretty rough. I don't want to offend any of your guests." His Emily Post was showing, and his concern was laudable and touching.

"You have always offended everybody," A.J. pointed out. "You may be the most offensive person who ever lived. The only difference now is that you're thinner. You were getting a little paunchy anyway."

"I wouldn't talk," Eugene countered. He was rolling a generous joint while he talked. "Unemployment has gone right to your hips." A.J. looked down. He might have picked up a pound or two, but he believed he carried it well.

"Keep it up, and I'll tell Angel where you hide the dope," he responded. "Now, how about it? Are you coming?"

"Tell Maggie May I'll be there unless I feel rotten," Eugene said slowly, almost grudgingly. "But I'll probably feel rotten."

"If you don't when you get there, you will after you eat the Indian pudding."

"Oh, God," Eugene said. "Is she bringing that?" He, too, had sampled the dish.

"No, I fixed it," was A.J.'s response. "But beware of anything that has lime Jell-O as the main ingredient. That's her fallback."

"Knowing Estelle, she'll whip up a bowl of lime Jell-O and horse shit," Eugene observed.

They grew quiet, and A.J. realized Eugene had once again drifted off. He got up and threw a couple more chunks on the fire. Then he went inside to secure a bowl of Angel's soup. He was sitting on the edge of the porch waiting for his portion to cool when Wormy arrived in Mom's Taxi. He got out and cast a look in Eugene's direction, then came over and sat.

"Get some soup," A.J. suggested.

"I might have a bowl in a little while," Wormy replied. He unscrewed the cap from the pint bottle he had removed from his jacket pocket and took a lengthy sip. "Want a taste?" he asked when he was through.

"No, better not," A.J. declined. "If I go home with liquor on my breath, Maggie might beat me with a stout cane."

"And the downside would be?" Wormy asked with a twinkle in his bloodshot eye. He had obviously been spending too much time in the Purdue presence.

"You're getting quick," A.J. noted. "I may have to tell Maggie you're having discipline fantasies about her." Wormy looked alarmed.

"Lord, Lord," he said with concern. "Don't do that. I really like your wife. I don't want her to be mad at me." He looked like he was about to cry.

"You just don't want to get uninvited to supper," A.J. said.

"I don't guess we're coming anyway," Wormy said sadly. "Eugene doesn't think he'll feel up to it." He sighed. "I could almost taste that turkey, too." He looked off into the distance as if he could see it out there: tender, roasted poultry, forever just out of his grasp.

"I got him to agree to come," A.J. informed him. "If you don't let him back out, you'll still get your drumstick."

"I'll try," Wormy said doubtfully.

"Don't try. Do." A.J. pointed out in the yard to the sleeping figure by the bonfire. "He doesn't have long. This could be the last time he gets out. If he won't come, pick him up and put him in the van." Wormy looked at Eugene and nodded.

"All right. I'll get him there somehow." He took another sip. "You're right, though. He's sliding. And it's taking more of everything to keep him out of pain." He lit a smoke. "More booze. More pills. More morphine."

"What do you think about all that?'" A.J. asked.

"I think it's his business," Wormy said without hesitation. "I say let him have at it. I've seen a lot of people die, and there is no good way to go about it." The wisdom of the ages as spoken by an

271

alcoholic helicopter pilot. A.J. decided to broach a subject that had been lingering since Eugene had taken his latest downward turn.

"I know you like Eugene, but it's starting to get a little rough now." He considered how best to continue. He wanted to convey that if it was time to hat up, no one would think less of Wormy for going. "If you, uh . . ."

"Don't," Wormy said. "I finish what I start. It's kind of like flying the helicopter out of the road after the crazy guy shot me down. Anyway, Eugene is my friend just like he's yours."

"Okay, then," A.J. said. "I won't mention it again."

"Anyway, I've got no place else to be and nothing else to do," Wormy said. "After he goes, I'll be moving on. I don't know what I'll be doing, but it won't be flying."

A.J. thought about this for a moment. An obvious solution occurred to him.

"Don't tell Eugene I told you," he said, "but he's leaving the beer joint to me when he dies." Wormy nodded, as if to say it made good sense to him. "I don't want it," A.J. continued, "so I'm going to give it to you. You seem to have a knack for the work." Wormy held up his hands, warding off the compliment and the largesse. Both were much too grand in his scheme of things.

"I'd just screw it up," he objected. "And what about Bird Egg?"

"You have to keep an eye on Bird Egg until he goes to the big card game in the sky," A.J. said, resolving another problem. He was on a roll. "After that, it's all yours. How can you screw it up? You buy alcohol, sell it for more than you bought it for, pay off Red Arnold every now and then, and play poker the rest of the time. It's not brain surgery." Wormy looked doubtful. He seemed resistant

272

to making the executive move. Then his eyes lit up.

"We can be partners," he proposed. "You be the boss, and I'll run the business. We can split the money." This wasn't quite what A.J. had in mind, but it looked like it was the best he was going to be able to manage. He supposed he could reserve his half for charitable works, like sending the children to college. One thing was for certain; he would have to present to Maggie her new status as the bootlegger's wife in the best possible light.

"Okay," he said to Wormy as he held out his hand. Giving him half a beer joint was better than giving him no beer joint at all, at least for the time being. They shook. "We'll try it for a while. Once you get your confidence up, you can buy me out." Wormy nodded.

A.J. felt a little better. In one fell swoop, he had dispensed with the problems of what to do with Wormy, Bird Egg, and the beer joint. He looked at his watch. The day was long into afternoon, and he needed to be going. He stood and clapped Wormy on the shoulder. They walked out to the bonfire. Eugene stirred, and it seemed he might awaken. Then he settled into a deeper doze.

"I think he's out for a while," Wormy said.

"If he's still asleep Thursday, he'll be easy to load," A.J. observed. Wormy nodded. Apparently he hadn't thought of it. A.J. exited the clearing. He could see Wormy standing by the bonfire looking to be deep in thought, perhaps on the subject of the load out if Eugene did not awaken. A.J. knew he would ponder the problem until he had worried a solution.

That night, he sat with Maggie at the kitchen table and talked about the Finn Hall. The house was filled with the aromas of holiday baking, and the three pies currently in the oven—one pumpkin and two cherry—were adding to the already mouthwatering composite of smells. Maggie and Eudora had baked themselves haggard, and their offerings were stacked casually throughout the kitchen. Eudora's new husband, Carlisle, had not contributed to the ovenfest. But he had grown weary, nonetheless, while reclining on the sofa watching bad movies and eating cheese puffs. So he and Eudora had retired early, ostensibly to sleep.

"Sleeping, my foot," said A.J., as they heard a crash from upstairs. John Robert and the children were gone to the drive-in, so unless there was a large badger wandering the second floor, he knew what was up.

"Hush," Maggie said. "They're newlyweds." They heard a yell.

"Damn," A.J. said.

"Don't talk about it. That's my sister up there." They heard one more yell, a loud one, and then it grew quiet.

"I don't know about you, but I could use a cigarette," A.J. said.

"Quit it," she said.

"I'm going to have to get with Carlisle tomorrow and get a few pointers," he continued.

"I hate to break it to you," Maggie said, "but Carlisle was the one making all the noise."

"All right," A.J. said. "You go, Eudora." This was getting better all the time.

"But feel free to get with Carlisle on those pointers," Maggie added. She got up and removed the pumpkin pie from the oven. The scent of nutmeg wafted across the room. "A few more minutes on the cherry pies and we'll be done," she said as she regained her seat. A.J. started back in on the subject of the Finn Hall.

"I just don't know about Truth," he said. "She seems human now, but what if she reverts?"

"Then you quit," Maggie replied. She looked at him and continued. "But I have to tell you that no one besides you seems to have much of a problem with her."

"So you're saying it's me?" he asked incredulously.

"Some of it is you," she confirmed. "If you keep your ego reeled in, you two can get along. I think you really want the job."

"I do," he said.

"So do it," she said. "Truth is very mellow these days. She's in love."

"With Diane?"

"With Diane."

"I can't believe you invited Truth over for Thanksgiving," he said.

"I was simply being polite," she said absently, checking her pies. "I don't see what the problem is."

"The problem is Diane and Eugene and Diane's girlfriend all sitting at the same table. Eugene will slit his own throat."

"You fret too much," she replied, pulling the cherry pies out of the oven. Their aroma was heart-warming.

"If they kill each other, I'm not burying them," A.J. stated emphatically. It had been bad enough with Plug.

"Let's go to bed," was Maggie's reply as she turned off the light. She patted his head when she walked by, obviously not gravely concerned over the upcoming Thanksgiving Day Massacre. He stood and left the darkened kitchen, heading for a nod.

The big day finally arrived, and A.J. was up before dawn but not before John Robert. When he arrived downstairs, his father was outside stoking his smoker with seasoned hickory. He had decided at the last minute to add a couple of smoked pork loins to the menu, just to be on the safe side. It was a chilly morning, and A.J. could see John Robert's breath rise in steamy puffs as he closed the firebox door and began to walk toward the house. He noticed a small limp on the older man, a little hitch in the get-along he had never seen before. John Robert stepped onto the porch and entered the kitchen.

"Just about ready to smoke these loins," John Robert said as he removed the meat from the refrigerator.

"I saw you limping," A.J. said. "Did you step on a nail?"

"No, I'm just a little stiff on the cold mornings these days." John Robert carried his roasts in a pan. "I'll be back," he said as he backed out the door.

A.J. watched his father gimp across the yard. Because of Eugene, issues of mortality were on his mind, and the sight of John Robert shuffling to the smoker saddened him, but he shook off the moment. He had a turkey to roast and a house full of people circling, ready to land. The larger meanings of life and the absolute futility of it all would have to wait until he had more time.

Thanksgiving Day at the Folly was not a fixed event. Rather, it was a continuum through which the various participants flowed, each bringing according to means and taking according to need. The first to arrive were Eudora and Carlisle, who had come two days earlier and intended to remain for the week. The next to arrive were the Alexanders—Carson McCullers; her husband, Karl; and their two boys, John Steinbeck and William Faulkner. He liked Maggie's younger sister and her husband, and the boys were good lads, although John was underrated by his peers, and it was often difficult to place William in time. They arrived around nine o'clock, bearing the makings of the Thanksgiving breakfast—country ham to fry, sausage balls to bake, and enough eggs to stock a henhouse. The biscuits would be conjured by John Robert. Hugs and greetings were exchanged, and the boys ran off in search of their cousins.

"Stay out of the guest room," A.J. hollered at their retreating backs.

"What's going on up there?" Karl asked. He was a quiet, slow-talking man.

"Eudora and Carlisle are taking a nap," A.J. replied as he sliced the salty, cured ham.

"Taking a nap at nine in the morning?" Carson queried.

"Never mind," advised Maggie, cracking eggs into a large green bowl.

Next in was the Smith family: Maggie's sister, Agatha Christie, and her husband, John, as well as their children, George Orwell, Ray Bradbury, and Madeline L'Engel.

"Uncle A.J.!" Ray yelled as he grabbed a leg and held tight. He was a sweet child but a loud one. "Are we having turkey?"

"No, baby, there was a problem with the turkey," A.J. said as he tousled the boy's hair. "Rogues from Texas broke in last night and got it." Ray looked concerned. "Don't worry, though," A.J. continued. "We've got plenty of hot dogs." The boy looked askance for a moment. Then he grinned and ran out of the room. He knew well the ways of his uncle.

Carlisle wandered in looking pale and drawn. He appeared to

be having trouble concentrating. A.J. poured him a glass of orange juice and handed him a jelly biscuit. There was no use in letting him get poorly.

Mary Shelley Hensley and her husband, Gary, arrived around noon, accompanied by the matriarch and patriarch of the Callahan clan, Emmett and Jane Austen. The Hensleys didn't have any children and intended to keep it that way. A.J. considered childlessness an abnormal condition, but to each his own. Gary and Mary were nice people despite their decision to not breed, and they were quite well-to-do, a condition easier to achieve in the absence of progeny.

The last of Maggie's sisters to arrive was Jacqueline Susann Stewart. A.J. called her The Apostate, because she had broken doctrine by not naming her children after authors. She and her husband Geoffery had named their large brood Glen, Peter, Carol, Russell, and Zachary, or Zack for short. The name for the imminent sixth child had not yet been determined. Interspersed among the entrances of Maggie's sisters and their families were the arrivals of the other guests. Estelle came over for breakfast wearing her pink flannel robe and furry slippers. She bore a huge lime Jell-O mold infused with chunks of carrots, celery, cheddar cheese, and bell pepper. She had outdone herself, and as A.J. accepted the offering, he was forced to concede the Indian pudding hadn't been that bad, after all.

"Estelle, you shouldn't have," he said, meaning every word.

"Better get that in the icebox," noted Estelle as she loaded scrambled eggs onto her plate. "We don't want it to get too warm."

"No, that's for sure," he agreed as he slid it way in the back of the refrigerator, out of sight but not quite out of mind.

More guests arrived throughout the morning and early afternoon. Doc Miller and Minnie whisked in with a bottle of fifty-year-old brandy and a vegetable tray. Minnie had made certain the assortment contained white radishes, which were one of A.J.'s favorites when served with a little salt. Hoghead landed with twenty pounds of Swedish meatballs, each a small study in Hong Kong tastiness. He was accompanied by Dixie Lanier, drive-in patron and recent divorcée after her husband, Pitt, accidentally shot her in the head through the side of the trailer while squirrel hunting. Pitt had been truly sorry over the incident and had begged Dixie for forgiveness, but the twenty-two slug buried just behind her right ear was not a transgression she could pardon. So she cut Pitt loose and sent him back to his mama's house to hunt squirrels. Dixie and Hoghead seemed to make a nice couple, and since the old cook was not a hunter, maybe the relationship would blossom.

The Folly filled as other visitors wandered in. Slim Neal came bearing deviled eggs, and in recognition of the general gaiety of the day, he had left his sidearm in the cruiser. Jackie came with Bernice Martin on one arm and a sweet potato casserole on the other, and A.J. was touched to learn he had turned down double-time-and-a-half to come to the revelries. Charnell Jackson was there with his German chocolate cake, and Ellis Simpson arrived with Raynell, the children, and four bowls of potato salad. Brickhead and Cyndi Crowe arrived with their brood and with Cyndi's famed baked beans. Billy from the Chevron came. He was no one's idea of a cook, so he brought several cases of cold drinks, belly-washers for the children, as he put it.

Bird Egg showed up, and when A.J. saw the old retainer, he

had to take double. Bird was scrubbed clean. He was shaven and barbered, and he appeared to be sober, although he smelled quite strongly of mouthwash. He was wearing a suit, mostly, and the fact that it looked like it had been excavated at the boneyard did not detract in the least from the gesture.

"Bird, you look sharp," A.J. complimented. The sleeves of his suit coat stopped about two inches above his bony wrists. "You must be here looking for women." Bird Egg produced a hangdog grin and stared at the floor, shuffling a bit, looking shy. A.J. made a mental note to steer him clear of the opposite sex, lest misunderstandings occur. "Who's watching the beer joint?" A.J. asked.

"Eugene and Wormy stopped by awhile ago. Told me to shut 'er down and take the day off."

"A day off with pay?" A.J. quizzed. "That's like having benefits. Next you'll be going on the insurance plan and signing up for the 401K." Bird Egg guffawed before wandering off in the general direction of the Swedish meatballs.

Diane arrived with her boys, Cody and Ransom. Truth was conspicuous by her absence, but A.J. suspected that his luck would not hold. The boys were subdued, which was understandable given the circumstances surrounding their father, but they seemed to forget their troubles as they joined in play with the other youngsters. A.J. had talked to his older two about being particularly nice to the Purdue boys, and why, and the girls had taken a solemn vow to see to it that they had a good day. As the children all went off to romp, A.J. sidled up next to Diane.

"I sort of figured you'd be coming with Truth," he ventured, hoping something had come up. Sometimes things just worked out, and maybe this was one of those times.

"She'll be along in a while," Diane said. She seemed to be in good spirits. A.J. sighed before broaching a delicate subject.

"Your ex-husband may be coming," he began, wishing he had thought to soften her up with some Swedish meatballs before venturing into the minefield.

"It was nice of you to invite him," she said cheerfully, missing the entire point.

"Yeah, I'm a nice guy," he said, regrouping. "The thing is, he doesn't know about you and Truth. He's still sort of . . . pining away for you, and I'm thinking that he might get . . . upset." He saw her eyes flash like black lightning.

"A.J. Longstreet, are you telling me that Truth is not welcome here?" Her dander was up.

"No, I'm not saying that," he responded. "What I'm asking is that if he does come, you and Truth cool it. There's no use killing him on the spot."

"Let me tell you something," she began, "I feel really bad for Eugene, but my life with him was over long before he got sick. I spent fifteen years trying to be what he wanted me to be, fifteen years of feeling like shit because I wasn't quite the little Barbie doll he wanted, and I'm through doing that for anyone." She was breathing hard, and her eyes shone when she continued. "I know you're trying to help him, just like you always try to help everyone. But I am who I am, and I feel like I feel, and if you and Eugene don't like it, you can both kiss my ass."

A.J. considered her words, and he had to concede their validity. The simple fact was that she was right. He had been out of line.

Her life was her business, and he felt bad for upsetting her, even though his intentions had been pure.

"Truce," he said, holding up his hands. "I'm wrong. You're right. I apologize. Don't hit. I swear I won't be this stupid again for weeks."

"You'd better make it months, after this one," she replied. Her tone was still stern, but her eyes signaled a reluctance to kill. Just to be on the safe side, he decided to leave her vicinity and stepped out for a breath of fresh air.

John Robert saw him and hailed him to the smoker. A.J. waved at Marie Prater as she came down the walk. Since she possessed the only good back in her family, she was carrying a large casserole dish while her disabled husband and boys shuffled dutifully behind.

"How goes life at the sawmill, Marie?" he asked.

"Life as we knew it has changed for the worse," she replied. Her voice sounded as tired as her eyes looked. A.J. felt for her. His professional demise had been relatively painless, but she was obviously suffering. He looked over at John Robert.

"How are those loins coming?" he asked his father. "We're running out of Hoghead's meatballs."

"The meat is ready," John Robert said as he speared the roasts into his pan. "Let's go feed the company." As they walked back to the Folly, A.J. saw Truth's Mercedes wheel in at the end of the drive-way. She exited the car and waved him over. He walked up, and she turned and smiled.

"A.J., I have two cases of wine and some turkey pie," she said. "Can you help carry some of it?" She was as nice as a walk on the beach at twilight, which he had to admit was preferable to her pre-

282

vious incarnation as one of the Horsewomen of the Apocalypse.

"I'll get the wine," he volunteered. He was about to hoist the Chablis when he noted the arrival of Mom's Taxi.

"I'll be right along," A.J. said to Truth, who had already started toward the house. The van door opened and out stepped Wormy. He walked over to A.J. Eugene appeared to be asleep in the van.

"I was just kidding when I told you to load him up and bring him anyway," A.J. said.

"No, he was in pretty good shape when we left," Wormy said. "He sort of faded out at the beer joint." He shrugged.

"How much help did he have fading?" A.J. asked.

"About a quart," Wormy admitted. He looked as if he was in pain. A.J. sighed. He had apparently wanted this day for Eugene more than Eugene had desired it for himself. He supposed he was a fool for even making the attempt.

"Take him home, Wormy," he said. "I don't want his boys to see him this way." Wormy nodded, as if he agreed. "I'll bring you both a plate tomorrow," A.J. continued. Wormy hung his head in disgrace. His shame was a burden upon him. A.J. patted him lightly on the shoulder. "It's not your fault. He's a hard man to control. You couldn't stop him if he wanted it. Now, go on." Wormy plodded slowly to the van, started it, and left. Eugene never moved. His last Thanksgiving was a bust despite A.J.'s best efforts, a total failure rivaling the first and final voyage of the *Titanic*. It was a pity.

Later, A.J. sat in the parlor in his favorite chair and viewed the fruits of his labor. Some of his pleasure was diminished because of Eugene's lapse, but it was still a good day. Family and friends were all talking, eating, and generally making merry. It was Thanksgiving at the Folly, and he had gone the extra lap to make it memorable, an observance that would be held as a standard for years to come. He broke from his reverie. Standing before him was Diane. He had not talked to her since rousing her ire earlier in the day.

"Where's Eugene?" she asked. "Truth told me he was here awhile ago."

"He was feeling pretty bad," A.J. lied. "He made his regrets and went home to bed." She considered this, and he was unsure whether she believed him or not.

"I was going to do it, you know," she said. Her voice was sad, and she was looking him directly in the eye. "I was going to be nice." He could sense it was important to her that he understand this.

"I know you were," he answered. "I knew it all the time." She sat next to him, and that was where Truth discovered them some time later, two old friends sharing the sweet sadness of daring to breathe.

"Are you okay?" she asked Diane with concern in her voice. Diane nodded.

"She's a little low," A.J. offered. "I think it was the lime Jell-O." Truth bent down and pecked her cheek.

"Maybe we should go," Truth said kindly.

"Yeah, I guess we should," Diane answered. She stood. "I'll go get the boys." She looked at A.J. "Thank you," she said, then left. Truth sat down in the chair Diane had vacated.

"What about the Finn Hall?" she asked, her tone friendly. He thought about it one last time.

"I'll do the job," he said, offering his hand.

"Fair enough," she said, and they shook. "How much?" she asked.

"Not a penny more than it's worth," he replied. The shrewd

real estate genius and the idle country boy took each other's measure. Then she nodded.

"That sounds reasonable," she said. Diane caught her eye from across the room, and she stood to go.

"I'll call you Monday," A.J. said. "My wife is tired of me being unemployed." Truth nodded and left to rejoin Diane while A.J. sipped a taste of Doc's good brandy and considered his new career. It could be worse, he supposed. He swirled the amber liquid in his glass and took another nip. Yes, it could be worse. He noted that the afternoon was waning, and many of the guests were making ready to leave. He stood, stretched, and threw a few sticks of wood on the fire. He was standing with his back to the flames when Hoghead came up to make his farewells.

"I've got to go, A.J.," he said. "But it was great. Did you get any of my meatballs?"

"They were superb, Hog," A.J. replied. Hoghead beamed.

"How about that turkey pie?" the old cook asked, pumping for just one more compliment.

"I've never had better."

A.J. maintained his post and monitored the exodus. There were handshakes given, compliments offered, and pleasantries exchanged as the guests left, each as full as a tick on a hound's ear. Finally, everyone had departed except for Eudora and Carlisle. A.J., Maggie, and John Robert sat in the darkened parlor and watched the fire prance. They sipped the coffee that John Robert had brewed.

"Good Thanksgiving," John Robert noted.

"Yes, it was," agreed Maggie. A.J. nodded.

"Did you try Estelle's lime Jell-O?" the elder Longstreet asked of no one in particular.

"Uh-uh," said Maggie.

"I wanted to be sure there was enough for our guests," A.J. said. John Robert chuckled.

"Well, somebody ate most of it," he said.

"I need to check with Charnell," A.J. observed. "We may be liable." They sat quietly for a while. Then he yawned.

"I think you may need a nap," Maggie offered. She looked at him. Then she looked at the crack in the ceiling.

"I think a nap may be just the thing," he agreed. It was the perfect ending to a mostly flawless day, a Thanksgiving Day to remember.

Take care of my brother, and don't ever throw away that green sweater.
—Excerpt of posthumous letter from
Eugene Purdue to Maggie Longstreet

A.J. STOOD IN THE CLEARING ON EUGENE'S MOUNTAIN
and warmed his hands at the fire. It was a wintry day, New Year's
Day, and arctic air scoured the mountain. His breath steamed in
the lengthening shadows as he inched closer to the blaze. Rufus sat
next to him but offered no belligerence, an oddity over and above
the general dementia of the day. This passivity was just as well,
since A.J. was unarmed. The venerable Louisville Slugger was ac-
cidental fuel for the flames before him, a bad way for a fine piece of
ash to go. The small inferno sizzled and popped, mingling orange,
yellow, and blue. Somber smoke drifted skyward.

He shuddered and took a small sip from the bottle he had
brought for Eugene. The spirit burned all the way down, amber
solace for a bleak day. He sighed and squatted, forearms resting on
thighs in the manner of old men whittling. He held up the bottle in
salute before sitting back cross-legged on the hard-packed dirt.

"Well," he said quietly to Eugene, who did not answer, being otherwise occupied burning up in the cabin. It had been a long and tiring outing, and A.J. was beset with weariness. But the vigil was over, and Eugene's time of travail was past. He had cruised the tributary, had caught the big cable car. He was now up close and personal with whatever awaited the departed.

A.J.'s mind traipsed back to the day after Thanksgiving, when he had brought a movable feast to the woebegone boys in the clearing—turkey and ham, dressing, boiled carrots, green beans, a jar of gravy, two pies, the remainder of the lime Jell-O for color, some Swedish meatballs, and one of Eugene's absolute favorites, deviled eggs. Eugene was sitting in the clearing in the La-Z-Boy warming his toes at the fire when A.J. arrived. He looked rough.

"If that's food, I don't want any," he said, gesturing at the plate. A.J. removed the foil wrapper and carefully selected a deviled egg. He popped it whole into his mouth and savored the morsel before speaking.

"I brought the dinner for Wormy," he said as he placed the plate of eggs in Eugene's lap. "I brought these for you." Eugene hesitated a moment before choosing one of his own.

"This doesn't mean I'll sleep with you," he mumbled around a mouthful of egg.

"Well, then, give it back," A.J. said, reaching for the plate. Eugene shifted sideways to protect his treasure. His left hand came out from under the blanket with a .45 caliber automatic pistol, which he rested lightly on his lap next to the eggs.

"Expecting an attack?" A.J. asked.

"I just want to be ready in case the South rises again."

They fell silent, and after a few minutes, Eugene fell asleep. A.J.

slipped the tray of eggs from his grasp and relocated all of the food to the kitchen. He wondered why Wormy and Rufus hadn't been standing their watch when he arrived. He walked back to the middle of the clearing and chunked up the fire, then sat next to his sleeping brother. Suddenly, Eugene startled awake. His eyes were wild, and he looked pale and afraid.

"Easy," A.J. said. The dramatic awakening had caught him by surprise.

"Shit," Eugene said, voice quavering. He fumbled for the ever present bottle of bourbon and took an extended drink, then another. After a moment, he calmed.

"Bad dream?" A.J. asked, giving voice to the obvious.

"Real bad dream," Eugene replied. He pulled back the slide on the .45 and checked his load. Satisfied, he placed the pistol back in his lap. "I've been dreaming about being dead. I don't like it."

A.J. nodded, granting the point of view. He wondered about the pistol, though. It was as if Eugene were awaiting an adversary, a physical entity he could fight. A.J. had no doubt that if the Grim Reaper walked into the clearing right now, Eugene would blow off both of his kneecaps before sending Rufus in to finish the job. Under those conditions the odds would be in Eugene's favor, but it wasn't going to work like that. Death would steal in like a mist on a moonless night. There was no defense. The fix was in, and no one got out alive.

"Do you think there's a heaven?" Eugene asked. A.J. was unsure how to respond. He didn't anticipate streets paved with gold, but he did believe in a reality after this one where the life force gathered. His grandmother was there now, and his mother. So he knew what he believed, but he didn't know if it was what Eugene needed to hear.

"I think we go somewhere else when we finish here," he said. "I'm not so sure it's like the Bible says."

"So you don't think the Bible is right?" Eugene asked. "You don't think God judges us, punishes and rewards us?" He seemed extremely interested, no doubt due to the fact that he would very soon be finding out for himself the true nature of the greater mysteries. A.J. groaned inwardly. Why in hell was Eugene consulting him on these matters? He ought to be talking to the Reverend Doctor Jensen McCarthy or someone else of like mind. Even Hoghead would be a better source of information on the mystic realms, once the menu was weeded out.

"I don't know, Eugene," he said, floundering. "I think that if there is a God like the one in the Bible, then there are too many things I can't explain. How can He let a tornado wipe out a church full on Easter morning? How can He let a shit head like Hitler annihilate His chosen people? How can He allow a drunk driver to kill a baby?" These were the questions of the ages, and A.J. couldn't answer them.

"You're a lot of damn help," Eugene noted.

"You're asking the wrong guy," he said lamely. "Do you want me to get a preacher up here?" It was a sincere offer. He was willing to go and bring one back by force, if necessary. Surely he could find a man of the cloth. If nothing else, he could hide at a church and grab the first one that came up.

"No." Eugene looked at him. "I think it's kind of like you think it is. There's something after here, but I don't know what. As for the Bible, there are a lot of things in there I can't buy either. I guess everyone takes it as true because it's so old. Hell, I bet if you buried a *Penthouse* for two thousand years, someone would think *it* was sacred when you dug it up."

"Wormy thinks it's sacred now," A.J. pointed out. He had no illusions that they had solved the Big Imponderable, but Eugene seemed to feel better as a result of the conversation. "Speaking of Wormy, where is he?" A.J. asked. "And Rufus?"

"They went hunting." Eugene settled back in the La-Z-Boy.

"It'll be squirrel stew for you, this evening," A.J. observed. Eugene hated squirrel about as much as he loved deviled eggs.

"Wormy never shoots anything," Eugene said. "He just likes to walk around in the woods." Shots rang from the west. A.J. looked at Eugene.

"Squirrel stew," he said.

"I'll eat the eggs," came the response.

A.J.'s mind snapped to the present, to the cold New Year's Day in front of the remains of a burning cabin. The blare of a siren and the roar of an engine under strain indicated visitors. He arose from his station on the ground, peeved at the intrusion. The last thing he wanted was a dose of Honey Gowens and the fire brigade, but the encounter was inevitable. The fire truck thundered into the clearing piloted by Honey and manned by Skipper Black, Luther Barnette, Ellis Simpson, and Hoghead, who had shut down the Jesus Is the Reason for the $3.99 Mexican Feast Drive-In when the call to action came. The wagon rolled to a halt and Honey and Hoghead leaped from the cab. Slower to respond were Skipper, Luther, and Ellis, who were nearly frozen and mostly beaten to pieces. Hanging on the back was good duty in the summer months, but the spots were less coveted during the cold season.

"We saw the smoke from town!" Honey yelled breathlessly as he yanked at a hose reel. Hoghead was shrugging into his fireman's coat, and the boys on the back were grimacing as they slowly disembarked.

"Hold up, Honey," A.J. said. "It's a total loss. Let it go." It didn't seem decent to wash Eugene's remains into the woods.

"I don't know," Honey replied, looking skeptical. He was not a man to go home dry when he had come to shoot water.

"Let it go, Honey," A.J. repeated. Honey looked at his grim demeanor. Then he looked at the cabin. Slow reality dawned on the careworn quencher of flame.

"Shit," he said quietly. "Was he in there?"

"He's still in there," A.J. said. "It was burning when I got here. I guess he was smoking in bed. I couldn't get him out." This version was not the gospel truth but was fairly close by some standards, and there was no sense in burdening Honey with details that would make him unhappy.

"Damn," Honey said quietly. There was not much else to say.

"I'm going to stay here until it burns out," A.J. said. "How about sending Red Arnold up here when you get back to town."

"What about Slim?" Honey asked.

"God, no," A.J. said. He pointed at the wreckage. "You can see the bus now. I don't want him trying to arrest Eugene's ashes." Honey nodded. The motor coach had slipped his mind.

"You want me to stay with you?" Hoghead asked

"No, but I appreciate the offer. I'll stay here with the dog until

Red comes." It was decent of Hoghead to volunteer, but A.J. needed solitude. The fire brigade reloaded and departed without incident, although the three junior members of the corps looked a mite mutinous as they began the return leg of their excursion. Alone again, A.J. squatted back down on the hard-packed red clay. His mind took flight and came to ground eight days earlier in the same clearing. He had journeyed up on Christmas Eve to wish the boys well. Eugene was pretty much dead by that point and knew it, but life is a hard habit to break, so he lingered on.

Since Thanksgiving, Eugene had taken several giant steps in the direction of the Fun Home. First, there were hard bouts of nausea. Then there was incontinence. Finally, the pain quit sand-dancing and heaved its grisly head in earnest. With each new development, A.J. rushed to Doc Miller for the cure. Doc repeatedly reached into his bag of tricks, but he had to reach deeper each time. But Eugene's torment was stubborn and would not abate.

"I need more morphine," A.J. told Doc a week prior to Christmas Eve. The old doctor raised his eyebrows.

"What are you doing, washing him in it?" he asked testily.

"No, I'm not washing him in it," A.J. replied in kind. "Tell you what. Come on up and listen to him moan awhile. Come listen to him scream when he sleeps too long and the pain wakes him up. Then tell me we're giving him too much." It was a bad day for Doc to be calling the tough ones from the cheap seats.

"He can't survive a higher dosage," Doc said stubbornly.

"And the downside is?" A.J. asked. He found the conversation frustrating. "He's in bad pain. Nobody is trying to kill him. Just give me the damn stuff." He stopped and took a deep breath. Doc was not the enemy. "Please," he said. Doc sighed and left the room. When he returned, he carried a small white paper sack.

"There's enough in here to put an army mule permanently out to pasture," he said. "Don't give him a drop more than he needs to stay out of trouble." He massaged the bridge of his nose. "Christ," he said, almost to himself. "If there's ever an autopsy, we'll both be in jail."

"There won't be," A.J. said quietly.

So it was with Doc's consent but not necessarily his blessing that Eugene's pain medication was increased. Thankfully, the result was not immediate death followed by autopsy and imprisonment. Rather, Eugene just slept most of the time, a deep, restful slumber. And this was what A.J. was expecting when he arrived on Christmas Eve morning. He pulled up next to a tired-looking Wormy warming his hands in front of a much abbreviated fire in the middle of the clearing. Eugene had not been out of bed in two weeks and would not likely arise again, but Wormy was not one to alter custom. So the fire persisted, but the La-Z-Boy remained empty.

"Rough night?" A.J. asked, handing Wormy the cup of coffee he had brought.

"Rough as a night in the Waycross jail," Wormy responded quietly.

"Is he asleep?" A.J. asked.

"Yeah, he's asleep." Wormy sipped his coffee.

"Why don't you take a break?" A.J. suggested. "I'll stay with him." He had big doings coming up later in the day, but Wormy needed relieving. The Christmas Eve festivities would have to wait until after he stood his watch. Maggie was heading up Christmas this year anyway. Eugene's waning days had left A.J. with very little

Yuletide spirit.

"Was the drive-in open when you came through?" Wormy inquired.

"That's where I got the coffee."

"If you don't mind, I think I'd like to go get a little breakfast."

"Go eat," A.J. said. "Sit and tell a few lies with Hoghead." Wormy nodded.

Gratitude was etched on his features as he headed for town. A.J. entered the cabin to check on Eugene and was surprised to find him wide awake and staring at the ceiling. He looked over and produced a bare hint of a smile. The effect was grotesque on his emaciated features.

"Is it Christmas yet?" he asked. His hand gestured at the small tree Wormy had installed in the corner. It was actually a Christmas bush, but it was the thought that counted. It was decked with an odd combination of handmade ornaments—beer cans on strings— supplied by Wormy complimented by a selection of more traditional baubles contributed by Angel. She still came daily and was due later that evening.

"It's Christmas Eve," A.J. said. The room reeked of illness.

"Better give me my present while you can," Eugene whispered. It was an unadorned pronouncement of fact. A.J. stepped to the tree and returned with the bundle he had placed under it. He handed the gift to his brother. Eugene's hands shook so badly he had to help him unwrap the offering.

"It is a fine gift," Eugene croaked. There were tears in his eyes as he hefted the beautifully restored Navy Colt with both hands and sighted down the barrel. "I wish I could shoot it," he said sadly.

295

"Have at it," A.J. said. "I bet you ten dollars you can't hit that wall."

"I ought to take your money, but I don't want to kill Wormy if he walks by."

"Wormy's gone to town." A.J. reached over and steadied the big pistol. Then he cocked it. "I think you need to shoot the wall." Eugene grinned and squeezed the trigger. The noise was deafening. The pistol kicked so much in his unsteady grasp that the hole was more in the ceiling than in the wall, but it was an impressive cavity nonetheless.

"Damn, that felt good," he said as he dropped the gun onto the bedspread. He had shot his last. "You owe me ten dollars," he said. A.J. paid up. Eugene clutched the bill like a miser, and A.J. realized how significant his gesture had been, how satisfying it was for the dying man to take one last tenner off his brother. It was a noble gift. But the gods were not in a charitable mood that day, although it wouldn't have cost them a dime to show a bit of mercy, so the fine moment was cut short. Eugene made a gagging noise. Then he began retching violently. He was doubled in hurt, and the severe vomiting spell caused his bowels to loosen. When it was over, he began to cry. The tears of wretchedness were pitiful to behold.

A.J. began the task of cleaning Eugene hindered by tears of his own. His task was made difficult by the obvious suffering any movement caused Eugene, and by his own notoriously weak stomach. But it had to be done, so he swallowed the bile at the back of his throat and kept to his work. Finally, mercifully, the job was over. Eugene was calmed, clean, and heavily medicated. A.J. was a mess, but life is hard and soap is cheap.

Eugene looked at A.J. His eyes were beginning to unfocus as the chemical cavalry found its way to his brain.

"I never wanted you to have to do that," he said. His voice was clear. "I'm tired of this shit. I'm ready for it to be over." He held his brother's gaze until he drifted off. A.J. looked at what was left of him. It was time to fish or cut bait.

He reached suddenly and retrieved the Navy Colt. He hefted it, felt its cold, blue weight. Then he cocked it and pointed it at Eugene's head. He gritted his teeth, took a deep breath, and willed his finger to squeeze. The trigger moved ever so slightly, then a bit more.

His arm jerked up at the last instant when the blast erupted, and when the smoke cleared there were two holes in the cabin. He was disgusted with himself for being a coward.

"I'm sorry," he said to his comatose brother. He dropped the Colt to the floor and sought saner latitudes. He was standing at the fire when Wormy returned. Their eyes met, Wormy nodded, and A.J. left without a word. He was quiet the remainder of the day, not because he had almost shot his brother, but rather because he had not managed the task.

But that was Christmas Eve, and it was now New Year's Day. A.J. returned to the present and found himself in front of the smoldering remains of the cabin. The afternoon shadows had become long, and he stood close to the glowing ashes for warmth. Nothing in them was recognizable but the unmistakable shape of a gutted school bus. No sign of Eugene could be seen. The fire had done its job well in that respect. A car door slammed. He turned toward the sound and saw that Red Arnold had arrived.

Red was getting long in the tooth, but he still cut an imposing figure as he gaited slowly across the clearing. He arrived at the fire, and he and A.J. stood and warmed their hands in silence. Finally, Red spoke.

"Honey said Eugene was in there," he said. He had turned around and was heating the Arnold hindquarters. Red's homespun mannerisms aside, A.J. knew he was being questioned, and that the answers needed to satisfy.

"Yes."

"Said you ran him off," Red continued. "Told him to let it burn." He lit a smoke and left it on his lips. He stuck his hands in his pockets and gazed at the sky.

"He told you the truth."

"Talked to Wormy yesterday," Red noted. A.J. was already aware of the chat. Red had come by the beer joint for his Christmas present. "Told me that Eugene was bad. Real bad." He turned back around and began to warm his hands again.

"Real bad," A.J. agreed. Red flipped his cigarette into the ashes and peered long at him. Finally, the old lawman nodded slightly.

"Damn shame," he said. "Eugene was a good boy." A.J. had to agree. He had had his ways, but plenty of worse specimens had strolled down the long corridors of time. Red began to walk to his car. Halfway there, he stopped and turned. There was a rueful smile on his lips.

"If Slim sees that bus, he'll be wanting to shoot somebody," Red observed.

"He does tend to be high-strung," A.J. allowed. "If you can keep him out of here a day or two, I'll take care of it." He intended to dig a pit with the dozer and fill it with the remains of the cabin and its occupant. Then he proposed to raise a large mound. It would be a funeral ceremony in the old style—about two thousand years old, in fact—but he figured it would be just odd enough to appeal to Eugene. Red nodded and climbed into his car. He U-turned and headed for the lights of the big city, leaving A.J. alone in the twilight with the ashes of his brother.

A.J. had arrived at the clearing that New Year's morning struggling with a sense of premonition, and he had been somewhat out of kilter since blowing the hole in Eugene's wall. As he pulled up, he saw Jackie sleeping in his truck, so he fully expected to encounter Angel when he entered the cabin.

"A.J., you look pale," she had said with concern. "You better sit down and have some of this soup." Death, taxes, and Angel's soup were the three constants of life.

"Maybe just a small bowl," he agreed, banking on its medicinal properties to clear his head.

Eugene awoke and was bathed and medicated by Angel with help from A.J. Then he went back to sleep. Wormy checked in but had to immediately leave. He was having labor difficulties down at the beer joint. Bird Egg was plastered and in the spirit of the season was attempting to give away all of the stock. He had plenty of takers.

"We really should let him go," Wormy said. Management was coming easier all the time to the former pilot.

"We don't pay him," A.J. pointed out. "How can we fire him?" Wormy shrugged in the time-honored tradition of middle management and left to go keep an eye on the grizzled retainer before he literally gave away the store. Angel and Jackie departed shortly thereafter, but not before securing A.J.'s promise to remain until

Wormy returned.

So he sat at Eugene's bedside and read the *1941 Yearbook of Agriculture*, which he had removed from under one of the legs of Eugene's kitchen table. At his feet sat Rufus, who had apparently temporarily forgotten that he hated A.J.

A.J. was rocking quietly while reading about the effects of deforestation when the trouble began. Eugene groaned and startled awake. He began to pant, and his eyes had a hunted look. A.J. twisted the top off of a vial of morphine and dosed his brother. He calmed as the medicine did its work.

"That was a bad one," Eugene slurred. His eyes were closed.

"I know," A.J. said with sympathy.

". . . getting worse," Eugene croaked as he drifted back off.

"I know," A.J. said quietly, lamely.

Doc had said the pain might become unbearable before the end, and just as Doc had predicted, it was taking Eugene a while to shut down, and his pain was becoming devilishly hard to control. A.J. picked his book back up but could no longer enjoy its contents. Beside him lay Eugene, suffering mightily through his final days. He moaned and gasped, twitched and panted. A.J. could smell urine, and knew Eugene had once again lost control of his bladder. The cruelty of the situation was absolute. Nobody deserved an exit like this.

He sighed and stepped out for a cigarette. He knew what he should do, what he should have already done with the Navy Colt. He was sick at heart. He had never actually agreed to kill Eugene, but the task had fallen to him, nonetheless. He had failed in his duty on the first take, but his responsibility was not relieved. Rather, it was increased, somehow. The pact had been made somewhere along the road, and now was the time to be his brother's keeper.

His cigarette pack was empty. As he rifled through the glove box of the truck for a fresh pack, his hand struck an object. It was the bottle of pills Doc had given him before Thanksgiving, the ones he had indicated would end Eugene's pain. A.J. shook them out. They were small and blue. He looked at them for a long while. Here was his answer. He knew it in his heart. Doc had never mentioned them again, had acted as if he had completely forgotten them. But the old man had known what was in store, and A.J. held the contingency plan in his hand. He dropped them back into the bottle. His cigarette stretched to three while he steeled his resolve. Then he reentered the cabin.

He put on some coffee to brew. While it was warming, he dumped all of the tablets onto the countertop. He ground them fine with the handle of Eugene's butcher knife and brushed the resultant powder into a coffee mug. The coffee boiled, and he poured the steaming liquid. Then he added two spoonfuls of sugar and set the potion aside to cool. He resumed his seat by the bed and waited for Eugene to awaken. Rufus had followed his every step.

Eugene drifted awake, and A.J. made short work of the necessary cleanup thanks to the diapers Eugene now wore. He slid him up to a semi-sitting position and gave him a cigarette. Eugene accepted it gratefully.

"How are you feeling?" A.J. asked.

"Feel great," Eugene responded slowly. "Let's go bowling." His face was pinched with effort. His right eyelid drooped, and A.J. wondered if he had suffered a stroke.

"What you need is a good cup of coffee," he said, moving to the counter. His affect was not even nearly right, but Eugene was too far gone in several senses of the word to notice. He sat back down with the cooled coffee and held the cup while Eugene took several sips.

"Your coffee really sucks today," Eugene noted. Then his eyes closed. The cigarette fell from his fingers and dropped to the floor. His chest rose and fell a few more times. Then his breath rattled to a stop.

A.J. was surprised it had been so quick. He had thought they might chat awhile, maybe speak at last of their brotherhood. But it was not to be. He sat for a long while. He had done it, but he held no feelings or thoughts on the matter. He was a blank page, an empty vessel. It had been too terrible and too easy to do. Finally, he arose and crossed to Eugene's desk and retrieved the unmailed letters. They were addressed and stamped, and he had every intention of mailing them. He placed them in the truck, then stepped behind the cabin and returned with the two five-gallon cans of gasoline Eugene always kept there for emergencies.

He reentered the cabin and began the business of finishing what he had started. First he cleaned Eugene, who had fouled himself when he left this world. He had to run out in the yard twice before the job was done, but he was determined Eugene was not going on to the much-touted better place in an embarrassed condition. Next, he slid Eugene's Grateful Dead jacket onto the pitiful, bony arms. In the pockets he placed a pack of Pall Malls, a Zippo, and pictures of Diane and the boys. He cradled a bottle of Jack Daniels under Eugene's arm and placed the grips of the Navy Colt in his lifeless left hand. Finally, he laid his hand on Eugene's brow.

"Sorry it took so long," he said. He lingered while he looked at Eugene's face, ravaged but now at peace. Then he doused the cabin with ten gallons of high test and sent Eugene out in style.

A.J. emerged from this reverie and found that it was dark in the clearing. The glowing embers before him were the only remnant of the earlier makeshift crematorium. Honey and the boys had come and gone, as had Red, and only he and Rufus remained. He sighed and made for the truck. It was cold, and it was time to go. He supposed he would drive home via the beer joint and break the news to Wormy.

He stopped when he reached the truck. Something was nagging at his mind. Then he knew. He turned and looked at Rufus, formerly the hound from hell and now just another unemployed dog. He held the truck door open.

"Are you coming with me?" he asked his old nemesis. The dog looked at him a moment, then trotted over and hopped in the truck. His business in the clearing was finished as well.

A.J. SAT ON THE PORCH OF THE FINN HALL AND
awaited the arrival of his employer, Truth Hannassey. From his
perch on the side of the mountain, he oversaw a valley of color. It was
early spring following a long winter season that had marked many
transitions, Eugene's departure chief among them. So he rocked
and considered the months just past, reflecting on the changes, the
endings, the beginnings.

Eugene was gone, of course, and the earth was heaped over
him in superb style. His barrow was the finest funerary mound
raised in those parts in five or six hundred years. A.J. thought it
had turned out well considering he had built only the one. Grass
was planted there now, and wildflowers had sprung up in recent
days. It was a pretty spot, and Angel spent a good deal of her time
there when she wasn't keeping house for Jackie or divorcing Johnny
Mack. The French are a tolerant people except when it comes to ignorant Americans, and Johnny Mack had finally gone too far when

305

he refused to make his peace with Eugene before the end. Angel had set him adrift right after her son's passing. Jackie still rode out to see him upon occasion, but most times Johnny Mack was an outcast. He was left with his Bible, his bourbon, and his bulldozer.

As for the estate, there actually was a will, as A.J. discovered when he was contacted by Charnell Jackson after Eugene's passing. In his role as executor, A.J. had many loose ends to tie.

"Eugene left you his mountain," Charnell said, his glasses down on the end of his nose. A.J. knew this was coming and had given ample thought to the inheritance.

"Deed it over to Angel," he said. "When she dies, it goes to Diane and the boys." Charnell was scribbling notes.

"Eugene left you the beer joint," Charnell continued.

"Wormy gets it." The pilot was doing well in the alcohol and poker business, and he and Rufus needed a place to live anyway.

"There's money in a box somewhere," Charnell plowed on. "You're supposed to know where. Says here for you to dig it up and give Angel, Diane, and Jackie each fifty thousand dollars." He looked pained. It was the lawyer in him, and A.J. knew it couldn't be helped.

"Check," he said. Charnell fumbled around and came up with a sheet of paper. It appeared to be a list of some kind.

"As Eugene's lawyer," he said, "I advise you that he wanted you to take care of the items on this list for him. There should be money enough in the box for it." Charnell looked at A.J. "As *your* attorney, I advise you to throw the damn thing away. Some of it is illegal." A.J. shrugged.

"Everything Eugene ever did was mostly against one law or other," he pointed out. "Why should he stop, now that he's dead?"

THE FRONT PORCH PROPHET

So A.J. executed the last will and testament of Eugene Purdue. When he dug up the infamous box, he found that it contained a gold pocket watch, a pistol, a pound or so of marijuana, the keys to the Lover, a photograph of Diane that featured all of her tan, and enough cold, hard cash to fund Eugene's final requests. He loaded all of the booty into the truck except the photo, which he decently buried in the side of the mound.

There were many remembrances to be dispersed, and he tried to honor the intent of the wishes as much as possible, although the man named Sonny who lived in Memphis did not receive the pipe bomb Eugene had specified.

Thus the book that was Eugene Purdue was closed, but the world took scant notice and continued to turn.

Slim Neal suffered a small heart attack after a spare tire fell out of the lawn-mower shed and attacked him. The excitable constable managed to subdue the assailant and get three slugs into it before collapsing from the excitement of the hunt, but it had been touch and go for a while. A.J. felt kind of bad about the incident and wondered how much the second bus had contributed to the infarction. Not the original bus, which was spending eternity under the mound with Eugene. The coach in question was the replacement he had purchased and parked on Slim's front lawn at the instruction of the departed as atonement for sins long-since committed.

Hoghead married Dixie Lanier, vowing to love, honor, and abstain from squirrel hunting. Bird Egg went to the big beer joint in the sky after being hit by a log truck bound for Alabama Southern. A.J.'s old pickup died. And Maggie was pregnant.

"We're going to have another baby," she had said when she broke the news. She was smiling. Of all the wonders in the wide world, Maggie liked babies the best.

"What are you reading these days?" had been the proud father-to-be's response.

It seemed to A.J. that the season of transience had ended. He had lost a job and gained another. He had inherited a fortune and given it all away. He had acquired a brother, then killed him. A child was on the way to fill the void in the life force. He supposed he had learned a lesson that he already knew. Permanence was an illusion, and nothing really mattered but *now*. So he vowed to make the most of the present and let the future lie. It was a belated New Year's resolution, one he hoped to keep. His other resolution, made late on New Year's Day, was to avoid killing anyone during the coming year. He had high hopes for that pledge as well.

A car door slammed. He looked up and saw Truth Hannassey coming toward him. As she stepped on the porch, he noted she was wearing a simple gold band on her left hand.

"Whoa," he said, shaking her hand. "Did Diane make an honest woman out of you?" Truth smiled and nodded. A.J. had to admit that Diane had been good for her.

"Yes, we got married." The happiness in her voice was obvious.

"You must have gone to Atlanta for that," he kidded. All of the local preachers were notorious for their conservative bent. "Around here, you are an abomination in the eyes of God."

"I just hate being one of those."

"I wouldn't lose too much sleep over it," A.J. responded, leading her to view a completed room. "He's looking elsewhere most of the time."

*photo by
Kiela L. Beam,
Cedartown, GA*

Raymond L. Atkins resides in Rome, Georgia, with his wife. They live in a 110-year-old house that they have restored themselves, and they have four grown children who drop by from time to time. Raymond has had a variety of occupations during the past thirty-five years, but now that the children are grown, he is pursuing his lifelong ambition of being a novelist and writer.

His hobbies include reading, travel, and working on the house. His stories have been published in *Christmas Stories from Georgia*, *The Lavender Mountain Anthology*, *The Blood and Fire Review*, and *The Old Red Kimono*. His columns appear regularly in the *Rome News/Tribune* and *Memphis Downtowner Magazine*.

His second novel — *Sorrow Wood* — will be published by Medallion Press in August 2009.

www.raymondlatkins.com

Flight to Freedom
D.J. Wilson

I KILLED MY HUSBAND, A TOWN HERO, and then called the police and turned myself in. "He's dead as a doornail," I said to the officer and then spit on Harland Jeffers' bloody, dead body.

With my head held high, I allowed myself to be escorted to a squad car outside my house. A house which had been more of a prison than the cell I was headed for.

Cameras flashed.

"Why did you kill Harland?"

Because he needed killing. And I, Montana Ines Parsons-Jeffers did just that.

So begins the rest of what's left of Montana's life. Not that she ever really had one.

Now she's headed for prison. There's no escaping it. It was the ultimate destination in her Flight to Freedom.

But one man might be able to help . . .

ISBN# 9781933836379
Trade Paperback
US $15.95 / CDN $17.95
Available Now
www.doloresjwilson.com

For more information
about other great titles from
Medallion Press, visit

www.medallionpress.com